RIGHT WITH YOU

A SMALL TOWN ROMANCE

CLAIRE CAIN

Cover design by Jess Mastorakos - Jess@jessmastorakos.com

PRINT ISBN: 978-1-954005-62-4

EBOOK ISBN: 978-1-954005-61-7

For anyone who has lost it and dared to find it again. For anyone who has felt crushed and healed and bloomed again. For anyone who loves donuts.

CHAPTER ONE

Elise

How does this man eat donuts three to five days a week and look like that?

The thought wasn't new. I had it approximately three to five days a week, every time Jean-Luc Doux entered my donut shop, ordered a plain glazed, and sat with a book at a small bright white table to eat it.

No coffee from next door. No milk. Not even water.

Just a donut. Like a monster.

Well, to be fair. Donut and a book.

A book he read using glasses he slipped on surreptitiously and tucked away again before he stood up to leave, usually ten minutes after arriving. The titles were usually in French with unfamiliar covers, which only heightened the air of mystery he carried.

Today, he waltzed in looking as impossibly handsome as always. His dark brown hair styled in a careless sort of mess that somehow still looked polished, his facial hair the perfectly short length so it wasn't quite a beard nor quite stubble, and his gray-green eyes set against the dark fringe of his lashes and brows. He wore a simple-looking jacket of plain black and under it a cream-colored Henley-style shirt with the top button undone, which seemed rather French of him. Not that I knew what was or wasn't French, but his style always looked a touch more careless and yet composed than his friends and coworkers at Saint Security.

Sometimes, I imagined he was a famous pop star hiding out in the safest place he could find. Other days, I wondered what it'd be like to discover he was on a secret mission from the government. Still other times, I fantasized about discovering he was some kind of fairy lord who ran a secret realm everyone assumed was bad but was actually an equitable and lovely place.

Lovely little fantasies that don't mean a thing.

I had a rich inner life, one might say. I'd never been a quiet person, but these last few years, I'd drawn inward, where it was safest. I had an outlet with my closest friends in some ways, but otherwise, I tucked myself away and focused on work, which suited me just fine.

"Hello there. What can I get you?" I asked, as I always did, because I was a normal person and not someone who let how severely beautiful this man was, or how often I imagined secret lives for him, show through our interactions. My secret world would remain secret, please and thank you.

Predictably, a dramatic pause followed. He read the menu as though he'd never been in before, then eyed the sign for specials.

I braced, knowing what was coming.

His gaze shifted to meet mine. My stomach swooped,

but I pasted on a smile. We'd been through this dozens of times now.

Keep calm.

"One plain glazed today."

Ah, the plain glazed. Definitely his favorite, if I had to guess, though he did sometimes opt for our specials or the daily. I often changed the flavors when feeling inspired or during the height of tourist season, but now that the ski season had ended and we'd entered the shoulder slow down, I'd eased off.

Maybe that was also due to my total lack of inspiration, my complete exhaustion, and a general sense of impending doom, but who wanted to think about that? It was so much easier to imagine fantastical scenarios where this beautiful man and his friends were secretly actual superheroes destined to save the world from alien invaders.

Or whatever.

"One plain, gotcha. Anything else I can get you?"

We didn't offer much beyond donuts, except bottled water and locally sourced milk that came in adorable glass bottles. Since we were directly next to Joe, an amazing local coffee shop, it would be silly to compete. Most people brought coffee here and settled in with a donut or vice versa.

Not this man.

"No, thank you."

I ducked my chin in acknowledgement, ignoring anything happening in my chest cavity or stomach because there should be no flutters or flips. An attractive man buying donuts was not uncommon around here. Silverton had something that lured men of a certain age and sexiness to the area, and one need only look at the roster of former military guys working for Saint Security to confirm it.

Add to that the plethora of other handsome men floating around and it was simply ridiculous.

Cut to: a film titled There's Something in the Water *where we find out there's literally something in the mountain run-off that pulls men via their genetically near-perfect makeup here.*

Sadly, it had also pulled men like Callum, my garbage pail ex, so... they'd need to work on that in storyboarding.

Despite the silly theories and logical banishment of such things, little zings and flares of heat still popped up whenever I saw Jean-Luc Doux, aka Cookie, much less sold him a donut.

"Here you go," I said, handing him a bright pink bag containing his donut, *Glazed* emblazoned in white across the front of it.

Wait for it...

"Thank you, Elise."

His gaze lingered, and I could've sworn there was some kind of twinkle in his gorgeous eyes. How could he make that simple phrase sound soft and alluring and flirty?

I nodded, swallowing down the riot his words started. Cells in my chest and synapses in my brain threw a party as the sound of my name in his low, smooth voice hit my ear drums.

Elise.

Good gracious, he said it every time, and I'd never loved my name more than when it slipped from his lips with his French pronunciation making it sound so beautiful. A crisp *eh* instead of the variable American approaches to the start that so often sounded like *uh.* And then the firm *se* almost like a z, a far cry from the wispy *ss* sound of my native language.

Okay so I had no linguistic training to properly explain

the sounds his glorious French tongue made of my name, I just knew I liked it.

A little too much, weirdo.

That helpful thought shoved me back to work just in time to see another customer wander in, keeping me from the oft-visited story my brain had come up with where Jean-Luc's glorious light accent had the ability to command anyone in its hearing, not unlike a vampire glamour. Nay, there was no time for that.

The absence of a line when he arrived was depressingly indicative of business in the last two weeks since Silver Ridge Mountain closed for the season. I might've loved spring in Utah—the timid blooms peeking out, the bright pink skies that began emerging, and the glory that would be fields of wildflowers come June, but... ugh. It sucked for business.

I helped the new customer and staunchly refused to enjoy the view of Jean-Luc sitting at my table eating my donut and reading with those thick black frames. It would do nothing for me, and I had prep to do for tomorrow.

He wasn't a lonely college professor, wishing for the right donut-making woman to take her coffee break and chat with him. He wasn't a bedraggled single dad sneaking a moment for himself and discovering the perfect woman standing right in front of him.

I knew very well these things weren't true, but what harm was there in a little imagination? Lately, it was all the creativity I had, and it was safe. No risks involved when the game afoot was merely me, myself, and I telling stories in the silence of our mind—to us.

After bustling around tasks and wiping down counters, I moved to the back to prep for a quick inventory of supplies so I could send in an order. By the time I checked back in the dining area, Jean-Luc had gone.

Ignoring the twinge of something I couldn't name, I finished tidying up and set chairs on tables. With no one coming in and only twenty minutes left, I felt fine about it. Since we opened early and the tourist traffic had tapered off thanks to the end of ski season, I'd started closing before noon.

Maybe it made me a crap business owner, but my desire to stay chipper and welcoming right up until closing time had fallen by the wayside right about the time I'd had to start trucking donuts to the homeless shelter every day rather than selling out. After a few days and realizing it wasn't a fluke and the traffic really had died off that abruptly, I'd adjusted how many I made and didn't have the same surplus.

On the way out to the dumpster around the corner, a shout halted my progress.

"Elise, stop."

Uh-leess. My heart sank.

"What do you need, Callum?" I asked, turning to face my ex and demanding my knees stand firm and my strength hold.

"What do *I* need? Leesy, it's what *you* need, and we both know it." He crossed his arms and looked at me, a mixture of pity, censure, and cruelty in his eyes.

Anger and fear warred as I gritted out, "I don't think so." I stepped away from him as he moved closer. My spine stiffened and my stomach clenched.

"You need me and what I've invested in your little shop. And if you want that investment to stay put, you'll do as you're told. You're mine whether you acknowledge it or not. It's that simple."

Fury ignited in my veins and my teeth ground together, because right at its heels came fear surging past all my best efforts at walling it off. Familiar, ugly, shameful.

Talk about the opposite of a fun fantasy.

"You—you don't get to tell me what to do. I'm not yours and I haven't been in months." My back hit the brick wall as he got closer and his hand reached for me. I craned my neck away, trying to melt back, to escape. But there was none, was there? Not where Callum was concerned.

"You'll do—"

His words cut off. I opened my eyes to see him sneering as he turned, someone grasping his arm and halting his progress toward me.

"Hey, you can't—"

"No. *You* can't. You won't."

Jean-Luc.

Holy crap, that was his murderous growl as he shoved Callum away from me and prowled after him. The normally quiet patron of my donut shop, and friend of my friends, wedged his forearm under Callum's chin, pressing onto his neck and pinning him against the other side of the small alley.

"You will not touch her again."

Callum cowered, but managed to spit out, "Who... who the hell are you?"

"Her boyfriend."

Her... boyfriend?

My boyfriend?

Um, wait. What?

Before I could process this fantastical announcement, Callum sputtered an expletive and made to move forward.

Jean-Luc simply leaned in, cutting off the air enough to silence him.

"Touch her again and I end you. That simple. You understand, or do I need to explain it?"

Forget about the "her boyfriend" thing for a second. How had I forgotten this man was a former special operations soldier in the Army, just like most of the staff at Saint Security? He was deadly and skilled and trained to do all manner of things I knew nothing about. That wasn't make-believe storytelling, but a truth that only just now felt real.

Callum shook his head, apparently understanding his predicament more clearly.

"Good. Touch her"—he notched his head toward the side in gesture to me—"and you die. Easy."

Wow, not just super soldier vibes, but even I could believe he was defending the spurned honor of his woman.

Completely swoon-worthy if not for the bit where I was, supposedly, the woman in question.

He pushed off Callum who instantly spat at Jean-Luc's feet and sent me a furious look before stalking away, hollering "You'll be hearing from my lawyer!" as he went.

Jean-Luc turned to me, unperturbed by Callum's threat, the fury melting into something I could've sworn looked like panic. He reached up and I flinched, the reaction an unfortunate byproduct of what had just happened. The adrenaline cranking through me couldn't discern between the man who'd just stormed off—who was a genuine threat to me—and this one, who seemed to be intent on making sure my ex didn't hurt me again.

But it was over. Callum was gone. All thanks to Jean-Luc.

A flood of overwhelm washed over me, and I shuddered, eyes glazing with tears.

He held up both hands, gorgeous face masked in concern. "Elise, are you okay?"

CHAPTER TWO

Luc

She shook with adrenaline. Maybe fear, too. I couldn't blame her. The ex was a slimy little *connard*, but he was a fairly big man. Not quite my height, but maybe just under six feet, and considerably bulkier than me.

And, fool that I was, I'd just frightened her. Not only by attacking her ex, even if he was a scumbag, but then apparently making her fearful I'd hurt her. And why should she trust me? She didn't know me and couldn't possibly understand I would never, ever hurt her. If she'd been with that jackass for any length of time, she'd learned to expect violence when he was unhappy or at least suffering from an ill temper.

I knew the kind of man who'd just walked away—they didn't step back until they understood they didn't have access to what they imagined belonged to them. A show of force and a verbal claiming would do the trick, or so I hoped.

Elise was safe.

I'd been working in Europe on and off since starting at Saint when it opened, but after my maternal grandmother passed, I'd come back for the funeral and ended up staying stateside.

I'd noticed Elise from the start. Sometimes, I only caught glimpses. Other times, I got to witness her laughing and talking with Nikki and Jo and Winnie, my friends' partners, and Jess, our colleague.

But I'd also seen her grow quieter. Sometimes, she seemed like a shell of a person, like she'd retreated into herself, and I wondered how her closest friends weren't more concerned. Perhaps they were, and maybe they'd all talked to her, but the quiet persisted. Elise Cordero wasn't a shy woman. She wasn't quiet ... except when suddenly, she was.

It was a peculiar sensation to witness oneself in someone else, like they held up a mirror to certain qualities. Of course we had many differences. I didn't have her past, nor she mine, but I related to what I suspected was a lonely way of living. This tendency to present oneself in a way that kept the majority of questions—and therefore truths— at bay.

Even with Barbie, Stone, and Beast as close friends, there were key parts of me they didn't know.

Glazed had given Elise new life, it seemed to me, but whenever that useless idiot was skulking around...

Rage simmered in my gut at the thought of him.

"I—yeah. I am." She cleared her throat, and my ire diffused until nothing but concern remained at the sound of her voice.

"I'm sorry for interrupting," I offered, not sorry at all, but needing to acknowledge I had butted in.

Brushing some dark hair that'd fallen in her face away with a shaking hand, she rushed to say, "No, please. I mean, thank you. I—I'm sorry. I'm just..." Her lips pinched, and she shook her head.

I was not a man easily moved to violence, but right now I almost wished the coward would wander back and try to touch her so I'd have my excuse.

"You're alright. You're safe." Saying the words wouldn't make them true, but I couldn't stop myself from supplying them and hoping she'd recognize the truth.

She exhaled sharply. "Yes. Thank you."

"You could get a restraining order. He assaulted you."

"He didn't actually touch me. You stopped him." Her espresso gaze flicked up to meet mine and held there.

A slow drop of melted chocolate heat ran down my sternum. "I'll make a statement about what I saw."

She was already shaking her head. "No. Thank you."

"I'm happy to if you change your mind."

"Thank you. And, I'm sorry, uh..." Her face dropped, gaze on her feet, then rose to reconnect our eyes again. "Honestly, I don't know what to call you."

"What would you like to call me?"

It was a genuine question. I wanted to hear my name on her lips, but she'd never said it. In fairness, she may not even know my actual name since so many people in Silverton knew me by my Saint, and former military, nickname.

She huffed and brushed her hands down the apron layered over a soft, long-sleeved T-shirt and jeans. "Your name would be nice."

Her brows tented, seemingly baffled by my refusal to offer her my name.

"You know it, don't you?"

Her eyes narrowed. "Do I?"

I smiled, enjoying the way her mood had lightened, how her eyes danced with teasing merriment now, and I wanted it to stay put. "Do you?"

She bit her lip, a smile tugging at her full mouth. "Is it… shortcake?"

I laughed outright.

Her smile widened. "Wait, no. Croissant?"

I mock-frowned. "Are you making fun of my French heritage?"

Her mouth dropped open and she reached for me, grasping my wrist in her small hand before she released it just as suddenly, glancing at the audacious limb with an odd expression before speaking. "No, no. Never. I—of course not. I was just teasing you."

"Teasing me, Elise?" Saying her name seemed to flip a switch, and electrical currents snapped between us, just like they always had when our eyes met. It'd struck me the first time I ever held her gaze and it had never stopped. Sometimes, I had to remind myself not to linger there or I'd incinerate. There was nothing between us, a fact I should've remembered more often.

Her shoulders rose as she sucked in a breath. "Do you prefer Cookie?"

I ducked my chin. "Do you?"

She rolled her eyes. "Goodness, who knew when you decided to talk, this is what it'd be like?"

Grinning again, I took mercy on her. "Call me Luc, if you like."

She nodded, accepting the offer. And now, time for me to go. Especially before she brought up what I'd let slip earlier when addressing that jackass. I had no desire to explain why the lie had tripped so easily off my tongue in the moment.

"*À plus tard*, Elise," I said, then stepped away, not wanting to draw attention because by now I knew very well she wouldn't want that. For as entrenched in this community as she was, she was a private person. What'd happened between her and Callum, or me and Callum for that matter, was not something she'd want anyone knowing.

And again—so relatable.

The sooner both of us forgot this, the better.

"Bye," she said softly.

Though I didn't look back, it didn't keep me from thinking about her the rest of the day. Because those words I'd let slip, they hadn't come from nowhere. They stemmed from the impulsive lie I'd told my family about my relationship with her. Soon enough, I'd have to deal with it and shut it all down.

Or I'd have to tell her why my family thought she was my fiancée.

CHAPTER THREE

Luc

Kenny's voice reached me on Dorian's porch where I paced.

"Alright, baby boy. I know it's gorgeously springy out and that's good for the soul after a long winter, but you coming in here voluntarily, or do I need to drag you in?"

"*J'arrive.*" I didn't often use French with my friends, but Stone had started studying French in the last year, so I used it more often at his house, and Kenny didn't seem to mind.

"I'm not sure I've ever seen you pace, so you can skip the stoic Frenchman bit and let it out," Kenny said, leaning on Dorian's kitchen counter like he owned the place.

Dorian glanced up from where he was grating something on top of something else, likely a petit four or other delicate little bite we'd all share over tea this afternoon. So today wasn't going to be Bake Off meets Home Reno—he was nearly finished with remodeling inside the small cabin next door, and now that we'd discovered his project, we did the heavy lifting while he prepared us some vol-au-vents or other treat in the kitchen. We all enjoyed his baking habit, especially since he'd gotten quite good after moving here to Silverton.

At the threshold of the living room, I stopped in front of the regal Alaskan Malamute standing sentry. "Bear, *bonjour, Monseigneur.*" I leaned down and touched my forehead to his. He may have looked like a dog bred with a wolf, but he was, much like his owner, a sweetie inside.

"Did you just refer to my dog as lord of the manor or something?" Stone asked as he set down two platters of treats, and Kenny shuffled behind him with a little tray holding a teapot and teacups.

"Gosh, I needed this," Kenny said, slumping into the couch and leaning back, brushing a hand over his face.

"What's going on?" I asked, happy to not be talking about me.

"There doesn't need to be anything wrong for me to need some tea with my boys, but I'll admit I'm over this whole long-distance situation."

He sat forward and nodded when Stone held up a cube of sugar. Stone dropped it in, then handed him his teacup resting on a saucer.

"When's she back?" Stone asked as he poured my drink —straight up, no milk or sugar, because I was a man of principle and it would be a shame to mar a quality Darjeeling, unlike some at the table.

The satisfaction of being known bloomed in me, followed by a stab of razor-sharp guilt. Yes, these men knew me... in some ways.

"Four more days," Kenny grumbled, then flicked out his pinky and took a delicate but obnoxiously loud sip of his tea.

I chuckled, and Stone cracked a miniscule smile.

"Actually, I'm fine. I'm just whining. I found the love of my life and she's about to be done with all her out-briefings and CIA shenanigans in DC and will be moving back here and..." He sighed and leaned back against the couch again. "It's kind of unbelievable."

"Why do you say that?" I asked, sliding a tiny lemon tart from the tray in front of me into my mouth. The bright flavor burst on my tongue, and the buttery crust created a perfect combination. I held up the tray to Kenny, signaling he had to try one as I chewed.

"It's just"—he plucked a tart up with two fingers, then continued with a wry grin—"it's better than I could've imagined, you know?" He popped the little bite into his mouth and groaned.

I laughed. "I knew you'd love it. This is the best yet," I told Dorian. "*Je n'plaisante pas. J'en prendrais bien dix.*"

"You'd like ten? That's excessive," Stone said, his brow furrowing, but a pull at the corner of his mouth gave away his real response to the compliment.

He was an odd mixture of shy and bold when it came to his baking. He wanted people to try what he made, to enjoy them, but he struggled to accept the praise that inevitably came with it—an apt metaphor for the man himself.

We chatted for a few more minutes, Kenny updating us on Elizabeth's plans, and his failure to get her permission to propose, and then they landed on me. There came the guilt pulsing under my sternum.

"So, give it. What's with the pacing? I know you can be angsty, but this is unusual."

Kenny winked like a dope, but I loved him for it.

I was not particularly angsty, but he liked to joke that since I was half-French, I naturally tended toward feeling ennui and all the typical French feelings.

But this angst was real. And what I had to tell them might change things between us, so I couldn't just brush it away. I couldn't avoid this any longer.

It was time to let them know more—in ways I'd locked away. I'd resolved earlier in the day to be honest with them, and also to be more honest—more myself—whenever possible. Just thinking it made my eye twitch with dread, but it would be worth it.

I hoped.

Beast wasn't here. Like the good husband he was, he was taking care of his pregnant wife. I'd almost copped out thinking it'd be best to have all three of my best friends in the same spot when I delivered this speech, but that would make me a coward. I'd catch Jude at his place when Jess was out, or corner him at work or something.

I had to do this.

"I have a confession to make. I'm afraid it's going to upset you both, and I... I don't want to tell you." There. I'd said it.

Had to start somewhere.

Stone didn't move, but Barbie sat up straighter and patted my back. "Then don't tell us. It can't be important, and nothing's worth rocking the boat, right?"

I blinked at him, dumbfounded. "Really?"

He rolled his eyes and sighed dramatically. "No. Not really. Tell us whatever you have to tell us, and we'll take it in stride. We love you, man, and we're not about to run out of here because of... whatever this is."

I huffed out a breath, forcing my lungs to empty. My

stomach clenched, and I stretched my neck one way, then the other. "Fine. I'll just say it."

Stone nodded.

They waited.

I didn't speak.

"Mmkay, go ahead," Kenny prompted.

So I did. After years and years of keeping it all in, I told them the truth.

"My name is not Doux."

Kenny blinked. "Your name is not Jean-Luc Doux?"

My head shook slowly. "No. It's Jean-Luc Devereaux."

Kenny blinked again.

Stone slowly lowered his teacup to his saucer. "As in..."

I exhaled. "As in the primary shareholder of the conglomerate behind several major international—"

"Holy crap." Kenny's eyes were wide.

I braced. At least they had heard of the business so I wouldn't have to explain that much. It shouldn't have surprised me. They'd both spent time working in Europe and would be familiar with the brands all sheltered under the business conglomerate. A world-famous haute couture designer. A world-renowned champagne label. Luxury brands all housed under one billion-dollar company my family had founded and still owned the largest piece of.

"Your family is... insanely rich," Kenny said. "Sorry, that's like, uncouth or something, but I literally grew up in a trailer over here, so forgive my poor breeding." He stuck out his pinky and then knocked back the rest of his tea like it was a shot.

A chuckle slipped out, and relief hit me. He was joking, at least, and not storming out with betrayal etched onto his face.

"So... knowing you as Jean-Luc Doux?" he continued.

I winced. "Not entirely false. I legally changed my name before getting into the military, taking my paternal grandmother's surname."

"Uh, yeah, not like it was random or anything," he added with a mock-scowl.

No, it wasn't. It had been another jab at my grandfather, to honor her name and not his.

"Why tell us now?" Stone asked, no hidden meaning in his words that I could detect.

That wasn't really his style, yet I'd been expecting far more upheaval than this.

"I didn't want it to affect my relationships. Before I joined the Army, I did it on impulse to push my family away, a little tantrum twenty-year-old me thought would result in being effectively disowned. The name and prestige had no bearing on my life after that, and have only recently become an issue again."

Thinking back on the time when my grandfather made clear I wasn't welcome anywhere near him didn't hurt anymore. It was simply a fact of my past. That it ever hurt was ridiculous considering I'd tried everything I could to get that exact response, like a spoiled child stomping his foot, and yet I hadn't been immune.

I hadn't minded that he'd held my trust and all the money in it at bay while I served in the military. He'd changed the conditions of the trust so it would be released at his leisure, essentially, and now that I was out, he'd added a new stipulation.

Marriage to someone he deemed worthy.

I wasn't a money-grubbing man. I didn't mind working for a living, and I didn't need millions of dollars. That said, Saint Security was expanding, and it just so happened I had the capital to invest without needing an outside investor.

Before, I'd never had any vision of what to do with the money, so it hadn't mattered to me.

But now that I did, I wanted it. And my grandfather wanted me to marry someone I didn't know to get it. There had to be a way to convince him to ease up on this superficial requirement.

"And now?" Stone asked, nudging the tray of lemon tarts my way.

I took one and kept my eyes on it as I explained. "Since getting out of the Army, I've been re-owned, apparently. I also suspect that when my sister insisted my family start speaking to me again, they listened. And now, my grandfather has informed me it's time to get married, or the agreed-upon return of my trust is null and void. So, he chooses the bride, and I cooperate, period."

They both perked up at this.

"Like, an arranged thing?" Kenny asked.

I chuckled mirthlessly. "Apparently. Which is ridiculous, because I've made it clear for years I have no interest in playing their games. I'm not the next CEO or family rep on the board or any of that. But I guess my joining the US military didn't show them that clearly enough, and now he's demanding I marry some woman he's picked out."

Impulsive though it was, my choice to enlist had brought me so many good things, these two men included. I wasn't proud of how I'd behaved before or during that time of my life, but I'd been relieved to have a break from... everything.

Kenny reared back, and Stone's brow creased. "And you said, 'thanks but no thanks, Grandpappy Moneybags?'"

We all laughed at that, and I took a moment to eat the tart and appreciate my friend's humor bringing lightness to something I could hardly stomach. Because I also needed to admit this next part.

"No. I, uh, I said no, I wasn't going to do that... If I didn't care about the trust, I could ignore it entirely. But it's a lot of money, and I could do a lot with it."

"Yeah, I mean, if it's decent, you could be very comfortable," Kenny reasoned, though still not understanding.

"It's millions. And with it, I could invest heavily in Saint. All those blue sky plans Bruce and Wilder have been dreaming up? The adventure training camps and courses Doc's developing? Tristan's self-defense academy. Hell, even a more robust staff and bigger European presence, or a second location—I could fund it."

They blinked back at me, the depth of the resource slowly sinking in.

"What aren't you saying? Just say it. I can't take this suspense!" Kenny pleaded, practically crawling out of his skin.

Stone's gaze pinned me down, making clear he'd brook no further evasions either.

"I told him I couldn't marry the person he had in mind because I was practically engaged to someone here." Impulsivity in response to familial stress wasn't only confined to the past. And hopefully, he'd let me off the hook. The whole marriage requirement thing was so I'd show I could be responsible. Great, but it didn't have to be with someone he'd hand-picked.

Kenny clapped. "Oh, well that's brilliant. Way to throw him off the scent."

Stone's gaze narrowed.

"Kind of. I was pretty sure he'd buy it and now, I just heard he RSVP'd yes to the gala."

Kenny's mouth dropped open. "Oh, damn."

I nodded.

"And who did you tell him you're almost engaged to?" he asked, voice tentative.

I scrubbed my hands over my face and back into my hair, the full idiocy of my lie hitting me like a wayward shooting star.

"Elise."

CHAPTER FOUR

Elise

Half an hour left until I could shut down my work and freshen up before heading out to see my friends.

And maybe Luc.

Ugh, Luc.

A man who was apparently my boyfriend now.

In no fantasy of mine had I ever conjured that up. Except, maybe I had imagined those words during the Callum-Luc confrontation? Luc hadn't mentioned it again, so had I somehow hallucinated it?

For now, I had to finish the handful of tasks remaining in my queue for my virtual assistant job I did to supplement my income. I'd never fooled myself into believing I could quit my job outright when I opened Glazed, but I'd hoped to pull back on hours. Maybe go truly part time. Alas, as we straddled ski and summer seasons, the shoulder season had already confirmed quitting altogether this year was a pipe dream.

At least I still had two part-time employees and one of them, bless her, loved the early Saturday and Sunday starts. The first ten months after opening, I'd been at Glazed every single morning we were open at the crack of dawn. When I hired Marisol and discovered she genuinely wanted those early morning weekend hours, I could've cried.

Actually, I totally cried. A lot. Because I'd been stressed and exhausted but also proud and happy, and finally having someone *want* to take the toughest shifts had been a dream. I didn't want to go back to the place where I did the jobs of three employees, or what should be more like four during ski season.

Couldn't a girl just sell perfect donuts by day and read books and sip champagne by night? Was that not a reasonable expectation?

My phone buzzed, and Callum's name flashed across the screen. It should've been silenced altogether during my timed working hours, so I didn't answer. Zero temptation to talk to the man who'd been hounding me since Luc gave him the old *touch her and die.*

Gah. I mean… seriously.

Talk about fantasy meeting reality with bubble-shattering swiftness. I had spent so many mornings daydreaming fictional tales about the man, I'd somehow forgotten he was an actual badass. He just looked so… polished. Had it been Jess's beastly husband sitting there, there would've been no forgetting he was a soldier. Even Bruce, who was far more traditionally handsome than Jude, had this *look* that said he was a little rough around the edges and had maybe once been a man of violence.

A man whose nickname was *Cookie?* Who'd supposedly

spent time modeling and looked every bit like he knew his way around a skincare regimen but magically didn't need it? The whole "touch her and die" moment shook all my illusions away, and I saw him.

Him.

I couldn't get distracted with thoughts of sexy Luc yet again or I'd never get this stuff done, and I wanted to run away from my dingy little office and into the loving arms of my friends and a bustling pub and feel like a young professional launching into an exciting weekend instead of a woman strapped with responsibility and worry and an ex who still had his fingers twisted into her life. Call me Carrie Bradshaw and watch me trot across cobblestones in my ridiculous Jimmy Choos for drinks with the gals with my day job far behind me... though I didn't want Carrie's life or friends. I loved my girls, even if I didn't always let them in.

Twenty-seven minutes later, I sent the last email and shut off my timer, submitted my timesheet, and sighed.

My phone lit up again, and I squinted at it as though seeing it this way would make it less dreadful Callum was calling *again.*

No, you jerk. I'm not selling my shop, and even though you think you can coerce me into it, it ain't gonna happen.

See? I could be strong up against that egomaniacal tyrant. It just happened to be harder outside of my head.

Exhaling all of those messy thoughts out, I perked up and grabbed the phone, launching from the chair and hustling to the bathroom as I read the group chat pinging away. My friends were hyping each other up, clearly all more than ready for the weekend.

Except Jess, who couldn't drink or stand the smell of beer, and who was still struggling on and off with severe morning sickness and low energy, poor thing.

Dove called as I pulled out my makeup to give myself a refresh.

"Tell me you're coming and staying," she said, her sweet voice ragged through the speaker.

"I am. Are you? Are you sick?" I asked, swiping on some mascara, which I hadn't bothered with yet today.

"No, just dragging," she said, then chatted through her day while I continued getting prepped, jumping off once we were both ready to head out.

Why was I putting mascara on to meet my girlfriends? First, there was such a thing as dressing for oneself. Feeling good in one's skin. Liking the way one looked when one spent a fair amount of time with one's hair in a ponytail and one's clothes covered by a bright pink Glazed apron perfumed with the combined scent of fried dough and frosting.

So yes, I wanted to feel a little less schlubby and a little more put together.

But also... Luc would be there.

Our interaction after he'd stepped in with Callum didn't mean we'd talk or... do anything other than maybe make eye contact a time or two. I hadn't seen the man since the incident earlier this week. Kind of odd, so maybe he was avoiding me? More likely, he had work obligations pop up. It wasn't unheard of for him to go a few days between visits to the shop.

If I saw him tonight, not that I was counting on it at all, I'd ask him about the whole calling himself my boyfriend thing. I mean, it was situational, obviously, but it merited a conversation between us. Didn't it?

Still. Even if he wouldn't be there tonight, couldn't a girl want to look decent after a day slogging through boring emails and tasks?

Yes, she could.

Saint Security, Luc's employer and the entity where a few of my friends, and many of their partners worked, held a weekly cocktail hour where they socialized and let off steam. This worked perfectly since our girl group met at the same time, and many of us had paired off with Saint men to do the whole happily ever after thing.

Nikki, Winnie, Jo, Jess, and now our newest baddie babe Liz were all tethered to Saint men in various states of dating, engagement, marriage, child-growing. And God bless them. May their rings shine brightly and their wombs grow with... fruitfulness? Whatever. I was genuinely thrilled for everyone who'd found their person. Seeing the way these men loved their women gave me hope that good men still existed. Not even hope—it gave me proof.

As I loaded into my car, I reminded myself that it didn't change the fact that I wasn't heading down the same path. I thought I'd found the man for me in Callum. He'd had everything going for him, perfect on paper and even at first glance. Good looks, a secure job, the whole slick corporate former frat boy vibe to him. Somehow, I'd convinced myself he was right for me. I'd thought it even when we fought, even when he started finding fault with small things that then turned into essential things like how many moles I had or the size of my feet. I persisted in believing we were right for each other the first time he grabbed my arm so hard it left a bruise within hours. And when he convinced me to give him another try, that he'd changed.

At some point, the ignorance fell away and I said no. It was sometime after Adam nearly took a bullet for Jo, or maybe when my mom took off to Florida with her latest husband. It finally clicked, and I wouldn't look back.

I wouldn't get back together with Callum—not again—

and I wouldn't fall for the charming man sweeping me off my feet thing again. I'd even struggled to enjoy romance novels lately, instead favoring thrillers and books on business or time management to the happily ever afters I'd lived off of for years.

I'd quite literally lost that lovin' feeling, and I honestly didn't mind. It was more fun—and far less treacherous—to make up stories in my head or watch movies or worry about the fungal spawn causing an apocalypse than anything a real-life man could induce me to.

Shedding those heavy thoughts, I made my way inside Craic, ready to focus on my friends.

"Good to see you, Elise."

I gasped, Luc's low, smooth voice sending a thrill up my spine. I turned and braced myself for the sight of him—*oof, direct hit*—and nodded. "Luc."

Then I kept walking.

Because lingering near that man was not an option.

The first time since breaking up with Callum I'd felt something in my cold, dead little heart of stone had been for him, and it continued to react like this mattered. Fortunately, I'd learned my heart was not to be trusted when it came to the male species, and therefore I ignored the little floor routine going on in my chest and hustled to the table where my friends were.

Think of the fungal spawn, Elise. Think of the zombies!

"I tell you, that man is just pretty. And I mean that in the most masculine, Calvin Klein underwear model type of way," Dove said, raising a glass of water to the middle of the table.

Catherine chuckled softly and said nothing but touched her glass to Dove's. Nikki, Winnie, and Jo laughed and took sips of their drinks but didn't join in the toast.

"Come on, you know you want to." Dove waggled her brows and held her glass aloft, waiting.

I grunted, accepted a beer someone had poured, and clinked my glass with hers.

She grinned. "Knew it."

With a roll of my eyes, I took a long drink. "It's not like it's a surprise I'd agree. I have eyes to see. It also means absolutely nothing."

And that was just it. Luc was beautiful and seemed kind, even, but the hoops I'd have to jump through to get from where I sat rather comfortably in the "single and not at all interested in mingling" to the "actually interested in a human man" spot were endless and therefore impossible.

Dove raised a shoulder, currently adorned in the pretty little boat neck, baby blue cap sleeve of her dress, and agreed. "Of course. But sometimes, it feels good to say true things out loud."

My gaze cut to hers, but she'd already glanced away, eyes roaming the pub.

"Anyone know when Liz gets back?" Winnie asked, and Jo piped in, explaining her sister's plans. She'd apparently had to go back to tie up loose ends of her job with some super-secret CIA organization and then she'd be back.

As if on cue, Kenny Carmichael gestured wildly at the Saint table across the room, likely telling some fantastical story with his usual flair. He was either entertaining or looking a little like a lost puppy lately, and I kind of loved seeing the super cheery guy so obviously lovelorn.

Smiling as I watched Kenny, my eyes snagged on Luc's. He wasn't watching Kenny.

He was watching me.

His full attention bore into me from across the room, and my stomach swooped low. Good grief, Dove hadn't been joking when she said he was male model gorgeous. He was the kind of handsome that seemed airbrushed or conjured up by AI. He had to be the combination of all the best features of the world's most beautiful men whittled into one perfect-looking man with the most delicious hint of a French accent.

Painfully beautiful was exactly the right phrase, and the twist in my chest reminded me why those looks didn't matter. Reality was men being disappointing and me unable to trust my heart. Luc might as well have been a prince in a fairytale where everything worked out.

I tore my gaze away, focusing on my beer. I didn't even like beer, but Nikki mentioned Kieran the pirate bartender had sent our table a free pitcher.

"Um, hi. *Hi.* He's coming over here," Dove said, nudging my arm with a frantic edge to her movement.

"Oh, yes he is, and he's laser-focused on you, Elise."

Winnie's voice jolted me from my study of bubbles.

"What?" I said, eyes snapping up and seeing Luc walking toward me with that same intensity. Had he not ever looked away? Did he... what did he want?

When he reached me, he ducked his head close to my ear and spoke just loud enough for me. "Could we talk outside for a minute?"

More than a bit dumbstruck, I nodded, eyes catching Dove's as she bit her lip and raised her brows high. Then I followed him out.

CHAPTER FIVE

Luc

Too late to turn back now, I wove between tables, stoutly ignoring whatever obnoxious expression Kenny wore as we passed the Saint group and slipped out the pub's door onto the sidewalk.

He knew where we were heading—what I was about to do. He and Stone hadn't exactly cautioned me against it, but they'd expressed concern. I didn't blame them—appreciated it, even. But it didn't sway me from the task, undesirable though it was.

I'd set this in motion, and I wasn't going to be the one to stop it.

I turned, slipping my hands into my pockets, and waited for her to stop. Happily, the spring air was cool, but not cold. Most of us had shunned jackets in favor of being layer-free after months of needing to bundle up. I'd never noticed it in North Carolina, but here it seemed to be a particular mountain-life sensibility that had people in T-shirts come the low fifties, and shorts not long after. The sky was still light enough as the sun set with pink streaks across a purple-dark palette.

She wore jeans that did very nice things for her legs, and a black top I wouldn't allow myself to admire as much as I might like, with heels and her shoulder-length hair wavy and shining beautifully. Her lips were pouty with some kind of gloss I wanted to taste, and her eyes were stunningly vivid tonight.

She had never not looked beautiful, and tonight was no exception. She had always been alluring to me, but the kinship I felt with her in the way she kept herself walled off was what called to me.

Had I not heard her clearly state she had no interest in men more than once over the last year, I might've considered asking her out. But once I felt at home here and decided I didn't want to keep taking overseas assignments, even that became untenable because I wasn't in the market for someone long-term.

I knew what it looked like to lose someone, even though I'd watched it happen from a distance, and I couldn't imagine opting into the possibility. Plus starting something with anything other than long-term in mind in a small town like this just didn't make sense.

So. Enough with the starry eyes and back to the point.

"Thank you for stepping away with me for a moment," I said, gut tight with dread at how this would all go down, but knowing I shouldn't wait any longer. I had to do this... didn't I?

Yes. I did. I'd decided. I wouldn't walk this back.

"No problem. What... can I do for you?"

She crossed her arms and waited—not exactly in a

defensive position but certainly not open. Not warm like she had been with her friends.

"I need to tell you something that will seem strange."

She blinked. "Okay. Go ahead."

"My... past. It's... particular. And my family... is also particular." I could practically hear Kenny jeering at me.

Way to go, man. Way to really lay out the truth of the matter!

Her brow furrowed. "Okay."

She drew the word out, clearly confused about why I was telling her any of this. We'd hardly spoken, let alone about family dynamics.

Fair enough and exactly why I needed to cut the dramatic vaguery and get to the point.

"I don't know how to put this delicately, so if you don't mind, I'd just like to tell you," I said, evaluating her with every word that came from my mouth.

Her defenses were up, but not sky high like they could be. She was curious. "That's a good plan because I have no idea what's going on."

I exhaled through my nose, gut clenching tighter, and laid it out for her. "My family wants me to marry a woman from New York. It's a complex situation. But I do not want that, and in order to avoid their pressure to do so, I have told them I'm engaged—or about to be."

She blinked.

"To you," I added, finally telling the whole truth.

Her jaw dropped a bit, and her eyes darted from side to side, then her mouth clamped shut. She studied me as though to determine whether I was joking, and finally said, "To—to me."

I nodded.

"And you said that because..."

There might be a time for full honesty on this subject, but for now I would tell her the most basic version. "You're a kind person and you're well-liked amongst your friends. People who know you speak highly of you. As far as I'm aware, you're single. And obviously, you make a perfect donut."

In the dim light of the spring evening, I could see her cheeks pink, even as she said, "You told your family we're engaged because I make good donuts?"

I swore and rushed to explain. "I didn't give them any reasons. I simply gave your name. It really doesn't matter, but I need to tell you since it does involve you, or at least, your name."

"Why—" She shook her head like she was dizzy before continuing. "I'm sorry, I don't know what to say right now."

I ran a hand through my hair. "Understandable. I've been an idiot. I'm sorry."

"Wait! The other day, you said... You said you were my boyfriend. Was that—"

"Nothing to do with this," I rushed to clarify. "It just—" I shrugged, thinking of a way to tell her that claiming her like I had a right to would be what made her slimeball of an ex loosen his hooks into her. "I wanted him gone. We both did."

She nodded. "Yes. We did."

"It wasn't a test run."

At this, she guffawed. "It would be a good idea for all parties involved to be on the same page, no?"

I winced. "You're right. My bad. That was spur of the moment, obviously."

Though we weren't just talking of her ex now. It was everything.

"Can you just tell your family we broke it off or something?" she asked, bringing us back to the larger issue.

She looked pained, and I felt it like a jab straight to the diaphragm. Of course this wouldn't be good news for her, and I hadn't even explained the worst part.

"Ideally no. They'll come to Silverton, see that you exist, be generally dismissive, and leave." Best case scenario.

Maybe I should've mentioned the trust, but it could wait. No need to complicate things before she'd even agreed.

"So, you want them to continue thinking we're engaged despite our having virtually zero relationship beyond me being your donut supplier?"

A small smile broke through the frustration welling up in me because this was something I liked about her. She had this sharp wit and humor, even when I'd presented her with a problem she shouldn't have to deal with.

"I do want them to, yes. And I'm hoping you'd be willing to, at the very least, not instantly deny it if someone should ask you." My throat tightened, and I exhaled slowly to calm my nerves. "I think I can avoid all but a brief meeting."

I hoped. I would need to beg Aurelie for her help, but my sister would do it. I knew she would. And if her husband Michele came, we'd have reinforcements and distraction enough to keep Grand-père's attention diverted.

"Oh. Wow. Okay." She shifted on her feet and wobbled before righting herself.

My hand shot out, but I stopped just shy of grasping her arm to steady her, mindful not to touch her. "Are you alright?"

She folded her arms again. "Yes, I'm fine. It's just... I'm

not interested in dating. I don't date, and I'm not going to start. So this is..."

"I know. I—I'm sorry. I've heard you say as much, and in some way, I thought maybe it was better to choose you than someone who might want something real. This way, it's clear." And I wouldn't look too hard at the reasons I never even considered someone else. I wouldn't let that nag at me, or make me feel foolish.

"I guess that makes sense. But... is there anything I can do? I mean, this is weird, definitely weird, but you seem..." Her lovely dark eyes slid over my face. "You seem stressed."

A huffed laugh escaped.

She couldn't possibly be real, could she? Was she actually standing here asking how I was doing when I'd just foisted this mess onto her shoulders?

"*T'inquiètes pas*," I said. "Don't worry, please. This is a mess of my own making."

Our gazes held, the connection and her nearness causing my heart rate to triple as we stood there, not ending the conversation, but not continuing it.

There was more to discuss, of course, but now didn't feel like the right time. I needed to give her space to absorb everything, and in that time, I needed to see what I could control.

Then I realized perhaps she was waiting for me to say more—to do something to end this.

But I couldn't.

Not yet.

It made no sense, but being near her felt good—felt right in a way I'd never felt around anyone except Kenny and Stone and Beast, and even this was different. It was that same sense of understanding, and though I didn't have a right to it, some part of me gripped it in an iron fist.

I'd finally found the ability to speak normally—or somewhat normally—in her presence. Until the last few days, I clammed up around her, likely thanks to a spike in adrenaline and a sense of foreboding. But I'd evidently pushed past that thanks to my stubborn determination to maintain my lie to my family. Seeing that jerk trying to lay a hand on her while she cowered into a brick wall had also loosed something in me. Of course it had, or I wouldn't have claimed I was hers. Abandoning the mediocre conversational skills I'd rediscovered now felt like a cruel joke, even if this was dangerous territory.

"How are you? Not, about this." I shook my head, an odd fluster of feelings piling up. "Has he been back?"

She swallowed, the long, smooth line of her throat working. "No."

She gave me nothing more, and I had no right to the information, even though I wanted it. If he was bothering her, I wanted to take care of it. I'd seen no one else intervene on her behalf since I'd noticed the dynamic between them. I wanted to understand what was still linking her to him, why she would entertain him for even seconds, but again, it wasn't my right.

Nor should I want it to be.

"He's persistent, but I don't think he'll show up in person again." Her mouth quirked into a smile. "I think you scared him."

I shrugged one shoulder. "I regret nothing."

Not true.

I regretted scaring her, but the smile told me enough. My threat to him hadn't been what'd scared her as much as the whole situation.

"And Glazed? Do you love it still?"

She moved, almost flinched, at my question and leaned a shoulder against the brick wall next to us. "Of course."

This woman was passion and drive. She was loving and bold. This answer held none of those things.

"Hmm."

One brow raised. "Hmm what? You have something to say?"

I shrugged again. "I don't know you well enough to be certain, but I suspect you aren't being truthful."

She gaped at me, then after a beat said, "You are not what I expected."

Every ounce of my self-control activated in order to keep from stepping close, backing her against that wall, and lowering my lips to her ear and begging her to tell me what that meant. If I wasn't what she expected, then that meant she'd expected something. Somehow, this struck me as an incredible leap forward from not thinking of me at all.

This didn't matter in the scheme of things. She'd just made clear she didn't want a relationship, and when I was thinking logically, neither did I. The wreckage love brought with it wasn't something I wanted after witnessing my father, a man I'd loved and respected, become a useless jerk in the wake of losing my mother.

Now, the only important thing was getting through this. But it wouldn't hurt if she liked the prospect of spending time with me to some degree.

"I hope you're pleasantly surprised," I offered, sounding miraculously nonchalant. She needn't know how much I hoped we could make this work and convince my grandfather.

She laughed softly. "I don't know what I am other than a stressed-out small business owner and, apparently, your fake fiancée."

Dove Jensen's blond locks caught my eye behind Elise, and she waved. "Everything okay out here?"

I gestured for Elise to head inside, not wanting to detain her any longer. If her friend was here to check on her, that likely meant none of them trusted me with her. I didn't like this, though I respected it. Unlike the other Saint men save Stone, they didn't know me very well. And we were done, at least for now.

"I'll be in touch soon, if that's alright?" I asked.

She glanced over her shoulder. "Sounds good."

Once she was out of sight, I sent a text to Kenny notifying him I was leaving. I couldn't stand at the table and laugh at jokes and pretend my attention was on anyone but the woman who'd just slipped back inside.

I needed time to think, and I needed to call my sister back tomorrow and get her advice right before I begged her to come distract my grandfather from the unsuspecting woman inside.

This hadn't gone as terribly as I'd expected, which only spoke to Elise's generosity.

Part of me chafed at that—she shouldn't give me the time of day, let alone be asking how I was feeling about all of this. We hardly knew one another even if I felt... whatever this was for her. And yet another small part of me, perhaps the voice that'd spoken her name over the line to my grandfather in the first place... that voice was absolutely thrilled.

CHAPTER SIX

Elise

Dove's eyes grew so wide, I thought maybe her bright blue irises would pop out of her head and take flight.

"Engaged?" she whisper-hissed as though anyone would overhear us in my cramped apartment. Occasionally, my neighbors banged on the door, but they wouldn't now due to it being a level conversation in the middle of the day.

"Yes. Engaged."

Her eyes narrowed. "I knew you were being weird. The whole time after you went outside with him, I knew something was up and I should've pushed."

"You did push, but I didn't cave. I don't want anyone to know." I shifted on the couch, curling into a ball and wrapping my arms around my knees. How often had I felt this same thing? The dread and even fear that my friends would find out the truth about the real dynamic with Callum? Or the fact that Glazed was very close to floundering, and I was trying my best not to be miserable about it?

Or even, the truth about my roots—the reality that I came from a woman who used men for their bank accounts, then moved on when they were emptied. That I worried I'd end up just like her.

Dove didn't even know about the altercation outside Glazed, when Luc pinned dirtbag Callum to the wall with his forearm and called himself my boyfriend. He could've said 'her knight in shining armor' and it wouldn't have been any less true, because in that moment, that's what he was. It was just all so... unreal. And the boyfriend thing paled in comparison to the fiancé situation.

"No one would care. It's not like you said he was your fiancé. That'd be embarrassing. But this? This is like... this is like some hot Mayfair Duke dreamboat randomly selects you as his bride."

"Are you reading historical romances again?" I asked, already knowing the answer.

She fanned herself. "I will never not blush when a hero slowly removes a woman's glove. There's just nothing like it in contemporary."

"True." Though I hadn't wanted the fluttery feeling that came along with those soft, simple moments in years. It'd be nice to *want* to feel it again, but I just... didn't.

Dream about Luc in special ops agent soldier guy mode? Sure.

Relive the moment he shoved Callum into the wall in defense of *me*? Also yes, though that one was more than a little dangerous considering it had nothing to do with fantasy.

"So, okay. He told his family, we don't totally know

what that means except they're coming here and will meet you, but it sounds like... not a big deal?"

The perplexed tone in her voice spoke clearly of her confusion, which I echoed.

"He was apologetic that he got me involved but told me because they would be coming here, and he refuses to admit we aren't engaged." Saying it out loud sounded absolutely ludicrous.

She smacked the coffee table in front of her dramatically. "Wait, does this mean he's rich? Like, normal families don't make their kids marry."

My head tipped side to side. "Not super common in the US, for sure. Maybe it is in Europe, and they just don't talk about it?"

She frowned deeply. "Lame. But worse, I feel like what you're telling me is there'll be no reason to pretend you're engaged beyond meeting his family and therefore no reason for you to cozy up with gorgeous Luc and eventually have his babies."

I barked a laugh. "You know I'm not interested in having anyone's babies."

She slumped back into the couch. "Maybe that's what we should be discussing." She paused to take a sip from her water bottle, ever the faithful hydrator, then continued. "Is Callum trying to weasel his way back in?"

Shame bubbled up and popped, a sharp burst of pain in my chest. If I hadn't experienced it more than once, I might've thought I was having some kind of medical event.

But no. That was just the fallout of a relationship with Callum.

"No. It's not happening." He wanted to get back together, but I wasn't going for it again.

A crawling sensation crept over me, the discomfort of

this conversation a perfect reminder of why I didn't like talking about Callum. Even when we'd been together, I didn't tell my friends much about him. That should've been sign enough our relationship wasn't healthy. Of course, not everyone shared every detail of their dating lives, but watching the way Nikki and Winnie and then Jo and even Jess had gushed or just *had* to share how wonderful their people were... it should've registered as a warning sign when I experienced a swarm of guilt and shame and unease sharing anything about Callum, even when we were supposedly fine.

"You know, none of what happened with him is your fault, right?"

Dove's soft voice drew my attention, and a humorless laugh escaped my lips when I turned to see her brows pinched and her lips turned down with concern.

"Sure."

She grabbed my hand and squeezed, then retreated back to her own space. "I mean it. I know you hate talking about it, but I also know you have this twisted idea that because he talked you into getting back with him, it's on—"

"More than once. He talked me into it more than once. I was weak enough, despite an incredible support system, that I went back." Emotion hit instantly as I added, "Even after he'd showed me who he was and what it would be like in no uncertain terms. I still caved."

I pressed the cuffs of my sweatshirt against my eyes to absorb the tears and attempt to calm myself.

"You say that like it makes it *more* your fault, but I want you to hear me. Look at me, please."

She was soft as rising dough at times, but she had steel in her. When I gave her my eyes, reluctantly, she continued.

"You are an amazing woman who deserves to be treated

with kindness and respect. With gentleness and love. You are not at fault for how that crap heap treated you, nor are you guilty of anything but trying to love someone who wasn't right for you. That's not a crime."

Grief washed over me, and I shook my head. "Sometimes, I feel like I've dealt with all this. That it's all behind me. But then random stuff happens, and it comes right back up."

Dove inched closer. "You need a hug, right?"

My tears burst fully, and I spoke through sobs. "Of course."

I pulled her in, clinging to her, breathing through my tears that felt so all-encompassing, I grieved that, too. Eventually, I huffed out the frustration and anger and sadness and leaned back, the comforting, sweet scent of her shampoo still lingering in my nose.

"Guess I needed that," I said, chuckling as I wiped at my eyes.

"It helps." She dabbed at her own eyes with a tissue while handing me one. "And I'm not convinced it's because you haven't dealt with a lot of what you needed to. Maybe you should go to therapy again, but maybe it's just part of being human. Most of us don't fold up our feelings and tuck them in a drawer, never to see them again. We take them out and wear them around from time to time. Sometimes, we decide we hate how they feel, and we get rid of them for good. But other times, we keep them in that bottom drawer."

I grinned. "What a metaphor."

She tucked a long lock of hair behind her ear. "Thanks. I tried."

We laughed at her prim retort, and I shifted our focus. "What's the latest with everything?"

She instantly knew what I meant. "Oh, did I not tell you? We got a spot at Silverton Springs. I have like, a month to get everything ready." Her smile pulled in a way that looked strained, but her eyes held their sparkle.

"It's expensive, right?" A stupid question. Silverton Springs was a gorgeous retirement community that also had a nursing home section for when residents needed medical care, too. It was highly sought after, and Dove had been waiting over a year for a spot to open up for her grandmother.

She chuckled. "Yeah. I'm... I mean I've been working, as you know, but seeing it in reality..." She shrank a little but sniffed and perked up. "It'll be fine. It's going to be amazing and I'm so excited. But I may not sleep more than four hours for a while."

Another laugh snuck out and amazingly, it didn't sound forced. I slipped my hand into hers and squeezed, knowing she craved the contact.

"You're an amazing granddaughter. I wish I had some way to help." The inability to assist in any way—whether offering some work or giving her a loan or anything—chafed more than ever.

She patted the back of my hand and offered me a soft smile, her eyes glistening. "Thank you. I know. Maybe if you marry a duke, you can hire me as the on-call nurse." She swung part of my cream-colored throw blanket over her head and wrapped it around like a bonnet. "Or a part-time maid."

We both cackled at her ridiculousness, but my heart weighed heavy in my chest.

Before I could stop myself, something pushed me to admit something I hadn't admitted fully to myself, let alone told anyone else.

"I'm not sure I can do it again—not with Luc so much as... ever."

She eyed me, trying to catch up to where my mind had gone. "Date?"

I shook my head. "Love."

Her eyes shone with a fresh round of tears, but she simply nodded. "Well then, maybe a hot half-French fake fiancé is just the ticket."

CHAPTER SEVEN

Luc

My sister's grin was so wide, it hardly fit on the screen of my phone.

"Don't look so happy," I demanded.

"Don't look so sad. You're an almost-engaged man!" She clapped and cackled like the little she-devil she was.

"I had no idea you were so desperate for me to get engaged." The glare I sent had her sobering up after her gleeful giggles. I was more than a little uncomfortable about lying to her, and I didn't want to embellish anything I didn't have to.

"I'll have you know I've always wanted you to get married so I have a sister. And after finding my own wonderful husband, I want you to find that, too."

I sighed. "I don't think I'm interested in a wonderful husband, but thanks."

She grumbled. "Wonderful wife, in your case."

"I'm not interested in that, either, if it's someone Grand-père picks out."

To someone who didn't know anything about our family dynamic, such a statement could sound incredibly juvenile.

"Ye of little faith. Grand-père set me and Michele up." She glanced to her right and hearts jumped into her eyes as she looked at the man in question, no doubt.

"And I'm grateful to him in this one instance because he seems to have chosen a mildly decent person, but—"

A dark head of hair swooped in and pinned me with a fakely outraged expression. "*Che cosa dici, fratello? Sono magnifico!* How dare you suggest I am anything but perfect for your goddess of a sister?"

Proving himself to be as irresistibly charming as ever, I laughed and rolled my eyes. "Alright, alright. *É vero. Sei il migliore.*" *It's true. You're the best.*

I couldn't argue because Aurelie's husband *was* actually the best. Our grandfather had found this outrageously kind and loving Italian man for my sister, who also happened to be the heir to his own family's fortune and the lynchpin in a deal Grand-père had orchestrated to add a major Italian brand to the family portfolio.

Gérard Devereaux had managed to marry off his granddaughter and actually make her happy while getting exactly what he wanted. Because it'd worked with Aurelie, he seemed to believe it would work with me.

Deep down, I knew he cared about us both. He was shepherding an entire dynasty of business and wealth and familial obligation he built, and he was doing it without his son. Since my father had abdicated any business duties when my mom passed and he basically quit functioning, my grandfather's focus had shifted. The next generation naturally felt more of the weight, and Aurelie had done precisely as he'd wanted because it also happened to be what she'd wanted.

Sometimes, I wished I'd wanted the same. But I hadn't. And the shift between us, that bitter distance that'd opened wide when I'd joined the Army and doubled down on the chasm by changing my name... I wanted it bridged. As I'd gotten older, I understood more. I didn't agree with the pressure he'd put on me or his methods, but I didn't want to cling to my anger and hurt forever. So here was a chance to try and rebuild or maybe, begin something new.

Just not enough to marry someone I'd never met.

"I'm not like you, though. I've never been the grandson he wanted, and I don't see why he's trying to force the issue now, but he's made clear he is. During our original conversation, he made clear the clock was ticking." Hence my lie, and now the situation.

Aurelie had always been dutiful and taken the path expected of her, partly because she had the older sister obligation gene, and partly because she enjoyed it. I would never cease to be grateful this was the case.

I had done so many things against the wishes of my family and particularly against the patriarch. Why would he think I'd do as I was told now? When my mother passed the year I'd finished school, my ability to care about his wishes turned to ash. My American mother had always been the subject of his scorn, and at seventeen, I'd committed to continuing her legacy. His disdain and frustration fueled my revelry, and I did whatever I could to push him.

Yet even now, I wasn't simply saying no to his nonsense. He'd taken it too far—a call to heel, and I wasn't his lapdog. I answered to him, yes, but not without question. I'd made up an excuse—told a lie—rather than reject the idea of marriage entirely. He saw me as aimless and drifting outside the military, and marriage, according to him, would settle that. Settle me. I didn't need to prove myself, but I was giving him an inch with this whole engagement. It showed I had commitment in my life, direction, a purpose, even if it was all a sham for the purpose of his visit.

Granted, I had several other reasons to want to appease him in some way, but not all the way. I couldn't turn my nose up at the trust anymore—or yes, I could, but I didn't want to. That very juvenile satisfaction at shoving his wealth back in his face years ago had grown into something more fraught. As a teen, I convinced myself I couldn't have cared less. As a grown man with a solid chapter of his adult life behind him, I understood the complexity of relationships and resources. I could use the money. And in some way, I recognized the way the trust reflected the relationship with my grandfather itself.

Damn, but it was all tangled.

"Luc, sweet naïve child, Grand-père will never give up on you. He may have given you space, but I guarantee he viewed your time with the Americans as a dalliance."

"Oh, dalliance," Michele chimed, waggling his thick brows to make the word sound even more salacious.

Aurelie giggled, then continued. "He's likely expecting you to return to the fold, a prodigal come home. Since you haven't done so willingly, he'll bring you to heel via marriage."

"I've gathered as much." He'd made it clear. It wasn't as though he'd kept his motives from me.

"Is the woman he has in mind so awful?" Michele asked, his jovial tone softening. He might've been a jokester, but he wasn't uncaring.

"I don't know her. But I don't need to."

"Ah." He nodded.

Michele thought he understood me, but I doubted he ever could. His parents were still alive, still happily married. He'd grown up anticipating an arranged marriage, and had walked into it willingly. For him, it'd worked out beautifully.

He was also such a sweetheart in the most genuine sense, I would lie to them for his sake more than for Aurelie's. I didn't want Aurelie to have to lie to our grandfather, either. Keeping her from understanding the situation fully allowed her to avoid having to choose between her loyalty to him and her allegiance to me. I might've disagreed with our grandfather's machinations, but it didn't mean I felt the need to cause turmoil in Aurelie's life.

"Wait. What does that mean? You don't want to be forced into anything which is nothing new, but—"

"His heart already belongs to someone else," Michele explained as though he knew.

Aurelie gasped, her nearly black hair swishing around her face. "This girl you said you're almost engaged to is real?"

I scrubbed my hands through my hair and launched into rapid French. "She is real. She's impressive. And since he's placed this spotlight on me, I'm going to propose. I hadn't planned to do it just yet, but now I will."

This was the lie I'd use for Aurelie and Michele so they understood the newness between me and Elise. They couldn't know we'd only been dating for hours and it was fake. They couldn't know any of it except that my grandfather's plan had accelerated the timeline.

Aurelie exhaled a giant breath. "I can see why you're concerned. Is it too soon? Should you consider meeting Grand-père's woman and—"

"It's not too soon." Inwardly, I cringed, but outwardly, I simply nodded. "It would've happened, just not *now*. So I need your help to keep the meeting simple so she doesn't feel bad about the timing, or even better, I'd like to avoid it altogether. And *that* is why I'm calling you. I need your help."

I spent the next few minutes working to convince my sister and her husband to intercede with our grandfather on my behalf—to charm him the way she always managed to and induce him to let me come visit in a month or so when my schedule was clear. I could excuse Elise's absence with her devotion to Glazed, and he'd have to respect her entrepreneurial spirit because he had some himself.

Aurelie burst out laughing. "You realize now that you're engaged, there's no way he's not coming?"

It didn't come as a surprise. Of course I knew this, even if I'd hoped she might have insight or some magical avenue I hadn't thought of that would halt all of this in its tracks. "Oui. I know."

Before we hung up, she promised to try and do what she could, which was all anyone could do, wasn't it?

And the next morning, she confirmed what I'd suspected all along. There would be no avoiding a visit from Gérard Devereaux. But she delivered worse news—he'd decided to come to the gala in three weeks *and* bring the woman he expected me to marry, despite my claiming to be nearly engaged to someone else.

We wouldn't manage a quick meet and greet. This had all just become a great deal more complicated.

So. Time to see Elise.

CHAPTER EIGHT

Elise

Luc entered the shop at his usual time on Tuesday morning. I didn't actually see him come in because, thank goodness, two people stood in line ahead of him.

I just... knew it was him.

Sure, sure. Not normal to have a radar for a man like him. Too pretty, too appealing, and evidently, too much of a liar.

Because honestly, who told their family they were engaged to someone they'd barely spoken to?

Our conversation last Friday had been the longest interaction we'd ever had several times over, and the second place went to a few days prior when he'd threatened Callum on my behalf. Any other moments between us had been just that—moments built from seconds, not minutes.

Yes, he came into Glazed for donuts and sat for a little while to eat a few times a week. But we didn't talk. He ordered, usually using my name once and as few other words as possible. If I hadn't seen him talking and laughing at Craic during happy hour, I would've thought he was shy based on how he behaved with me.

I filled a wax-coated paper sack with Dr. Daniels's order and handed it to her across the counter. "Have a great day, Doctor. Thanks for confirming donuts are not bad for our health." I winked at her—the joke tired by now, but why stop?

A smile brightened her already lovely face. "Every now and then isn't a problem. Moderation isn't just an old wives' tale."

"See you next week," I said, and she laughed.

"I hear you calling me out. That's just fine, Elise Cordero. I know where you live."

She waved as she exited and left me with the next customer. I heroically did not look past this person to get a glimpse of Luc.

The desire to do so gripped me, but I avoided it. My next patron ordered, and I happily filled a box with a dozen donuts, then said goodbye, keeping my eyes on him as he left and not the man now standing directly in front of me.

When I couldn't justify not looking at him any longer, I met his gaze.

"Hello, Luc."

His lips twitched, which I did not take note of because I was not looking at his lips. Nay, I was hardly seeing their surprisingly soft-looking shape. I wasn't noticing the way his bottom lip was a bit fuller than his top one, and how his scruff for today seemed a touch longer than usual, high-lighting said unignorable lips.

"I apologize for taking a few days. I would've called or texted, but I don't have your number."

His gorgeous gray-green eyes didn't stray from mine and therefore, he held me captive. "Okay."

"Unfortunately, I'd hoped to dissuade my family from visiting so you wouldn't have to deal with this mess—this lie I've told—at all."

This lie he emphasized as though I might not know what he meant.

Oh, yeah that. I practically forgot about the whole thing.

"But?" I prompted, needing him to get to whatever bad news I could see written on his handsome face.

"They are coming. And I—"

"Hey, sorry man, can I just grab a quick half dozen?" John Wallace jogged in, apologizing to Luc as he stepped up to the counter.

"What's the urgency?" I asked, glad to see my old friend, and frankly, a little relieved to interrupt whatever Luc had been about to say. I didn't know why he made me so jittery and self-aware, but having someone else here gave me a moment to breathe.

"It's kind of an anniversary for me and Dahlia. I brought her donuts when we were just starting out—when *you* were just starting out, too, and—well, anyway, it's a good day to take a little walk down memory lane." He smiled and gave me his order.

While I slipped the six donuts into a box, warmth suffused me at the memory. "I remember you ordering them. I was still using the old boxes and twine, right?"

It'd been when I was running the shop part-time for special orders only. I'd do ordering ahead and deliver on certain days, working out the proof of concept and building the addiction to the donuts, so by the time I opened, everyone would desperately need them regularly.

Or so I'd hoped.

People like John and Dr. Daniels and so many other locals kept me in business.

Luc wandered to a table, so by the time I finished with John and wished him luck, I'd regained my equilibrium. I grabbed a glazed donut and took a seat across from him, sliding the pillowy sweet delight his way.

"Merci."

It shouldn't have charmed me or sent my pulse racing to hear such a basic word in his native tongue, but it did. Call me a simple woman, but hearing this man speak French gave me a weird thrill. It reminded me I didn't know him— he wasn't from here. In fact, he had likely lived at least part of his life in Europe. A vastly different experience than mine, and that was before we ever touched his military service or the fact that he seemed to have a sibling and living grandparents.

Cut to a ship where a version of Luc is wearing a billowy pirate's blouse open at the chest. Maybe he's got an earring and hair is long, pulled back in a queue because it would definitely be called that and not a braid in this period piece. He's holding a swooning woman in one arm, her bosom heaving, and he's whispering French into the curve of her neck, her collar bone, her breast—

Nope. No. Vivid and not a terrible casting, but simply not acceptable territory just now.

"You were saying something before John interrupted," I said, not sure how to clear my mind of the fog foisted upon it by his single utterance of French.

Goodness help me if he were to actually speak it to me for more than a second. I'd probably expire on the spot.

"Yes. So. I have a proposal for you."

I chuckled, smiling at his joke.

But he wasn't smiling.

"Oh, not a pun, then?"

One side of his mouth pulled up. "A missed opportunity I hope you'll forgive me for. But, no." The intensity of his gaze settled into mine, and he leaned his forearms, beautifully displayed thanks to the rolled cuffs of his blue and gray plaid shirt, against the table. "I would like you to consider being my fiancée for a while. A temporary arrangement."

I opened my mouth to speak but promptly shut it when it received the *we have no idea what to say* message from the rest of me.

"It's unconventional, I know. I wouldn't want you to feel like you were lying, so my hope is that we would embrace the temporary but real nature of the agreement, without being personally invested or serious."

"I'm not sure I'm following." Read: was definitely *not* following.

He shifted forward in his chair, straightening his already perfect posture like he was preparing for a presentation. "I propose that you become my temporary fiancée. In name, yes, but also with the idea that we behave as an engaged couple—or, while perhaps without the affections of a real relationship, but with the protection, the care, and the fidelity of one. All outward signs of engagement. And yet, of course, it'll be fake. No real feelings, no actual commitments beyond the parameters of our agreement. Nothing serious."

His words plunked down against my skull and slowly seeped in like rain on a parched landscape. The initial resistance I felt to being his *actual* fiancée was already ebbing, a curiosity for what exactly this would look like rapidly taking root. This would be pretend. Not reality. Entirely fake. Make believe, even.

"So you don't want to kiss me, but you want to beat up my ex-boyfriend?" I asked, wishing he'd state it clearly.

He coughed and cleared his throat. "For the purposes of this discussion, that is an exaggeration, but not inaccurate. My point is, we would be faithful. In appearances, we would be affianced. I have no desire for anything serious in real life, but that wouldn't matter in this context. And I would"—he cleared his throat again—"forgive me, I would make it worth your while."

Cue the record scratch and halt all softening to the subject. "How so?"

"We could agree on an amount that seems fair. I'm happy to pay you for your time as we go, or in lump sums at the beginning and end. We can even—"

"Can I ask you why you'd suggest paying me for something that seems like a favor?" My cheeks flamed, and the pit in my stomach opened wide, wide, wide.

He couldn't know how I was scraping by right now, could he? I hadn't complained about my finances with friends or anyone. It was a point of pride, admittedly to a fault, that I didn't talk about money with people. When you grew up with a woman who jumped from one man to another following the gravy train, you learned what desperation looked like. I wanted nothing to do with it.

The fact that I'd let Callum into anything regarding money, let alone this business, was the last vestige of pain I felt about our relationship. And this... this with Luc just wouldn't work.

Before he could speak, I stood and thanked God for a customer approaching the door. I practically ran toward the counter as the bell rang, cutting off whatever Luc might've said, and my need to halt the shame spiraling through my chest. Shame and an unreasonable amount of anger, though I couldn't be sure who it was for.

CHAPTER NINE

Luc

Well, that went perfectly, and now I had to get to work.

As soon as one person exited, two more slipped in. Elise was buried behind a line of people eager for her donuts. I stepped up to the glass case and waited for her gaze to land on mine.

No chance at reading her expression, I mouthed, "Later," and she nodded an "okay." I hoped it genuinely was. Her upset at my suggestion had been rather unexpected.

Two minutes later, Kenny caught me as I was mounting the steps at the front of the Saint building.

"How'd it go?" he asked, clapping me on the back in his affectionate way.

"Poorly."

He startled. "Really?"

I scowled at him, evidently channeling Beast. Speaking

of, the giant of a man plodded down the hallway with a mug of steaming coffee and slowed to greet us as we passed Reception.

"How's our baby?" Kenny asked him, plucky as all get out and grating on my nerves.

I didn't normally struggle with his cheery nature because I knew, lately better than ever, what a genuine person he was underneath it all. He chose joy even when it didn't get served up to him naturally, and I admired it.

But my jaw had locked tight when Elise's cheeks had burst into flame and her eyes cast down. My gut had dropped into the ground as I'd read the broadcast she sent out with her shoulders curving in just like they used to do around her awful ex.

Shame. Embarrassment.

And I'd been the cause.

Stupid!

"*My* baby seems to be perfect. And my wife is, too." Jude's face softened. "She's starting back next week if the rest of this week goes well."

"Heck yeah!" Kenny held up a high five and Beast begrudgingly slapped it. Then he held it up in my direction, and I met his with my own hand with zero enthusiasm.

"Even when you're grumpy you'll show up for me." He looped an arm around my shoulder and pulled me in like he might give me a noogie, then waltzed us toward the break room. "Let's get you some caffeine."

Allowing him to guide me down the hallway and past Adam, who gave us a chin lift, and Bruce, who raised one brow at Kenny's steering embrace as he spoke into a cell phone, we arrived at the well-equipped break room in less than a minute.

Kenny reached for two mugs and poured coffee into

them, then doctored his, and left mine black. He delivered the mug to the table in front of me and sat.

"Tell Ken-Ken."

I groaned, then laughed. "I love you, man, but Ken-Ken is not happening."

He chuckled, shrugging a shoulder. "Made you lighten up a bit, though, didn't it?"

"True enough. Let's go."

He stood and waved a hand, signaling I should start talking as we walked back toward our offices.

"I told her we should be engaged but temporarily. That we should act in a way fiancés would minus the emotional involvement, but including protection, care, etc. because she has a dirtbag ex who she might need help looking out for. And I mentioned I could compensate her."

Kenny's eager, bright blue eyes shut in slow motion and he cringed. "Well, there you go."

I waited for more, but he didn't elaborate. "There I go what? How do I go? What is so obvious?"

The look he gave me was all disappointment. "You embarrassed her."

"How is this embarrassing for her? *I'm* the one who lied and is now coercing her into doing something for me because I acted like a child in order to avoid having my trust taken away again, and still can't bring myself to deal with my family any other way." The edge in my voice was unusual as I tended to be fairly level-headed, but Elise's reaction had unsettled me.

"*Au contraire, mon frère*, which, can I just say, is so much more fun to say to *you* in particular?"

I glared at him.

He huffed and leaned against the edge of my desk now that we'd entered my office. "Point is, you're wrong and I can't emphasize this enough. Just... completely wrong. So wrong it's amazing you—"

"Please. For the love of everything good in this world, please just spit it out."

When I looked up again, the little turd was grinning. He crossed one ankle over the other and replicated the movement with his arms. "I don't know Elise super well, but I've observed her enough to know she's strong and proud and works hard for what she has. She's survived the jerk of an ex, and you offering to pay her to essentially exist *can't* have gone over well. Even if she doesn't realize you're basically a European prince—"

"I am not a prince, and—"

"Like I said, *practically* a French royal—"

"I am *not* royalty. My family is—"

"Nearly a direct descendent of the Sun King himself..."

He trailed off and waited for me to react, but I'd known the little twerp long enough to be sure it'd only escalate.

He flashed his brows up and down, doofy smile still in place.

"No," I sighed. "I am not in fact related to Louis the Fourteenth."

He sniffed and glanced at his nails as though they were perfectly manicured and not just neatly trimmed. "Well then why are we even here?"

"If you weren't nearly engaged to a CIA agent, I would consider plotting your accidental demise."

He cackled, throwing his head back with all the careless ease of a man who'd found the woman he loved and gotten everything he wanted—or was well on his way. He deserved every bit of it, too. But right now, he might just find himself at the wrong end of something sharp if he didn't get it together.

"Okay, okay. I see it. I get it. You need me to focus, and I will." He unfolded himself and paced toward me where I'd stopped near the doorway. "You gotta go be honest with her. Not the formal, fancy version of honest, but the uncomfy one. The 'I have a weird dynamic with my Grandpappy and need to placate him somehow but I don't want to marry someone I hardly know, so I'm begging you to let me be your fake boo and dupe him, and because I know that may be horrendous as I am horrible-looking and rude and generally smell like garbage covered with Axe Body Spray, I want to fairly compensate you for your time under duress.'"

I turned and walked out.

"Hey! That was good advice!" he whined, trotting after me.

I kept going, straight into the conference room because he'd babbled for long enough—our meeting was starting.

Bruce had organized the schedule for the next two weeks and presented a tentative task matrix for the duties surrounding the Silver Ridge Charity Gala coming up soon. This event brought hundreds of visitors, and among those would be celebrities who needed protection. Sometimes, the local PD would contract with Saint to help with events like this, too, though it sounded like so far we didn't have any of those obligations. All of this proved to be a great distraction from Kenny's irritating—but possibly good—advice, and the fact that my family intended to accept their invite to this very event.

After seeing my assignment, my mind dragged me back to Glazed, and I worried over what to say and how to make things right with Elise. I didn't know her well enough to gauge how upset she was, but it felt like ants under my skin knowing I'd upset her at all.

Was it pathetic how this ate at me, knowing she

might've been insulted by what I'd said? She couldn't fully understand how much her wellbeing mattered already because it didn't make sense. Of course it didn't. But I liked her, and it certainly didn't help my ability to swallow the fact that I'd hurt her.

As soon as my lunch break came, I'd head back there. If she was already gone for the day, I'd figure something out. I needed to make sure she was okay. Make sure she was good. Happy.

And worse, but perhaps most pressing, I needed her to agree to be my fiancée.

CHAPTER TEN

Elise

A knock on Glazed's front door pulled my attention from my task. I'd been sealing fifteen boxes full of donuts with Glazed stickers starring my smiley pink glazed donut mascot.

My pulse raced.

I'd kept busy for the last few hours, first with customers, then closing up, then working on the special order someone had made for the PTA meeting this afternoon at the elementary school. My brain had been grabbing at Luc's words and expression—searching through every second of our time together to suss out his intentions, but nothing worked.

As I walked toward the door and flipped the lock, I promised myself I'd stay calm and hear him out. I wouldn't assume he was lying to me or keeping things from me. I wouldn't assume he'd use whatever I said against me later.

I wouldn't assume he was just like Callum.

"Do you have a few minutes?" he asked, his eyes downright soulful as they inspected my apron and a large smear of frosting stretching from one side of my chest to the other.

Not my finest work, but the edge of the industrial mixer had been coated when I leaned in—it didn't matter. I was a mess and in some ways that made me feel better. There was no pretending I had it all together. If he had somehow detected I was financially stressed, then... so be it.

"Sure."

I tipped my head to the side and turned back toward the kitchen. A small swell of pride burst as we entered the space where the three stacks of five boxes each full of a dozen donuts waited for me to finish. They looked beautiful, and inside, the donuts were fresh and delicious. These would reach new clients who didn't have time to come downtown in the mornings, and maybe they'd set up a standing order for their PTA meetings.

Note to self: find a way to suggest this as a recurring arrangement.

"These look beautiful. That's a lot of donuts." He kept his hands tucked into his pockets but his eyes traveled over the neat stacks.

"One hundred and eighty. All glazed and ready to go." I moved to the sink to wash my hands, then dried them so I could finish the task of sealing the boxes. He simply watched in silence.

Ugh, this man. He was naturally quiet and yet he sent my blood pumping. He smelled so good and clean, he was still too gorgeous to look directly in the eye, and he was driving me insane with his quiet company.

He's a fantasy.

I shouldn't forget this.

A low rumbling sound filled the space, and my jaw dropped as I looked over to see him press a hand to his stomach.

"Was that you?"

His grave countenance and wide eyes spoke of how uncomfortable he felt. "I am so sorry."

I laughed and reached for one of the remainders on a rack. "Here. You need lunch, but we need to talk, so how about you eat this and then you can go drown yourself in protein shakes or whatever you do to stay so fit."

Ope. Yeah. So. *Way to be obvious.*

One of his dark brows arched. "Drown myself in protein shakes? What about me eating your donuts several times a week gives you the impression I like protein shakes?"

The hint of a smile at the corner of his mouth was, let's be honest, a little alarming. Because there was confidence in that expression, and he'd relaxed in the wake of his post-tummy-rumble mortification.

I flicked a hand like my comment meant nothing. "I'm just saying, some of us eat donuts regularly and it shows, and for some of us, it doesn't." I cheekily glanced down at my body, then over to him, promptly shifting so my back was to him, busying myself with the delivery bags a second later.

His voice dropped low when he said, "Please tell me you're not suggesting you are anything less than exquisite."

A jolt of surprise stopped me, and I turned to see his face somber and almost... well, if I had to guess, I'd say almost upset.

I rushed to clarify. "I... I mean I'm not sure I'd say I'm *exquisite* but thank you for that. I mostly just mean you look like you're about to audition for the next Superman movie."

Mmkay and had I imagined such a thing? Yes. He'd look great in the suit and basically already fought crime like a boss. But...

An awkwardness descended and coated me in regret. I didn't particularly struggle with body image—or I didn't used to. I'd realized what a blessing it was to own the way I was made and the changes that'd occurred over my thirty-four years on the planet, but the knot in my stomach now was real. I'd gotten into the habit of putting myself down in front of Callum as a way to build him up—a pattern I'd adopted after being on the receiving end of his negativity and insults. And my throwaway joke felt a little too close to the habit I'd worked to forget.

Luc had spotted it instantly.

He shook his head slowly. "I'm paid to stay in shape, so I do. I also have decent genes, based on how my parents aged. But I don't live for working out or anything like some of the guys do. It's an important part of my life and has been for a long time, as is feeding myself, but I find I struggle to enjoy the food that fuels me best."

My eyes narrowed on him. "And so you come here for a fix a few times a week."

His mouth pulled into a smile. "Yes. You and Stone tend to be my suppliers for my sweet tooth."

I laughed, enjoying that this man who, rumor had it, had been an actual model at some point in his adult life, had a sweet tooth.

And then it hit me. *Cookie.*

"Wait, is your nickname related to food preference?" I slid one stack of boxes into a bag, then another.

He huffed but it sounded good-humored. "Yes. I love most sweet things, but cookies are my true weakness. And when people in assessment and selection for EMU way back when figured that out, I had my name."

I bit my lip, trying to hold back a true laugh. The idea that this stunningly hot, muscular, half-French man ended up with the nickname Cookie because *he likes cookies* was just too adorable.

He waved a hand between us. "It's alright. Go ahead and laugh. I embrace it and I'll be happy to see your smile."

The laugh that would've shot out with his permission got caught in my throat as his words registered, and yet again I was left with a fuzzy, warm, and imminently alarming feeling. With a rough clearing of my throat, I grabbed the last stack of boxes and slid them into a bag.

"I need to get these delivered soon," I said, unsure what to do with him or myself or anything.

"I apologize for interrupting. I wanted to ask if I could take you to lunch or dinner sometime soon. We could nail down what this would look like more specifically. The obvious caveat here is that if you don't want to be involved, please say the word and I'll forget about all of it."

He stayed rooted to the spot where he stood, hands tucked into his pockets.

This was a slightly odd posture because I could've sworn I'd noticed him being a fairly handsy talker. When I'd caught him joking or laughing with Kenny and Beast or even working, he used his hands in an interesting way. But any interaction we'd had thus far, they'd been tucked neatly away.

"I'm still willing. But I won't take money for it. I'm not —I don't need—"

He held up his large hand—good confirmation they weren't actually stapled into his pockets.

"I'm sorry I suggested you needed money. You deserve

compensation of some kind for dealing with this situation, which is genuinely an imposition on you. I know you don't have time right now, but I can lay out more fully what it'll involve—again, if you're comfortable—and it will take time. So if you won't accept payment in a financial sense, maybe we can figure out a way this will be beneficial for you."

Something in there gave me pause and sparked a realization. "Now that I think about it, Callum seemed to shrink when you said you were my boyfriend. You being my fiancé might deter him even more. That's good for me."

I'd get him off my back, giving me space to breathe and figure out a way to move on ahead, and so I could face his threat to sell Glazed head-on. His stake in the business should've been paid back over time. If he was dead set on pressing this issue, I'd figure it out and remove any ability to pressure me or even pretend he had a hold over me. Get him out of my life as soon as possible.

I crossed my arms over my chest and eyed him, the uptick in my pulse easing off as I decided he looked earnest. He never seemed to be deceitful on purpose, but I couldn't ignore the context of this whole situation being rooted in deceiving his family. Then again, we'd both be lying in this situation. Pot, meet kettle.

"So you're thinking there'll be some public appearances? That kind of thing?" I asked, shrugging off this sleazy feel of using someone for my gain. Though it would be mutually beneficial here, not me being a parasite. I could take another minute and get some answers about how this would work. If I didn't, I'd end up driving myself crazy thinking through it tomorrow.

"Yes. At least two from what I can tell based on their schedule, but likely a few more. And before then, if we intend to make it convincing, we'll need to get to know each other a bit better."

"Okay. That makes sense." I wasn't clear on exactly when or how this would happen, but I could do this. Having a fake fiancé for a while would drive home my unavailable status for Callum, even if it only lasted a few weeks. It'd make clear I'd moved on and maybe he wouldn't have to know when we stopped spending time together.

Plus, I liked the idea of getting out of my own head and thinking about something else—some*one* else—besides myself and my business. It'd be a nice distraction from my work-focused reality, and also, Luc needed help. My help. I could grant it, and it wouldn't really put me out, so why not do it?

"Good. Then I'll text you to make our next plan, and in the meantime..." he said, his voice low and eyes that cool gray-green and the shadowy scruff on his cheeks looking just rough enough to scrape against skin in a delicious way, "...think of some way I can make this up to you."

"You playing my boyfriend is enough."

"Fiancé," he corrected.

I swallowed hard and nodded, a kaleidoscope of images flashing through my mind in a crush so vivid and stunning, I nearly choked. Luc's large hand cupping my face, Luc's soft lips on my neck, Luc's smooth voice whispering words into my skin in a language I couldn't understand...

Whoa. No.

That was not the kind of fantasy this would be. It simply couldn't be.

His brow furrowed like he might ask what was wrong, so I quickly turned and grabbed the bags for delivery. I would not explain how I'd just had an attack of fantastical physical interactions between us, as though my brain was suggesting that's how he could *make this up to me*.

No. *Just no, brain.*

I would do this for Luc to get Callum off my back, to get myself out of the funk I'd been in, to avoid stewing in my worry about the business, and to help a nice person. It would be a purely fictional pairing with this lovely man, a person I'd never partner with left to my own devices, and it would be a distraction. Maybe a little fun. Like living in a live-action romance book or something. Nothing else.

Period.

CHAPTER ELEVEN

Luc

E lise agreed to meet for dinner that evening.

I'd expected a longer wait, but was relieved to see her suggestion. We didn't know each other, and if we were really going to convince my grandfather I was in love with her enough to propose, and not simply in reaction to his desire to marry me off to an advantageous match and avoid losing the trust, we'd need time to do it.

Kenny had checked in about ten times this evening as though anything would've happened between getting home from work and changing into jeans and a fresh button-up. It wasn't fancy, but living in a resort mountain town in the West meant few things were.

I arrived early out of habit and with a touch of nerves, and paced along the sidewalk in front of Guac.

"Hey, sorry I'm late," Elise said as she came to a stop next to me, not quite looking me in the eyes.

I'd noticed she did this—didn't give me her full gaze and sometimes seemed like she was looking past me.

"You're right on time." I held out a hand to gesture her forward. "Shall we?"

Her hair swished as she turned, and I admired the curves of her body as she went, until I realized I probably shouldn't be doing so. I didn't want to stand here objectifying her or making her feel like an accessory. Yes, her jeans fit her perfectly, and she had on a dark top that tucked into her waist then flared out at her hips. No heels tipped her taller—she wore sneakers. Casual and comfortable.

The absence of pretense constantly refreshed me when it came to Elise. I'd had too many instances of women wanting me for my family's money when I was younger, and for my appearance once I joined the military. In either case, I hated it.

I didn't want to spend time with someone who wouldn't let me know them. Perhaps this was the height of hypocrisy considering I'd lied about my last name to my closest friends for years, and yet, they knew me. They knew the fabric of me, and I knew them. That mattered.

Elise didn't want me for any reason. She seemed to be only lightly interested in humoring this whole set up, for which I was grateful. The irony of wanting to create this ruse with someone who had no real interest in me wasn't lost on me, but I couldn't begrudge her anything.

It didn't keep me from forcing my hands to stay in my pockets instead of guiding her at the small of her back inside the restaurant, nor did it stay the pace of my heartbeat when I caught the soft hint of her perfume.

The reality here was simple. I'd been moved by something in Elise Cordero since the first time I set eyes on her well over a year ago, and in this moment, I saw the potential. A longing began to unfurl.

To know her. To touch her. To be with her. To be hers.

I'd never experienced such a desire, and in response to the inkling, I crushed it soundly. She'd made clear she wanted nothing to do with men—a statement which I'd heard in several variations countless times in the last year, and now to my face. Add to that my own reluctance to invite desolation by way of heartbreak into my life. It simply made no sense.

I didn't want to become my father, who'd hardly been able to function since my mother passed.

Still, my reaction to Elise was unlike anything I'd ever felt and had locked me up tight, jumbling the words I would've spoken to charm her, or the ways I might've attempted to impress her when I did encounter her. All of my usual calm and charm evaporated completely within a ten-foot radius of her.

Somehow, breaking the seal of communication between us had forced me out of that odd, futile place and into a more self-possessed existence. Maybe because before she seemed like an impossibility, and now she most certainly was. If she agreed to this, it'd be fake. If she refused, she'd probably dislike me haunting her store three mornings a week. Nothing had to change, though—we'd just go on like we had been, as dreadful as that sounded.

And yet, here we were, sliding into the bright red booth at Guac, knees brushing under the table, and ready to share a meal.

She stared at her menu for a moment, then took a big breath and pressed her hands flat against the plastic surface before leveling me with her dark gaze.

"Let's order, and then I need you to tell me everything

before we get caught up in something else. I want to work out all the details and talk through your concerns and I'll tell you mine so when I walk out of here packed with chips and guacamole and queso, I am also completely sure of what this looks like moving forward."

We couldn't have agreed more. Maybe not the chips and guacamole and queso part, but still. "Yes, please."

A smile cracked. "Good. But first, I do need to eat a little because I forgot to have lunch."

Ten minutes later, we had each helped ourselves to chips and salsa and placed our orders. I'd asked for a beer and, as though my ordering something other than water gave her permission, she tacked on a margarita.

She shoveled a few more chips with salsa, then sank back into the booth. "Okay, that took the edge off."

The waiter delivered our drinks and a large molcajete full of guacamole. I held my beer out to her and she grinned, touching the margarita glass to the neck of my bottle.

"To you, for showing up even though you didn't want to."

She laughed and shook her head, but took a sip of her drink, so I did the same.

"Alright. I need a little more than just that we'll meet the family together. I'm guessing you want to act like a couple, right? Like, we're showing up already engaged?"

I nodded. "Yes. I told my grandfather I was about to get engaged so it won't seem out of place that's done. I'll get you a ring because he won't believe it otherwise. He's insisting on bringing the woman he had in mind for me." I took another sip of my beer, nerves bubbling up with the next thought. "We'll need to be convincing."

She crunched on a chip holding a heap of guacamole

and chewed, but bobbed her head up and down like this statement didn't scare her away.

Dieu merci.

"I figured. But, can I ask why you won't tell him the truth? I don't mean to sound like I'm judging you for this because I know families can get weird, I just... I want to understand why you'd push through this with someone who is nearly a stranger, rather than be upfront with him." Her dark brows pinched together, and the concern in her voice rang clear.

Her question might've been something I'd prefer to brush off, but she wanted to understand, and if she was actually going to do this, she deserved to.

Plus, a not-small part of me wanted her to know I wasn't merely lying for lying's sake. I wasn't a habitual deceiver, and this was an unusual situation. I'd talked through some of this with Kenny and Stone, but she deserved the details if she was going to do this.

"My grandfather is an exacting person. He's hard-working and not cruel, but he does expect people around him to toe the line. He wants obedience and loyalty, and I have not given that to him in years." I took a breath, then a drink before continuing, unsure of how she'd feel about this next part.

"You know I'm not judging you for any of this, right? I mean, I know people say that—*no judgment*—and it's basically impossible. So I can't say I won't *ever* judge you in some way, but I'm not currently making a list of your failures. I'm not looking for choices you've made that are wrong and tallying them up. I don't want you to think that."

A pang of something brutal sank between my ribs at her tone and the gentleness in her eyes. How did anyone meet her gaze and not instantly stumble?

This was a rare quality—this genuine desire to hear and understand someone without instantly evaluating them. Her impulse to reassure me she wasn't seeing what I viewed as personal failures in the same way was nothing short of generous, to say the least.

I took another swallow of my beer. "Thank you. In that spirit of not judging too harshly, I'll tell you that I graduated from *lycée* at seventeen and staged my first rebellion. My mother had just died and my father disappeared into his grief."

"I'm so sorry, Luc," she said, stretching out a hand toward me before retreating.

The show of empathy brushed against me, alluring and innervating.

With a nod to acknowledge her words, I continued, knowing if I stopped for long, I'd struggle all the more to finish. "All my growing up years, my grandfather's expectations were clear. We would graduate at the top of our classes, then go to school in the UK or one of a few select prestigious schools in the US, and perhaps tack on a master's degree, and then come home to France and begin working in the family business. Soon after, we would marry someone advantageous from a list of possible people and from there, live out our days representing and furthering the family name."

"Sounds inflexible."

"Very. And I had planned to do as asked, but after my mother died, it all seemed so ridiculous. My father, after a brief period of depressive mourning, had launched off, constantly traveling for months at a time and sailing around the world. Doing outrageous things only super wealthy people did to keep him distracted from the reality that my mother was gone and my grandfather had no sympathy for it. He'd always hated her and hated that my father had chosen a poor American waitress when they met."

My heart ached saying the words aloud, as though giving voice to them made them matter. As though her job or financial status had anything to do with her value as a human being.

The waiter delivered our plates of food—her chimichanga slathered in queso sauce and my fajitas—and we both picked up our forks. She dug in, and I assembled my first fajita as I continued.

"So in the infinite wisdom of a bitter seventeen-year-old, I went a little wild. I partied and burnt money as fast as I could light it on fire in the dumbest ways, and then, once that only slightly ruffled my grandfather, who seemed to see it as a fleeting phase he could wait out, I flew to Japan and spent a year modeling there."

Elise coughed right as she was swallowing a gulp of her margarita and slapped a hand over her mouth. After a moment, she managed to get it down and dabbed a napkin across her lips.

"Sorry. I—" She cleared her throat and laughed behind her hand.

"My modeling is that hilarious?" I joked.

Her eyes fluttered shut and only then did I notice the trace of a blush rising to her cheeks. I straightened, deeply curious what was going on in her head.

"No. It's honestly not a surprise at all, other than maybe why you didn't make it a whole career. I just... there had been rumors you were a model. But you obviously look like that..." She waved her hand in my direction and her eyes darted around my face. "So. Yeah. Now I know they're legit."

I shifted in my seat, trying to identify why she wouldn't

look me in the eye now, and suppressed a grin. Call me a fool for enjoying that this woman found me attractive, but with as opaque as she was, at least there was that. I likely wouldn't have enjoyed anyone else being frazzled by my appearance, but for some reason, knowing Elise wasn't entirely immune to me gave me... hope.

What an odd thought.

Still, there it was. A tiny ember.

No idea what it was hope *for*, but I found myself cradling it close just the same.

CHAPTER TWELVE

Elise

My brain ran at a sprinter's pace.

I just told him how hot he is and of course he knows this but now I've made it incredibly awkward and obvious just how gorgeous I think he is and that's fiiiiine. It's cool, cool, cool, cool, cool.

His gaze rested on me, but I didn't dare look up and let him see the full blaze of my blush, so I kept my eyes on my food and hoped he'd continue.

Mercifully, he did.

"They are legitimate. It was an odd time in my life, but that didn't seem to faze my grandfather either. At that age, all I wanted was for him to acknowledge I had agency and should get to choose, but he'd simply say it was a passing fancy and I'd change my ways soon enough. Then I did something more drastic—leaning into my half-American heritage my grandfather disdained and, even better, joining the American military. He froze the trust that contains a fairly large sum of money I should've received at twenty-five and made it so I couldn't access it until I was out of the military. That time has come... and he's moving the goal post again. It never bothered me because I had no use for that kind of money."

I froze after crunching my latest guac-smothered chip. He laughed softly, this charming little wisp of air and flash of teeth, and shook his head.

"I was a petulant child and..." He looked down and tucked some grilled vegetables into the tortilla he'd been slowly filling, lines bracketing his mouth with his frown. "I'm afraid I've put you in this position because I still am sometimes. At the same time, I finally know how I'd use the money in the trust. I want to help Saint Security expand. We have a great investor now, but I'd love to shift that to someone who's employed there. I'd—all those details don't matter. The point is, I'm hoping this will appease him enough to stop him from dissolving the trust."

I swallowed my bite and studied him. Why did his admission that he'd been acting a fool about all this make me like him more? Even the knowledge that he wanted to help expand Saint brought me joy because so many great people worked there. Some of my very favorite people, in fact.

"No one is immune to family dynamics. I'm surrounded by people who have these beautiful, loving relationships with at least one member of their family, and I—" My lips snapped closed when I realized what a personal truth I'd almost offered him right on a platter with a side of rice and beans.

He gave me a few seconds to recover, each of us eating

our dinner with distant sounds of piped in mariachi music and the hum of other diners filling the space between us.

"You don't have to finish whatever thought you started, but if you want to, I'd like to know." His quicksilver eyes flickered back and forth between mine. "I'm under no illusion you're perfect because no one is. But I admire and respect you, what I know of you, and I hope you'll feel safe to tell me whatever you want."

The emotion attempting to leak from my tear ducts came down to exhaustion. And maybe the overwhelm of being a business owner in a niche market in a resort town with heavy seasonal market shifts.

Maybe it also had something to do with this man being so forthright with me about his own failings and welcoming me to be human.

"You're so sure I'm not perfect?" I asked, deflecting and hoping the tease would help me inch away from the ache at my jaw that signaled a potential onslaught of tears.

He flashed a grin before sobering. "I'm certain. And I'm glad. I could never be fake-engaged to someone perfect."

After another bite, during which I summoned both calm and bravery, I set down my fork. "I was going to say I'm not close to mine. My mom follows her heart on a whim and is currently married to husband number six. They live in Florida, and we talk maybe once a month."

I wouldn't explain everything there—the reasons why we don't talk more or why I couldn't stomach being around her when she was married or recently divorced or looking for someone new—so basically ever.

"I'm only close to my sister, whom you'll meet. She just confirmed she and her husband will be coming into town the day after my grandfather arrives."

"I'm glad I'll get to meet her. On that note, you just said fake fiancée, but the other day you said you wanted it to be real for all intents and purposes. I think I know what you mean by that—you want it to look real to everyone. That'll help the Callum situation, too. But... are you thinking we'll tell people?"

His shoulders rose and fell with a big breath. "I defer to you on this. I understand if you're not comfortable telling others. Perhaps you tell your close friends what's really happening, and everyone else will believe we're engaged as will, we hope, your ex."

"Tell them it's fake?"

He nodded. "You tell your friends I've been an impulsive child and lied to my grandfather and you are the kind soul helping me navigate the mess of my own making."

I chuckled, appreciating his self-deprecation even if it was a bit much. "I'm not sure all of that is necessary, but I would prefer to tell my friends. They won't say anything to Callum, for sure, and otherwise, I'm not sure who'd notice. And you can let me know if you'll be telling yours or—"

"Fair warning. I have already told Kenny and Stone."

My lips twitched. "I can only imagine what Kenny said."

His eyes shut slowly, Luc's flair for the dramatic hilarious. "You can imagine. And after tonight, assuming you're comfortable with the way forward, I'm sure he'll let you know how he feels about it."

I giggled at the thought of what Kenny Carmichael would say. The man was the most excitable, hilarious person and yet so full of what seemed like genuine love for his friends and the people around him, it was delightful instead of annoying or tiresome.

"I look forward to that."

He seemed pleased by this, but his expression shifted as I took another bite.

"Before we finish, let's talk specifics. One concern I have is the presentation of our engagement."

"As in... how we look together? If the main event is the Silver Ridge Charity Gala, I may need some help with what to wear, but I clean up okay." A bit of my self-esteem crumbled at his concern, but his hand shot out, stopping just short of mine on the table.

"I'm not at all concerned about what you'll wear, but of course I'll provide whatever attire is necessary. You won't incur any expenses in that regard. I meant more that typically, an engaged couple would touch."

His gaze found mine, and the meeting of our eyes combined with that word from his lips—*touch, touch, touch*—sent my pulse climbing.

"Oh, of course. But um, what were you thinking?" And had it gotten hot in here? Had Luis suddenly cranked the heat despite the spring air warming the evening already? Had my shirt shrunk to a size smaller than when I walked in?

We're standing in a packed ballroom and he's holding me close as we dance in what feels like slow motion. The crowd around us blurs and he's running the pad of his finger along my bare shoulder. I'm in a strapless ballgown akin to Belle's in the animated movie and he is, inexplicably, wearing a Phantom of the Opera *style mask. He dips his head and runs his nose along the line of my jaw, then—*

"We'd need to hold hands. I'd put a hand on your shoulder or back, maybe, to walk next to you. Normal things a couple would do in a relationship." His throat bobbed, almost like he had to gulp down anything else instead of continuing.

I took a large drink of my margarita and promptly found the bottom, ice clanking around in the glass, so I set it down and touched a napkin along my lips as though I were dainty and delicate and not someone who typically simply *wiped* my mouth. The prospect of being on display in front of Luc's extremely wealthy family suddenly made me mindful of just about everything.

Straightening my spine and pulling my shoulders back, I held my head higher and banished the slouch I favored too easily when sitting. When I met his gaze, he'd been waiting patiently for my response.

"That'll be fine. I'll just... I'll just need some practice."

Against my wishes, my cheeks heated *as a version of him in a mask with his dark hair slipping over his forehead in a roguish wave pressed me closer and coasted his lips along my neck in that make-believe ballroom in my head. He practices kissing me there, practices lacing our finger together, practices slipping his hands into my hair and dismantling the artful updo some kind talking wardrobe or feather duster worked hard on...*

Yikes, that's a lot.

I ducked my head to take another bite of my dwindling dinner, hoping he wouldn't notice.

"Of course. I will, too. It's been a while since I've been in a... relationship."

Fleetingly, I wondered if maybe I wasn't the first woman he'd been fake—or maybe even real—engaged to, based on that hesitation before *relationship*.

"Me, too." He seemed to know about Callum—or if he hadn't known before he interrupted our confrontation days ago, he certainly did now. If we were talking about a *healthy* relationship, I wasn't sure I'd ever been in one of those.

The waiter came to take our now-empty plates, and we

chatted lightly, not pushing back into the main topic of conversation. He took the bill and paid it before I could put up a fight, and I hated myself for being secretly relieved he'd done so.

Which was a great reminder of exactly why this wasn't a real relationship. I didn't want someone to take care of me, and the fact that I felt a twinge of relief was proof I was my mother's daughter. Until I managed to bury those roots completely, I wasn't in any shape to be someone's partner.

But in this scenario, I didn't have to worry about all of that, did I? I'd have the distraction of getting to know this beautiful man and the opportunity to help someone. I could shove the tendency for self-preservation down because this wouldn't put me in danger. This was all for a goal and it had nothing to do with my financial gain or marital status. It had, ultimately, very little to do with me at all, except that I happened to be the woman he'd asked.

We walked out of the restaurant, and I could've sworn the heat of his hand hovered just behind me, but with a glance, there was nothing. Outside, he turned to me, peering down and seeming surprisingly tall. Was it because we were standing closer than usual? Or had I just not noticed? He had at least six inches on me, maybe more, but tonight it felt more significant.

"We'll do this again. You tell me when you can so we can get to know each other better. Until then..." He held out his hand.

I swallowed and felt the pulse in my neck and at my temple in an instant, but I slipped a hand into his large, warm, dry one.

All that rushing, anxious energy in me ceased. The air around us must've stilled because the space between us, the sounds, the bustle... everything stopped. Our hands shook once, up and down, and I watched as though they belonged to strangers.

He released me. I swallowed hard and wished him good night, my voice all but missing, and walked home with his soft *bonne soirée* fluttering at my ears.

CHAPTER THIRTEEN

Luc

Twenty-four hours later, I'd reached out to Elise to schedule our next meeting.

Meeting. Right.

I'd offered to meet her anywhere she wanted, and she'd asked if we could avoid eating out again. I hadn't missed the twist of discomfort that'd crossed her face when I paid, but other than one protest which I refused, she'd gone with it. If she wanted to eat in, that was fine with me. The better to openly discuss things and... practice.

I'll just need some practice.

Her words and the pinch in her brows echoed through my mind. She didn't know how much her words had haunted me since we'd spoken. She was beautiful and kind and the fact that she needed to practice being touched made me want to activate some of the skills I'd tucked away when

I left active-duty service. It made me want to test Callum Davis's resolve and find him a cozy jail cell.

Clearly, neither one of us had dated recently, but the fact that she hadn't because her ex had been so awful was more motivation to let this ruse do double-duty. It could get me through this meeting with Grand-père and hopefully persuade him to release the trust to me, and it could also convince that idiot she wasn't his in any way.

The tension had crept into my shoulders and wound a knot between my blades, but I stretched my neck and breathed through the thoughts of her ex as I pulled up to an apartment building not far from downtown. It seemed nice, though I didn't like that I could see residents' doors from where I parked as they faced out, each nestled on a landing of a stairwell. A safer setup would be for her door to be on an inside hallway where a locked access door prevented just anyone from entering the building, let alone approaching her door.

Was she in the market to move?

I'd get that fixed somehow.

When my family arrived, we'd likely have to at least pretend to be spending a fair amount of time together. We could rationalize we were newly engaged so she kept her place, but the truth was, nothing but head over heels in love would make me propose. Which in turn meant I wouldn't want to be away from her. It was how he'd been with my grandmother before she passed. It was how my parents had been right up until the cruel reality of human frailty showed its hand and my mother passed from lung cancer despite never having smoked a single cigarette in all her years.

A familiar leaden quality filled my lungs as I banished those thoughts and shut my car door. I sent Elise a text confirming I'd arrived so I wouldn't surprise her, but as I stepped onto the stairway, movement caught my eye, and I peered at the window of a vehicle passing.

My brain went on full alert as I stepped back toward the sedan, which simply kept driving. But I'd seen him—I'd seen her ex here at her apartment complex. The odds of him visiting someone else seemed slim. I wouldn't barrel in and jump to any conclusions like I had a right to demand an answer from her, but I'd ask her.

Taking the stairs two at a time, I arrived at her third-floor walkup and knocked twice. It took her a few seconds to answer, during which I steadied my mind and heartrate. If that *petit con* had done anything to her—

"Oh. Hi, Luc." Elise stepped back from the threshold, pulling the door wide as our gazes connected. Her eyes darted away as she tucked a few strands of hair behind her ear, and if I wasn't mistaken, her hand shook.

"Was he here?"

Her dark eyes jumped to meet mine, then she turned and padded farther inside. I closed and locked the door, following just behind.

"Elise, was Callum here? Is that why you seem shaken?"

Her energy was all off. Maybe she was truly this nervous to have me in her home, in which case I'd leave right this second, but having seen that sniveling little jerk skulking away as I arrived gave me a strong suspicion he was the root of the problem.

Her lips slightly pursed, she scrubbed a rag along the countertop in her kitchen, then halted and her eyes shut. She exhaled slowly, warring with herself and likely wishing I wasn't there.

But I was, and I couldn't help but feel perhaps I could help. I knew something of their dynamic, having observed it, and more recently, interrupting it. I needed her to know I wasn't judging her, like she'd so kindly said to me.

"I don't blame you or judge you or... anything other than have concern for you, Elise. I want to know you're safe and happy, and you don't seem to be either."

She turned so I could see her face and my heart squeezed. She had tears limning her eyes and she looked so defeated.

Something monstrous rose up in me at this sight. I would tear the world down around her if it would keep her from feeling this way.

"He was here. I didn't let him in, and he didn't touch me. I think your threat is holding him off to some degree at least." Her arms wrapped around her waist, and she shook her head. "I just feel trapped."

My feet carried me closer, and by a thread, I managed not to pull her into my arms. She didn't want that, and I wouldn't impose it on her. But had I ever longed to hold someone and comfort them more?

Never in all my life. Nor could I imagine wanting it more than I did right now, as though every bit of sinew and bone in me was crawling toward her, pulling me into her with the need to hold her together and make her know she was safe. But this wasn't right—I wasn't here to comfort her, even if some primal part of me wanted it.

"What can I do?" I asked, desperation etched in every syllable. I hardly knew this woman, but it felt like a soul-deep imperative that I solve this for her. If I made the problem go away, then she wouldn't feel like this and then *I* wouldn't, either.

She smiled softly, resigned, and shook her head. "There's nothing to do. Hopefully, once we're at the gala, he'll see us together, maybe even before then, and it'll help."

Maybe before then, too. The little twerp had seen me tonight, just as much as I'd spotted him. Why would I be visiting this complex if not to come be with my girlfriend? The ruse must've worked already—he'd know Elise wasn't available, and if he wanted to get to her, he'd have to get through me.

Our gazes held, her eyes flickering back and forth between mine for a moment before she broke the connection and moved to the fridge to retrieve a pitcher. "Can I get you some water?"

I accepted the offer and the glass she handed me a moment later, then moved to the two-person table wedged behind a love seat next to the window. The space was small but tidy and welcoming enough. She had a bright teal throw blanket livening up a nondescript gray couch and small wooden coffee table. Her TV sat on a small stand. Bar stools at the side of the space connected it to the kitchen, and down a short hallway were likely her bathroom and bedroom.

"Thank you for agreeing to meet here. I thought it might be best if we keep our interactions simple these first few times." She grabbed her phone, then set it down without looking at it. "Sorry. Force of habit to grab that thing, but I'm trying to get better."

"I understand completely. Sometimes, I feel like it's another limb."

She smiled, small but genuine, and it eased a nameless ache that'd set up residence in my chest since arriving.

"I thought we could do twenty questions? We don't necessarily need to know every detail about each other, but if the goal is to make this believable, we need to know the basics, and I thought this could be the fastest way to get there."

The doorbell rang, and she startled so violently, it sent me to my feet, racing toward the door of her apartment and ripping it open.

"Hey man, how's it—"

I snatched the bag from the unsuspecting delivery driver and tossed him a twenty-dollar bill as I shut the door in his face. Generally, I had better manners, but I was tired of seeing her anxious. I set the food in the kitchen and unwrapped it, then searched for plates.

Elise approached, eyes wide.

"I didn't mean for you to order food. I—"

"I just ordered a few things I hope you'll like, and if not, we'll order something else."

My words emerged clipped and irritable, which I wasn't proud of. But I didn't know how to get what I needed from her—the truth. Recognizing my own idiocy, I exhaled and turned to her.

"I apologize for my curt response. I'm concerned for you. I realize you don't know me well enough to trust me with whatever is happening with Callum, but I worry for you."

Her shoulders slumped and she leaned a hip against the counter about a foot from where I stood.

"He has a stake in Glazed and he's pressuring me about it."

My eyes narrowed. "Pressuring how? What does he want?"

She huffed. "Great question. I think he's trying to use it as a way to push me into being with him, but I've made it clear that's not happening. So now he's..." She swallowed hard, grinding her teeth as she found the words. "I think he's trying to scare me with threats to sell the shop. At one point, he mentioned meeting with a chain out of Salt Lake, but I'm not even sure what all he can do. There weren't terms about me repaying him this quickly. I—" Her head fell back and she appealed to the ceiling. "I never should've involved him."

Her frustration was understandable, but all I felt was relief. Financial issues I could solve. That said, I'd learned my lesson the last time I offered any kind of assistance in that regard, even if it was in payment for her help.

"I'm sorry. That's awful of him and shows his character even more."

Her lashes fluttered and she seemed truly baffled by my response for a few seconds before her mouth tipped up at the corners. "Right? So... a fake fiancé won't be the fix, but it might help. Sure can't hurt."

The hint of a smile from her sent me into a full-blown grin, the triumph of having said possibly the right, or at least not the full-on wrong thing, a genuine reward.

We chatted as we dished up the food I'd ordered—sandwiches from the diner I may or may not have had Jess's help with selecting—and settled in at the table to begin our questioning. We covered favorite colors and movies and music and travel destinations. Every answer she gave made me want to collect a dozen more.

Despite vastly different upbringings, as adults we had a surprising amount in common. We both liked to read, both preferred running to other forms of exercise, and both liked the desert mountain climate of Silverton more than anywhere else we'd lived.

She talked about her friends and her love for them shone through so clearly, it hooked into my chest. She felt for them how I did for my friends—they were more than that.

As she relaxed into the comfort of conversation and

good, if simple, food, that fire of hers shone through, and it relaxed something in me.

It also solidified a plan.

I didn't know how to navigate building a relationship from virtually nothing so it'd be believable, but tonight felt like steps toward that. Small, but important steps.

Where I had no doubt was my plan to help her. She might not want to be paid, but I had resources at my disposal, and I could alleviate the threat of her ex with a little bit of maneuvering. I could neutralize him indefinitely, not just as a fake boyfriend or fiancé... and I intended to do just that.

CHAPTER FOURTEEN

Elise

The reading room at All Booked Up had never been so welcome.

Actually, that was a lie. I always looked forward to book club and I loved snuggling into this cozy room with my dearest friends and talking books and fictional troubles. It was the perfect escape from my actual problems and it reminded me I wasn't alone. I didn't often see all of these friends unless we were purposeful, so other than Friday evenings for an hour or two, it was this—the Silver Ridge Romance Readers Book Club.

Dove eyed me as I bustled in, feeling oddly refreshed considering how hectic the week had been. Having a man I was trying to get to know so I could fake-be-engaged-to-him was demanding enough, I'd started to understand why Luc had wanted to pay me. Of course I wouldn't accept anything for my time, and thus far, he'd insisted on feeding me at any chance he got, so I'd convinced him that was enough. Well, we also had the Callum angle, which was a tangible benefit at this point.

Jo popped the cork on some prosecco while Nikki and Winnie set trays of small finger foods on the table in the middle. It all looked fantastic. Catherine grabbed a small savory tart-looking item and popped it into her mouth, eyes shutting and a light groan of satisfaction sneaking out as she chewed.

"Sorry. I forgot lunch and I'm so hungry. I did two houses in The Ridge today." She sank back into the loving arms of the chair she always sat in and sighed.

"Two! Woman, what on earth are you doing working that hard on a Saturday?" Dove asked, eyeing her with disapproval.

"That's the pot calling the kettle black if I've ever heard it," I said just loud enough so Dove could hear me.

She grumbled. "Oh, yeah? Well you, too, are a pot... or a kettle. Or whatever it is when a third thing is saying a thing that's like two other things." She scrunched up her face in a scowl.

I chuckled under my breath, then gasped when Jess walked in looking radiant and so far from the sick, sad version of herself she'd been these last few months.

"Holy crap, hello pregnancy glow-up," I said, delighted to see my friend beaming.

She posed, letting her tiny protruding belly show.

Winnie clapped and Nikki let out a whistle. Jo laughed with so much happiness it practically oozed from her pores, and Dove had tears in her eyes.

"I feel human again," Jess said, eyeing the bottle of prosecco. "I would toast to myself and this baby if I could."

Jo popped up and moved to the small fridge behind the

sitting area, producing a variety of carbonated flavored waters for her. "Your selection, Madame."

Jess smiled, plucking up a cran-raspberry flavor and surveying the food. "We've gotten fancy lately. Are we all pitching in for this?"

"Ooh, so we have mushroom bourguignon tarts, goat cheese and red pepper mini tartines, a roasted spring vegetable medley with crumbled feta in endive, and... shoot, let me see what else he said it was." Jo swiped at her phone.

"He? Who made these?" Dove asked, sliding one of each of the delights onto a small plate Jo had set out.

Jo didn't look up. "So the last two are a cheddar and spring herb gougère and a mini white pizza with asparagus and peas, and then he gave us a sample of desserts."

"Seriously, who made all this? Did you pay for them?" I asked, biting into the mushroom thing and wanting to cry, it tasted so good. Savory umami partnered with buttery crust to form the perfect bite.

Jo's expression went cagey, and since she was essentially the worst liar of all time save the whole secret identity thing she somehow pulled off for the first year she was here, she wasn't fooling anyone when she said, "I'm not sure."

Jess rolled her eyes. "Jo. That's nonsense and you know it."

Winnie agreed. "What if we want to hire this person? The food is"—she took another bite of whatever she had sampled as though compelled, chewed quickly, and finished—"amazing."

Nikki and Catherine agreed, their mouths full.

Dove had slumped back into her seat, bliss written on her face as she chewed with her eyes closed.

"I can't tell you. He made me promise not to. But I'll convey your approval, if that's the message you want sent."

Jo slid a few items onto her own plate and smiled down at them.

"Approval, yes. Absolutely," I said, taking a bite of the gougère.

So. Good.

Catherine nodded eagerly. "Completely delicious and I'm just sad there isn't more."

Winnie echoed her thoughts, as did Jess, who still eyed Jo like she might be able to see through her to who'd supplied the goods. Dove had taken another bite and grinned as she said, "Tell him I'll trade my maidenhead for a chance to eat this food regularly, how about that?"

I coughed, prosecco nearly shooting out of my nose.

Catherine must've inhaled something because Winnie had to pat her on the back as she sputtered, her face bright red, while Nikki covered her mouth and Jo's fell wide open. Finally, Jess burst out laughing and we all joined in.

Dove's eyes fluttered open and she shrugged. "What can I say? The way to my... heart... is through my stomach?" She cracked herself up this time, and we all joined in, giggling at her outrageous words and dabbing mouths and eyes as we recovered.

"Well. I will never forget that, I have to say." I raised my glass. "To good food and great friends and the freedom to be sad or silly or sick or hungry or tired or *whatever that just was*"—I winked at Dove—"and still feel at home."

The "cheers" circled around the room, and my heart, the one that'd felt rather weary lately, took a breath. So much love reflected back in each of those faces, and I gathered it all up, tucking it into my chest so I wouldn't forget I wasn't alone.

So often with Callum, I'd felt alone. He'd managed to make me feel that way even when I had these women. After going through a fair amount of craziness together, I felt closer to them than ever, and yet I'd kept so much from them.

By the end of the night, I'd resolved to tell them what was happening with Luc, but I didn't want to monopolize the conversation, and once we'd launched in to discuss our latest read, I saw the way Dove shifted in her seat, checking her phone and worrying her lip.

"Everything okay?" I asked her quietly when we took a stretch break.

"Nan... she's not feeling well. I might need to go soon." She checked her phone again, tapping out a message before looking back at me. "Are you going to discuss..." she wiggled her brows and mouthed *Luc*.

I shook my head. "No. Not tonight, anyway. Are you going to tell them..." I didn't need to specify. She knew I meant her financial stress, the move to Silverton Springs, and all that meant.

She raised one sassy little brow. "Not tonight."

I huffed, but tipped my head to one side. "Fine, then we'll both be cowards."

She made a face, then glanced back at her phone, and soon, we started up again.

It wasn't cowardice keeping me from mentioning Luc's proposal to them, though. It wasn't wanting to isolate myself, either. It was simply that I didn't know how to describe it—I needed more information.

And maybe there was a small inkling that I'd like to keep it mostly to myself, at least for another little while.

CHAPTER FIFTEEN

Luc

With ten days until my grandfather's arrival, my stress levels had ratcheted up significantly. I'd tried reasoning my way into telling him the truth and pleading with him to respect my choice, but whether because of my stubborn pride, or that child in me who hated how he'd dismissed my mother, even in death, I couldn't bring myself to give in.

At some point, I'd have to swallow that pride and level with him. Maybe a few months from now, when all the drama from this visit had faded. Maybe we'd even have a few moments to connect while he was here and that would help.

And so, I made plans with Elise. We'd chatted more on the mornings I'd gotten donuts, at least when she didn't have customers lined up. And we'd gone to lunch once, I'd brought her coffee for another round of twenty questions, and we'd been texting. Nothing constant or formal, just... questions as they popped up.

Things like when we learned to drive—her at sixteen, me at eighteen since at the time, I was in France—and what our favorite subject in school was—her English and math, me, history. I asked her when her first kiss was and she took a full ten minutes to respond as compared to formerly instant back and forth, at which point she responded, *"I think we should meet up and practice."*

Practice... kissing?

My mind launched into a litany of explanations for what she meant, but I shut it down and asked her to tell me when. Tone and intention couldn't be read over text message, so I'd wait to clarify until we were in person. This way, she could lead the conversation and set the pace.

The combination of anticipation and anxiety made me drive a little faster to her house, then ease off and give myself a stern talking to when I realized I was rushing everything. I'd buttoned my shirt wrong, done a poor job of tying my left shoe, and I was certain that if I'd shaved, I would've missed half my face. Fortunately, I hadn't shaved, nor had it been a day to trim my facial hair, or I likely would've left a bare line in the middle of my chin.

By the time I reached her door, I'd promised myself I wouldn't continue this manic pace. I would be calm and receptive to whatever she wanted to practice.

"I already made dinner, so I hope you listened to me," Elise said as she stepped back, welcoming me into her space.

She'd joked more than once that I'd show up to wherever she was and foist food on her, but it wasn't all wrong. I liked feeding her. She'd fed me so many times, it felt right I should return the favor.

"You said you were making dinner, so I didn't bring anything." I held up a bottle of wine. "Except this."

She grinned and took the bottle. "Thank you. That was thoughtful."

"I can be thoughtful, despite what it may seem," I said, following her into the kitchen.

She eyed me. "Why would you say that? I haven't thought of you as anything *but* thoughtful." She set the bottle of wine on the counter and slid me a wine key.

"Family stuff, I guess. My grandfather liked to make sure I knew he thought I was thoughtless. To him, my refusal to do what he wanted translated into being a generally thoughtless person. Or maybe the even more unspoken thing back then was *selfish* person. But he said that outright to me when I joined the military."

She chuckled as she stirred something in a large pan on the stove. "Funny how going into the military could be considered selfish. It's a form of service."

I pulled the cork and filled two glasses with healthy pours of the robust red wine. I hoped she'd like it. "It can be. For some people, it's service. For some, it's a job when there's no other option. For some, it's an escape." I thought of Kenny, for whom it'd definitely become one. But he was also someone who *served*.

"They call it *serving* in the military for a reason. I don't think a person's motives have to be altruistic to qualify. There are naturally things that a person does in the military, things they give up and things they take on, that is different than anything else."

The edge in her voice, the way it sounded defensive of me and my friends and anyone else who'd served, sparked in my chest.

I stepped closer and held out her glass of wine, which she took. "Well then, to those who served."

Her lips slid up into a bright smile. "To those who served."

Our gazes held as we each tipped back the glasses and took our first sips. My eyes dipped to her lips as she pressed them together like she was savoring the flavor of the wine.

My stomach clenched and I swayed forward, then cleared my throat and pulled back, remembering myself. She turned quickly and spoke to the pan.

"Could you get the salad stuff out of the fridge? I have some field greens and a vinaigrette I made earlier. Nothing fancy."

Did she have any idea how long it'd been since I'd enjoyed a simple homemade meal with a woman? Maybe this didn't technically count as a date, but it should've. It did, in my opinion.

My friends and I often cooked for each other, especially during ski season when the restaurants were so full of tourists it made quick pop ins less appealing. But this... having her slide chicken and wild rice onto our plates then bustle to set them down at her tiny table while I brought the salad bowl and dressing along with my wine... it all felt so good.

A facile thought, maybe, but I couldn't deny that the simple domestic routine of preparing dinner together sent a needle of longing weaving in and out between my ribs.

"So, pretty basic. It's just chicken and some wild rice and salad. I'm sorry it's not—"

She waved her hand and I caught it, giving into the temptation to touch her. "This looks delicious. Thank you so much for cooking."

She pulled in a breath and I released her instantly, not

wanting to encroach, but certain I couldn't listen to her apologize for making me dinner. Even if it proved inedible, her efforts were genuinely kind, and I wouldn't think of demeaning them.

"Thank you. I mean, you're welcome." She pressed her lips together like she had to or she'd say something else.

We took our seats and dug in. Happily, the food was all delicious. Simple, sure, but flavorful and well-cooked. It was perfect.

"This is excellent, Elise. Thank you," I said, finishing my last bite. We'd hardly spoken, and I'd become ravenous after the first taste.

She finished chewing and studied me while she did. "I don't think I've ever seen someone eat an entire meal in five minutes."

I swallowed a sip of wine. "Then you've not spent much time with soldiers, I'd guess."

She chuckled and took a drink, too. "Maybe not. Or if I have, they've all been on their best behavior."

"That's it exactly. We tend to force ourselves to slow down and act decently fairly well."

"Should I be alarmed or honored you don't feel the need to slow down for me?" She leaned back in her seat, her shoulders relaxed, and her eyes soft.

Seeing her so comfortable brought me something more than relief—it brought me a bright, almost glowing sensation of pleasure.

"Definitely honored. Your food was so good, I forgot my manners."

Her laugh was deliciously disbelieving. "Of course it was."

"I'll always tell you the truth," I said, hoping she'd

believe me because I meant it. So far, I hadn't lied to her, and I didn't intend to. I wanted her to trust that.

"I think I believe you."

"Good."

Her dark eyes hooked into mine, and the thought that I could drown there flashed in my head. What a cheesy, useless thought, and yet the need to stay latched into her kept me glued to my seat, until she broke away and stood.

We cleared the table together, and though she refused to let me rinse dishes, she did let me help load her dishwasher.

Our hands brushed, and I counted each one. *One, two,* a slow slide of fingers as we passed off plates. *Three, four,* a delicious graze when I brushed past her to rinse a bowl.

And then it happened.

Those eyes drew me in and seemed to ask a question. They seemed to say, will you stop what you're doing and look at me? And I did. I paused my movement when we were face to face and just shy of bodies meeting in the small space of her kitchen. I dipped my head down and her chin tipped up so our gazes locked yet again and she breathed out slowly.

"Are we going to practice kissing?" Her words came out in a rushed sound slightly more than a whisper.

It was all I could do to keep from closing my eyes against the crush of wanting, against the assumption that this was an invitation, but I did. Because her pupils were a bit wider than they should've been, and even though she seemed to welcome contact, we couldn't *start* at a kiss.

I abandoned the bowl in my hand to the counter and set my palm next to her hip. Not caging her in but steadying myself and giving me a gauge for the space between us.

Drawn to her, I resisted connecting us from thigh to chest and gritted out a sentence I didn't like admitting.

"I don't think it's time quite yet." What I wouldn't say? *I don't think I can handle it.*

It couldn't be spoken, nor did I want to look the truth in the face. If we did kiss—*when* we did—I needed to be ready.

Her lashes fluttered and the dip between her brows formed. "I'm sorry, I—"

I took her chin in my hand, my touch soft but demanding. "I want to kiss you, Elise. Very much. But I will not do so until you tell me to."

CHAPTER SIXTEEN

Elise

My entire body liquified.

Honestly, it was miraculous that I didn't launch myself at him and kiss him right then and there. But the gentleness couching his words stopped me. Yes, it was sexy as all get out of him to say such a thing in the first place, but it was... thoughtful. The polar opposite of what his grandfather had accused him of being.

"Okay," I managed, holding his gaze and summoning all the courage I knew existed in me. The planes of his face were stunning, and at this range I could see, not nearly as perfect as I'd thought. Somehow, the small scar in his left eyebrow and the freckle inside his right iris made him even more appealing.

His head dipped ever so slightly, and I exhaled slowly as he backed away, moving all the way into the living room and taking a seat on the couch.

"Do you want popcorn?" Because we had to fill the space with something other than the sheer *wanting* still coursing through me.

"*Bien sûr*, thank you," he said, and even though I wasn't certain of the meaning, his inflection told me he meant yes.

But also, maybe he wasn't gentle and thoughtful? Because if he were, he wouldn't have spoken French just now. He wouldn't have held up a lighter to the already singed parts of me.

In a few minutes, I settled in next to him, our elbows brushing and highlighting just how small my couch—realistically more of a love seat—was. I didn't often host here because the space was cramped, and almost everyone else lived in houses with larger living rooms. Lately, the most time I'd spent with friends had been in the All Booked Up reading room, and I was just fine with that because it was delightful.

I'd left him to make a selection, and, to my surprise, he'd chosen *The Proposal*, a movie about a fake engagement destined for a marriage of convenience.

A bit on the nose there, sir.

I didn't make the point because we weren't getting married. In a matter of weeks, once his family had come and gone, this would all be over.

This thought settled like a thorn in my chest, but I pushed it away. I'd anticipated an action film or maybe something dramatic and sweeping, but here we were watching Sandra Bullock and Ryan Reynolds fall in love in the gorgeous setting of a small Alaskan town.

After their kiss in front of his family, which went from fake to real in a delicious moment of unexpected tension, my stomach flipped at the thought of kissing Luc.

"Perhaps we should try something," he suggested, resting his large hand palm-up on his thigh.

My heart thudded in my chest, but it wasn't dread or anxiety. It was desire pumping through me, and I let myself enjoy it. Not that it was so rare with him, but in the reality of my life, I hadn't wanted to touch a man in a long time. I simply hadn't. And every time I felt pleasure or anticipation at contact with Luc, it felt a little like magic. Like a small miracle.

I slipped my hand into his, my entire being lighting up at the contact of our fingers lacing, my palm resting against his large, warm one.

A simple touch, yet so much more.

He hummed softly. "This is nice."

I laughed, and if Dove had been in the room, she would've heard the low-key delirium lining the sound, but thank goodness she wasn't here. Hopefully, Luc couldn't hear the edge of hysteria as every nerve ending in my body played the maracas.

"It is," I said, as though I was hardly moved by the contact.

We stayed like this for a while until his thumb arced over my skin in a soothing and yet deeply unsettling movement. The pad of his finger was slightly calloused, and every swipe felt like he was plucking at an ever-tightening string.

My mind played tricks on me. It imagined his hands slowly but surely exploring my wrist first, then the dip of my elbow and up the soft curve of my biceps. It imagined him dropping his mouth to touch his lips to my neck, behind my ear, and—

"Elise, *mon cœur*."

His voice came in a raspy whisper, but then I was

shaken awake—a hand on my face startled me enough to open my eyes.

Endless gray-green eyes with that little fleck of a dark freckle to one side waited for me, staring back as I oriented myself to reality and not the dream I'd apparently crafted in a movie-induced sleep.

"I'm so sorry I fell asleep," I said, then realized my whole body was leaning against him, and my head had likely been on his shoulder.

"Don't apologize. The movie is over, and I should go."

The moment hung and some insane part of me thought about saying no, he shouldn't. Some other more confident woman—a version of me who knew what she wanted and understood what she had to give—that woman would've told him to stay.

But this person, the one who'd climbed out of the totaled car that was my relationship with Callum, she was still finding her way. No longer did she suffer from whiplash or aching knees or a bruised heart. It was simply that she didn't know if she could get in another car—if she'd ever drive again.

She was enjoying riding in a car, though. Not being behind the wheel, perhaps, but taking the ride—and that was why this setup with Luc was perfect. That was why there would be no asking him to stay, but also no brutal emotional fallout when the wheels fell off. I could take the drive as a passenger, let him do the driving of this fake... car? Okay, so the illustration got a bit murky, but the point remained. Wanting Luc wasn't the hard part. Liking him wasn't either.

And knowing those feelings would stay tucked away while we took this drive together was what would help me avoid the hard part.

I sat up and brushed my hair from my face. "Alright." I didn't want to sound too enthusiastic about it. I wouldn't have minded dozing here next to him until morning, but that would've been confusing, too.

I walked him to the door, wondering if I should apologize again. He slipped his hand into mine and towed me along with him, which made it feel like maybe he wanted me close, and I took that as an answer.

"Thank you for dinner and for the movie," he said, his voice a little rougher than normal with the late hour. "And for holding my hand."

He raised our joined hands and pressed a kiss to the back of mine.

My heart swooped low.

"Thank you for coming. And for being patient—for moving slowly." I hoped he'd understand, and when he nodded, I knew he did.

I'd shared about my mother and he knew about Callum —he'd witnessed it. But somehow, this moment made me feel more vulnerable than I'd ever felt with him. Had I stripped down in the living room and decided to walk him to the door naked?

I might as well have, for all the layers I had to hide behind now.

"I'll text you in the morning," he said, turning to go and releasing my hand, but I scrambled to get it back, clutching at his wrist as I said, "Could I hug you?"

Already emotionally bare in a way I hadn't expected, why not throw myself at his feet? And yet it was all for practice, all couched within the context of fakeness, so the risk felt more bearable than I would've guessed. Testing the waters without getting soaked, in a way. Remembering the feel of his hand on mine, on my thigh, it made me wonder what full-body contact with him would be like... And rather than drive this anticipation into levels of crazy restlessness and fuel for my overactive imagination, maybe getting on with it would quell the desire to some degree.

The half-smile tugging at his lips would've slayed me, but before I had time to fully register it, he'd slipped his arms around me and pressed me close. Instantly, I wrapped mine around him and stepped even closer, relishing his warmth and the firm planes of his body. He was so muscular and big and safe.

It clicked then.

I didn't know Luc all that well yet, but I knew he was safe. In ways Callum, despite how well I thought I'd known him, had never been.

What would it be like to be with someone who could be gentle and considerate like this? And why was that such a dreamy proposition instead of a given? I hadn't lowered my standards in theory, but in reality, my time with Callum had proved what I'd been willing to give up, and that truth burned through me.

If I ever did try with someone again—and I really didn't anticipate doing that—I'd want it to feel like this. Buzzy with possibility and a little longing, but warm, gentle, and safe.

I pulled away, fully aware my thoughts were taking me places I couldn't afford for them to go.

"Talk to you tomorrow," I said, and grinned when he sent me a wink.

He shuffled down half a flight of stairs while I watched, then turned and notched his chin up. "Lock the door."

I nodded, confirming I'd do it, but had planned to watch him until he disappeared all the way down the stairs.

He planted his feet, hand on the railing, then squinted.

I waited.

"Go ahead. Do it now."

I started to argue, then thought better of it, chuckling softly and closing the door as I did. I clicked the lock so loudly it had to have been audible for him.

Bossy, he could be.

But also safe.

CHAPTER SEVENTEEN

Luc

My grandfather arrived at the Silverton Regional Airport by private jet exactly on time. Dutiful grandson that I was, I stood waiting on the tarmac when he did. Fortunately, so was my dear pal and excellent buffer, Kenny Carmichael.

"Jean-Luc." My grandfather nodded regally at me, then extended his hand.

I accepted it, a hint of marvel gliding through me with the first contact between us in years. His hand was dry but the shake firm, despite the fact that he'd aged over a decade since we'd last touched.

"*Grand-père. Bienvenue à Silverton.*" There was so much to say, but this would be a starting place.

He nodded again, his three security personnel hovering at a distance, then turned to Kenny.

"Kenny Carmichael, sir. I work with your grandson at

Saint Security and we served together in the Army." Kenny extended his hand.

My grandfather accepted it and shook, eyes snagging on Kenny's left hand. He scowled and said, "You've lost your fingers."

Kenny's eyes danced and he gasped, clutching that hand to his chest. "I hadn't realized."

I cleared my throat to stifle a laugh, and my grandfather's scowl deepened. Behind him, his assistant tapped on a tablet and stopped at his right without ever looking up. She spoke softly in French, but too quietly for me to hear.

Grand-père nodded, then turned his silver gaze to mine. "We'll take a car to the resort now. Odette will arrive tomorrow."

My teeth ground together at his mention of the woman he had chosen for me.

"I hope she'll enjoy her stay," I said, unwilling to seem interested in her arrival or anything about her. She was undoubtedly a lovely person, but not someone for me.

His jaw flexed and his nostrils flared slightly. "Aurelie has told me of her plan for dinner tomorrow. Will you be in attendance?"

He meant the family dinner Aurelie had arranged for me, Elise, my grandfather, and her and Michele. No Odette, and no one else. "We will."

He might not have wanted to ask about Elise, but he'd be meeting her. In a small group with Aurelie and Michele to help defend and protect her, there would be no easier time to make the introduction.

My grandfather's eyes fell away, and he bid me a quiet farewell as he walked past us to a waiting black Land Rover SUV. The airport staff, all too used to wealthy flyers arriving and never so much as touching their luggage, hustled to load his and his assistant's bags into the back with the help of the driver. The security team had checked the vehicle, guided him in, and waited for him and his assistant to load in before also sliding in. Kenny and I watched as they pulled away within three or four minutes of exiting the plane.

"Well, he's warm and fuzzy. I see where you get your kindness and that unflagging commitment to sunscreen."

A laugh tripped out of me at his unexpected insults. My grandfather's skin was weathered and deeply tanned thanks to his propensity to spend his time working from a property on the French Riviera.

"He views sunscreen as a generational choice. I guess we'll see whether skin cancer is, too," I said, a familiar frustration with him rising.

His dismissal had been absolutely no surprise, but I still found his stubbornness to be most irritating. He wouldn't buy into the supposed sham of sunscreen, nor did he believe in marrying for love despite having done exactly that himself. He looked down on people without wealth and status similar to his even after his own son married a poor waitress from the States.

And yet, he'd extended his hand. That was something. And it gave me a modicum of hope that maybe all of this would work out. We'd left *la bise*—the French cheek kiss of greeting—behind a long time ago, but the handshake, it meant something.

"Wish I could be a fly on the wall at the old family dinner tomorrow. That sounds fun," Kenny said, steering my focus back to the here and now.

"Yeah. It'll be a blast. I just hope Elise will be okay."

We walked toward the car I'd driven to get us here, and

once we were tucked inside and navigating to wrap up the day at work, Kenny circled back.

"I know you're set on convincing Gérard you're engaged to Elise. I fully support not getting engaged to some rando you don't know whose main goal is to develop her portfolio."

I could feel a *but* coming, so I waited, curious to see what kind of wisdom he might lay on me.

"But, if you're that worried for Elise, maybe you need to call it. You need to put her first if you care for her at all. Sit down with your grandpa and see if you can reason with him about the trust instead of pushing this."

The engine hummed as we rode along as though he wasn't accusing me of using Elise. The worst part was, I couldn't deny it. She wouldn't either. I *was* using her. That was the entire premise of the agreement.

But.

I did care for her. I'd always liked her and noticed her, but the more time we spent together, the more compelled I felt to be around her. The more I wanted from and with her.

The more I wished maybe this wasn't all just a ruse.

But she didn't want that. And I wouldn't forget it.

"She's not going to get hurt. Anything that happens is about me and my grandfather, not about her. She knows I think the world of her."

But my words were false.

She didn't know what I thought about her at all. We'd spent our time checking boxes on lists of get-to-know-you questionnaires and practicing holding hands.

At the memory of her hand in mine and her head on my shoulder as she slept during the movie last week, my heart clutched. Her exhaustion weighed on me, as did the reality that she was choosing to spend her precious time with me instead of resting or doing other things she needed. I didn't take that lightly.

"Yeah, that's the thing, though. It *is* about your grandfather and you, but it'll also be about her. If she's standing in his way of you being with this other woman, he doesn't strike me as the kind of man who's going to tolerate her, let alone be welcoming or kind."

Guilt and dread swirled in my gut. "I know. I'll talk to her."

I'd more than talk to her. I'd make sure she understood that anything coming out of his mouth reflected on him and not her. Based on his complete refusal to acknowledge my engagement, which I'd told him via text had occurred last week, I wouldn't be surprised if he was a Class A jerk. Of course he'd be technically well-mannered, but he hadn't traveled all this way to be diplomatic.

Kenny kept me distracted with colorful commentary on my grandfather and his assistant all the way back to Saint. I managed to stay focused on my own work prepping for the busy week of celebrities in town for the gala this weekend, and reminded myself that in just a few hours, my sister would be here.

Maybe it made me weak for needing my big sister, but I did. I needed her and Michele as reinforcements and to stand with me.

Aurelie's dark hair hung in razor-sharp sheets down either side of her head. She looked fresh-faced and ready for the day when she opened the door to her suite and hauled me in for kisses on each cheek, then a hug.

She squeezed me and did her obligatory lean back and lift, though she could only get me an inch off the ground since I outweighed and had at least five inches on her.

"Did you get bigger since I saw you last?" she asked, tapping her chin.

I chuckled, my heart bursting to see her in person. "It's been almost two years, so it's possible." I certainly hadn't gotten taller, but being out of active-duty life meant I'd put on some muscle now that I didn't need to be quite as fast or ruck march forty miles at a time.

"Is that him? Is it our baby brother?" Michele threw the door wide and caught me in a signature Michele embrace complete with lung-compressing squeeze.

I cringed against his hold for show, then laughed outright when he kissed my head like I was a small child and not a man who was taller than him. When he'd married Aurelie four years ago, he'd dived in with more enthusiasm than I could ever have anticipated. He was my biggest fan—I was second only to Aurelie in his mind.

Honestly, he was like the Italian version of Kenny in more than a few ways.

Michele released me and cupped my face in his hands, shaking me a little bit. I wouldn't have been shocked if he'd kissed me full on the lips in his enthusiasm, but today he just looked like a proud dad as he gazed at me.

"Alright, love. Let him go and let's talk," Aurelie said, taking her husband's hand and leading him to the sitting area in the suite.

I followed behind and sat in a comfortable, stylish chair. The room was full of forest and sage greens and creams and golds. It was all very classy and crisp while somehow managing to be comfortable and not stuffy.

"So we meet her tonight? Have you prepared her?" Aurelie asked, already onto business.

"I'll pick her up a bit early and make sure she doesn't have any questions." We'd spoken about the situation enough that Elise understood my grandfather had an agenda for his visit. I'd need to make sure she also knew he might be quite rude.

"We'll do what we can, but he's very upset at you, you naughty boy," Michele said, winking at me as though he relished my disobedience.

"Are you enjoying this?" I asked him, leaning back in my chair and watching as they each filled small plates of fruit and pastries from a silver tray set on a low table in the sitting area.

"How could I not?" He balanced his small plate on one of his trouser legs and rested his arm along the back of the small sofa, grazing Aurelie's shoulder.

"He's only enjoying that you've told Grand-père no. It happens so rarely, it's something to note." She bit into her croissant, brows raising as she looked down to inspect the pastry. "*Ooh, c'est bon, ça.*"

"It's a pleasant surprise when Americans know their pastry," Michele added, shoving almost an entire croissant into his mouth.

"Anything else I need to know? Do you know Odette at all?"

I hadn't investigated my would-be bride because I hadn't wanted to. But now that the time had come, I'd realized this was short-sighted. I could use the Saint resources to dig deep, but ultimately, I didn't need dirt on her. I didn't need anything from her except for her to accept that she wasn't meant to be with me.

And Elise is?

The thought slipped in, poking at something I couldn't quite name. Of course Elise wasn't. I had no plans to marry for real, and neither did she. We were on the same page with that decision.

"She's a lovely girl. A bit young, if you ask me, but that *would* be Grand-père's choice, wouldn't it?" She held a fork aloft, a small strawberry speared on its end, and added, "As you can tell by the name, they've got deep French roots but immigrated a generation or two ago. They've got business holdings Grand-père is interested in now, so..."

It always came down to business. Well, business and family. But for my family, those two were intertwined and messy, and maybe they were for this Odette as well. I pitied her, because she wasn't about to make the match that would uphold her family's origins or whatever it was they hoped to gain here.

We sat and chatted a while longer before I had to get to work. I'd begin personal security detail for a client tomorrow and maintain that for fairly long days right up until the gala, so I had a few things to do before meeting with Elise this evening.

I bid my sister and Michele goodbye and gave them a few suggestions for what they could do with their time, then headed out. I'd formulate a way to tell Elise just how bad it might be, and I'd hopefully manage to make it worth her pain and suffering.

CHAPTER EIGHTEEN

Elise

Half an hour before closing, a gorgeous couple entered Glazed and instantly started beaming as they took in the bright pink walls and white, light pink, and black accents.

By now, seeing stunning people wandering the streets of Silverton, especially nearing a big event like the upcoming charity gala, had become par for the course. Or it should've been. I wasn't sure I'd ever get used to seeing big name celebrities around town.

These two weren't famous that I recognized, but I hadn't gotten a look at them straight on until they stepped up to the counter and the woman grinned.

"You're Elise."

It clicked instantly. "And you're Aurelie."

"Yes! This is my husband Michele. We're so happy to meet you!"

Her enthusiasm shocked me, as did the leap in my chest as she leaned over to air kiss to one side of my face then the other, despite the counter separating us, then took my hand and patted it as though it was a stand in for a hug.

I was genuinely happy to see someone who belonged to Luc—who knew and loved him in ways I never could but wanted to.

Wait. That had to be the frosting fumes getting to my head.

"The pleasure's all mine. Can I get you a donut?"

"*Si, per favore*, I need to eat at least two of these beautiful creations," her husband Michele said, eyes flittering from one donut to the next.

His accent was heavier than Aurelie's, and I could tell it was Italian, though that might've been only because I *knew* he was Italian thanks to Luc's run down of everyone in the family a fiancée would reasonably be expected to know.

"Luc has raved about your donuts." Aurelie beamed, eyes on my creations.

Why did knowing this give me a thrill? I knew he liked my donuts. He'd said as much, as had his behavior for the last six months of him being here at least twice a week, if not more.

"What does my *fratello piccolo* get when he visits?" Michele hit me with his wide, toothy smile.

He was certainly a handsome man. He had longish hair, wild with romantic curls, and yet somehow it made his deep-set dark eyes and olive skin seem all the more bedroomy and appealing rather than unkempt. He kept one hand around Aurelie's waist and tucked into her side, two fingers disappearing under her shirt.

More affectionate than American couples tended to be for sure, but instead of making me uncomfortable like PDA often did, I liked it. In fact, I loved knowing these two enjoyed each other so much they couldn't keep their hands off one another.

Um, okay, these two could totally be the stars of a pirate romance. Or maybe even an epic fantasy. She's the chosen one and he's the dark prince set against her... until he's not.

Mentally refocusing on the here and now, I started in. "Luc likes—"

"Ooo I like the way she says *Luc.*" Michele wiggled his thick brows.

Aurelie elbowed him in the side. "Please excuse him. He's just excited to be on vacation and he loves my brother."

This had me grinning. "I'm so glad. Do I say Luc wrong?"

Aurelie chuckled and Michele just smiled broadly.

"Not at all. You say it perfectly. He's just being... him." Instead of irritation or exasperation, she leaned close and pressed a kiss to his cheek.

Goodness, these two.

"Well, Luc loves the plain glazed and he often gets whatever is seasonal or special. I'm sold out of this week's special, but I do have a seasonal spring lemon blueberry cake donut."

Michele loosed a chain of words in rapid Italian I couldn't dream of understanding and Aurelie laughed.

"He's saying that sounds like heaven. We'll take two glazed and two of the lemon blueberry, thank you, Elise."

When she handed me her credit card, I shooed her away. She pursed her lips and gave me a perturbed look that was so like Luc, I had to laugh. If I hadn't already known they were siblings, that would've tipped me off.

I handed them their little sacks of donuts. "You're welcome to eat here, but if you enjoy coffee, I highly recommend stepping next door to get a drink from Joe." I gestured to the side where they could find the coffee shop and its charming owner. Ethan would get a kick out of Michele for sure.

"Thank you, Elise. And we'll see you for dinner tonight?" Aurelie asked as Michele yanked out a glazed donut, shoved half of it in his mouth, and groaned so loudly I felt like I should apologize for witnessing it.

My lashes fluttered as I tried to will away the heat rising to my cheeks and huffed a small laugh. "Yes. Yes, you will."

Aurelie chuckled, too. "This man loves food and he has no patience. Thank you for the donuts, and remember, our grandfather is all bark." She tilted her head to one side, then amended, "Well actually, he's bite, too. But mostly bark. And his problems with Luc are nothing to do with you—I can already tell you're lovely."

"Thank you," I said, not sure what else I could say. How should one respond when one's fake almost-sister-in-law warned one away from the very person one would be spending extended time with that evening?

Well, one probably stops referring to oneself in third person.

I worked on my computer for another half hour between serving clients, enjoying the fact that I'd met Aurelie and Michele. They'd be familiar faces at dinner tonight, and they were certainly kind.

By the time I shut down the shop, worked my assistant hours in the afternoon, and finally showered and got put back together, I had ten minutes to spare. In that time, I paced and sent Dove messages telling her she should come kidnap me before Luc arrived.

"Why would I do that? I want you two to go knock his grandpa's socks off."

A lovely thought, but even without whatever new information Luc would give me tonight, I knew I wouldn't do that by virtue of being anyone other than the woman he'd chosen for his grandson.

"Not likely. Plus, I'm all dressed up and what if he's disappointed?"

The moment I sent the message, I wanted it back. Just as quickly, it showed as *read* and response dots bubbled up. I wished I didn't care what Luc thought of my new cocktail dress or the way I'd styled my hair in loose waves to my shoulders. I didn't normally try this hard, and something about doing so tonight made me feel naked rather than armed with fashionable clothing.

"If he is anything less than speechless from you in that dress, he's an idiot and I will require him to come to my doorstep so I can slap him with a kid glove."

I chuckled at the image of Dove swatting Luc's cheek with an empty glove. She was definitely still in her historical romance era.

"Thank you. I just want this to go well. It's all pretty pointless if it's not believable."

I could accept I was pretty, but Luc had literally been a model. Aurelie was just about the prettiest woman I'd ever seen, and her husband matched her in an equal yet opposite way. Would Luc's grandfather take one look at me and instantly know I was a woman struggling to hold my life together? Would he see through me as quickly as I feared?

"You're amazing, whatever happens. I love you and I know you can do this."

Her faith in me bolstered my courage, and I took one last look in the mirror. Hair wavy but sleek-looking, makeup as expertly done as I ever managed with subtle cat-eye black liner and a little bronzer and blush to give me color I didn't naturally have thanks to my work schedule, and a cherry-plum lip color that matched the pretty maroon and fuchsia of my dress. It was bold, but the fitted shape highlighted my waist and gave grace around my middle. I wore wedges because I would likely have to wear actual heels for the gala, and I wasn't about to do that to myself twice in one week.

The doorbell startled me out of my perusal, and I shuffled to get to the door, pulling it open and working to calm my breath as Luc walked in wearing a black suit with a crisp white shirt and sneakers.

"Sneakers?" I asked, not able to eke out a full sentence since the sight of him winded me.

His facial hair was perfectly styled, short but purposeful, and his hair looked coiffed but not glued in place. The little piece that sometimes fell into his eyes currently rested on his forehead and I wished I could say it didn't happen, but it did—my stomach flipped.

He was just so stupidly handsome, it was unavoidable.

And the look on his face...

His jaw flexed and his eyes became nearly smokey as they slipped down over me, then back up, each inch set on fire with his gaze.

"You look incredible," he said, stepping closer.

My pulse jumped and I swallowed, practically vibrating with nervous anticipation.

"You do, too," I said, my eyes locked on his.

He swayed forward, and I lifted my chin, not far from begging for him to finally try out the whole kissing thing, when he straightened, his brow bunching as he said, "We need to talk."

Oh.

That's so much less fun than kissing.

CHAPTER NINETEEN

Luc

She was stunning.

Literally.

It felt like I'd been tazed as I walked in the door and took in her legs revealed under the flounce of her dress and the way it traced her curves... she could turn eyes on a normal day in her casual attire at work, so when she put in all this effort to be even more alluring? I was doomed.

And I'd nearly kissed her, which would've been both insane, and the worst way to break a promise. I'd told her I wouldn't kiss her until she asked me to, but damn did I hope she'd decide she wanted to ask me before all of this was over.

Something inside me sank at the thought, but I pushed that slump away. Right now, before I got confused about what this was, we needed to discuss what she should expect. Aurelie had sent me a text this evening reminding me I needed to be honest about who our grandfather was, and I planned to do just that.

"Should we sit?" she asked, fidgeting with her fingers and turning toward the living room.

"Sure," I said, determined to sit on the chair and not next to her on the couch. I'd want to touch her, and being knee to knee with her golden bare skin revealed by the skirt of her dress was not the right choice.

"My grandfather already—"

"I met your sister—"

"You what?" I asked, not sure I'd heard her correctly since we'd both spoken.

She tucked some hair behind one ear. "Your sister and her husband came to the shop today."

Aurelie had said nothing about meeting Elise, the little snake. "And... what did you think?"

Her face split into a wide smile. "They were lovely. I mean, physically beautiful, obviously, but they were so nice and Michele is..."

I laughed. "That said it all. Michele is!" I widened my eyes. "He actually reminds me a lot of Kenny. He's the Italian Kenny if Kenny had been raised a spoiled rich kid but found his heart when he met my sister."

"Aw, that's adorable. They were so sweet together. They really seem to adore each other."

I loved that she'd seen that in what had to have been a fairly quick interaction. I had no desire for such desperate love after watching my father grieve, but I was glad Aurelie had found it. Especially since she'd wanted it. She had her head on straight and if something should happen, I wouldn't let her lose herself like our father had. But that wouldn't happen to her.

And it wouldn't happen to me because I'd never put myself in the position to let it.

Because this... whatever this growing, blooming thing between me and Elise was? It was just for now. She didn't want anything for longer, so it made us a perfect match while it lasted.

Elise's expression turned thoughtful, but she didn't offer anything else.

"What are you thinking? Are you concerned?" The last thing I wanted was for her to want to bow out of this tentative agreement but feel obligated.

"After meeting them, I can't help wondering if maybe you should consider getting to know whoever your grandfather chose for you. If they're anything like Michele, it might be worth exploring."

"I appreciate the thought, but no." I had nothing else to say on the matter, nor would I. I didn't want that version of a marriage, and I couldn't imagine wanting anyone else besides—well. I couldn't imagine wanting anyone else.

Perhaps this was the juvenile response, but at this point, I was in it. Plus there was the matter of the trust being dangled like a carrot, the goalpost moving every time my grandfather lost his patience or disagreed with my choices. *That* had to stop, if nothing else changed.

She nodded ever so slightly, but didn't speak again, so I pushed into what I needed to discuss.

"My grandfather believes we got engaged last week, so it's new. He'll likely be dismissive of you or even both of us, definitely of the fact that we're engaged. He may even ignore you entirely. Please know that whatever happens, his behavior reflects poorly on him and means nothing about you." I hoped with everything in me she knew this. "I have to warn you that he's probably looked into your life to some degree. He may be quite pointed with how he speaks about your eligibility, to use an awful, outdated term."

I hated the reality of those words, but they were true. Kenny was right—she needed to have some amount of notice this could be brutal.

She inhaled slowly as though steeling herself. "I hear your concern and I want you to know, I'm not worried about what some man I've never met thinks of me." She laughed softly. "Easy to say, I know. But I'm mentally preparing knowing he's not happy about us. Plus, I'll never even see him again after this week, right?"

Her statement should've made me feel better, but it didn't. It was an easy claim to make, as she said, but knowing how vicious my grandfather could be when he wasn't getting his way, I worried. The niggling suspicion that something bigger was barreling toward me—toward us —sat heavy in my gut. *Maybe I never should've asked her.* Still, she was right. Why should she care what Gérard Devereaux thought?

"True enough. And we'll have Aurelie and Michele there to draw his attention away from us."

She stood and reached out a hand, which I took as I rose to face her.

"You seem very nervous, and I just want to say I'm nervous, too, but not to be next to you. I'm proud to do that. And I'll do whatever I can to play the doting fiancée with hearts in her eyes." She squeezed my hand.

"Thank you." I inched closer, drawn to her. "I should end all of this, but I can't. Even though it's so stupid, thank you for being with me. Thank you for... letting me claim you as my own for a little while."

As though the words became a spell once spoken, I felt them wrap around my heart and knot into a bow.

Claim you as my own.

I'd never said such a thing nor had I wanted such a thing, but the ache, the squeeze in my chest, hinted at a deeper truth I couldn't look in the eye right now.

"It's my honor," she said, soft and so generous.

A buzz on my watch alerted me to the time and broke the spell. "Time to go. Ready?"

She smiled and reached for a small clutch and the keys sitting atop it.

"*Allons-y.*"

Fifteen minutes later, we were escorted into a private room at the Silver Ridge Resort's finest restaurant. It was the only truly fine dining place in town, but most people preferred the more casual options sprinkled around Silverton. We entered the small room to find a round table set for five and my grandfather, Aurelie, and Michele already seated.

"There you are," Aurelie said and instantly stood to greet us. She kissed my cheeks, then Elise's, and Michele did the same.

I approached my grandfather, who'd risen to his feet and stood quietly after buttoning his suit jacket with one hand.

"Good evening, Grand-père. This is my fiancée, Elise." I settled my palm against her back in a gesture I hoped she would read as one of support as she held out her hand.

I held my breath, waiting to see how he'd respond. It wouldn't have been altogether shocking if he had simply looked past her, but instead, he took her hand and bowed deeply over it to press a kiss there. "Lovely to meet you, Elise."

"Thank you. I'm so glad to meet you, too, Mr. Devereaux."

Grand-père released her hand, and she gracefully sat in the chair I pulled out for her. I would've preferred to have her next to Aurelie, or even Michele, but after that almost effusive greeting, I had hopes he might be on his best behavior.

I wasn't giving him the benefit of the doubt here, but I hadn't been able to do that in so long. Since my mother passed, at least. He'd grown harder, and of course our relationship had gone from loving to strained to nearly nonexistent in the years since then.

That could all change.

It could. But first, we'd have to get through this dinner.

Once we were all seated, a waiter arrived with menus and we all talked with him while looking at it. He returned with a bottle of red wine he opened tableside and poured a splash for my grandfather who tasted it, sloshing it around and letting it roll over the sides of his tongue like a true connoisseur, and then nodded. The waiter poured the wine into pre-set glasses and we ordered.

Aurelie and Michele dominated the conversation, blessedly chatting about all manner of things happening in their lives. They were redoing a wing of the historic home they lived in now, each finding the process grueling. My grandfather spoke up to add his memory of renovating while my grandmother had been pregnant with my father, and how he could still smell the way the paint had permeated everything and made my grandmother sick.

I hadn't heard him speak about her, let alone any fond familiar memories, in years. Had he gone through some major life event in the last eighteen hours and decided not to invite Odette here? It seemed so at odds with the way he was almost jovially talking with Aurelie and Michele and occasionally sending winks to Elise.

"What did your parents do, Elise?" Grand-père asked.

And here it came. I'd thought it too soon.

Elise finished chewing a bite and dabbed the corner of her mouth with her napkin before smiling. The expression would likely seem lovely to anyone who didn't know her well, but there was no ignoring the strain around her eyes.

"I never knew my father, and my mother has primarily been a homemaker."

She gently cleared her throat and shifted in her seat—just enough to send my pulse up a notch. We hadn't talked much about her family, and I was kicking myself for that. Of course my grandfather would want to know her lineage, almost like a collector would demand the provenance of a painting. It was a sick thought, but accurate, and I had no doubt he'd done the same thing with my mother. I'd warned her he'd look into her past, but somehow asking her here at dinner, as though he didn't know, seemed particularly awful.

I had asked her—we'd broached the topic of family during our dinner at Guac, and it'd been obvious she didn't like talking about this. I hadn't wanted to be a mercenary jerk and push too much at the time. It wasn't the wrong move, but only my grandfather would make me pay for trying to be a gentleman.

"Interesting. And how did she engineer such a lifestyle for herself without your father?" He nudged a little slide of wagyu filet mignon onto his fork and raised it to his mouth.

Aurelie saved me from throttling him right there.

"Grand-père, what are you saying? How rude!" She set her fork down and the genuine outrage on her face would've cowed a lesser man.

He, however, flicked a wrist. "It is a question worth asking, is it not?"

I felt paralyzed with a slimy sensation of disbelief, disappointment, and regret. I should never have done this. I should've been man enough to say no to my grandfather, or to play his games while he visited and let the woman down privately. Whatever the case, it shouldn't have been this—putting Elise on the spot.

"I understand why you'd ask. I hope you'll respect my choice not to elucidate my mother's choices when they are not my own."

My head snapped to Elise, and she set her napkin at the side of her plate.

"If you'll excuse me for a moment," she said and rose.

Michele, Grand-père, and I all stood. I tried to catch her eye, but she wouldn't look at me. She walked with confidence out the door of the small room, and I whirled on my grandfather.

"How dare you ask such a thing? Why would that matter? How is that appropriate for a first meeting?" I wanted to take him by the collar of his bespoke suit and shake him.

No charming affect slipped into place now that she was gone.

"I voiced what I needed to. She's a gold-digger and I could see it a mile away. I'm shocked you couldn't, but maybe it's because you're being led around by your—"

"I'll go check on her," Aurelie said, cutting off Grand-père's crass words.

"Thank you." I watched Aurelie exit and turned to the man who felt so much like a stranger. "You'll apologize for being rude when she gets back."

Only a slight head shake, as though he couldn't be bothered to execute the full gesture. "*Non.* I will not, Jean-Luc. It is time you come to terms with reality."

CHAPTER TWENTY

Elise

Braced on the counter, I breathed through my nose and forbade myself from crying.

Don't cry. Don't cry. Don't let that dried up old raisin make you cry.

Everything in me pushed against the tears welling in my eyes, and I reached for a tissue from the shiny gold box on the counter. Dang, this place was classy. I hadn't been to the resort in a while, and I'd forgotten how nice and detailed every bit of it was.

The door swung open as I dabbed at the corners of my eyes trying to save my makeup.

"Are you okay? He's such a jerk." Aurelie let loose a volley of what I assumed had to be insults or curses in French. "I am so sorry."

She stood next to me and held my gaze through the mirror.

"I'm okay. I knew it wasn't going to be easy—Luc warned me. He just... he kind of went for the jugular, and I'm not even sure he realized it."

Aurelie scoffed. "Oh, he realized it. He knew. He probably ran a background check on you before he stepped on the plane."

The crush of embarrassment and sadness hit again, and I cleared my throat to banish it. Luc had warned me, hadn't he? Or, he'd tried. Who knew why I thought it wouldn't hurt to have that bruise pressed on.

I needed to explain, though. It wasn't all her grandfather's fault.

"It's just... my mom. She is one of those women who trades husbands for a bigger paycheck. She's probably the very thing your grandfather is scared *I* am, and I can't blame him if he looks at my family and sees a glaring red flag." I sniffed, begging my eyes to stop leaking. "It's silly I should care so much—" I stopped myself before adding *when this is all an arrangement, it's not even real*, just in time. The truth was, "It has me wondering if I'm like her."

My words were all but air by the end. She reached for me then, her hand finding mine, and she turned me toward her by the shoulder with her other one. She held me by the upper arm and dipped her head to speak right into my eyes.

"You are your own woman. I don't know what kind of person that is, but I know it's someone who loves my brother. I know it's someone who didn't ask for this treatment and who didn't propose to *him*, didn't initiate it for financial gain, and to me that means you aren't like her."

I sniffled again but kept my jaw locked tight, afraid if I opened it to speak I might let loose a full-on sob. The combination of my shame, her kindness, and the overall opulence of the setting driving home the stark disparity in my life and Luc's… it hurt.

"My grandfather's motives are clear. He doesn't want Luc with anyone but the person he chose. That's why he's leveraged the trust, let alone forced the issue by coming here. He should be respecting Luc's choice and respecting you, but I'm sorry to say he isn't. I'll be having a word with him about that, but for now, please tell me you're okay. Tell me you believe his nastiness doesn't mean anything about you."

With a huff, I tried to absorb some of her certainty. "I'll try. I really will. I don't want—" My voice cut out again, but I cleared my throat and willed myself to get through it and lock up those tears. "I don't want Luc to suffer because I'm upset. I just want him to feel like he's done what he needed to do." Maybe that was too close to the truth…

Impossibly, Aurelie's gaze softened even more than it already had. "I don't know your mother, but I suspect you are two very different people." She squeezed my shoulder and dropped her hand. "You're a strong woman for doing this, Elise. A few tears don't change that."

This to her must be dealing with her family. I wondered if she'd be so charitable if she knew the truth—that I didn't love Luc and he didn't love me. Didn't that make it worse?

She leaned toward the mirror and checked her lipstick which was perfect. When she leaned back and found me watching her, she winked. "Thank you for being here for my brother. Now, are you coming?"

With a fortifying breath, I nodded. "I'll be right out. Just need another minute."

She left without another word, and I took a moment to wash my hands and go through the familiar routine of drying and tossing the luxurious paper towel in the trash.

Voices just outside the door had me taking my time—I was not interested in running into anyone before I was fully ready to rejoin the dinner. I'd regained my composure and felt like I could reasonably return and plaster a smile on my face, and maybe even withstand another round of sly questioning from Mr. Devereaux.

I'd fallen into a familiar trap of thinking about myself this way—poor me and my gold-digger mom, right? But Aurelie was right, and she hardly knew me. I wasn't the same person as my mother. I didn't have a secret motive to get money from Luc let alone marry him for his wealth. In the end, this was all fake and it was all because he'd asked. I wasn't getting paid for this—something *I'd* insisted on. He offered and I refused—absolutely the opposite of what my mother would've done.

Luc needed to be the focus. I could lean into this messy situation and help him and stop feeling sorry for myself— about my mom's choices, my financial situation, my stupid ex, or my awareness that I didn't fit in this world or this role Luc had asked me to play, but if he still wanted me for it after tonight, I'd do it.

Wasn't I done letting men push me around? I'd vowed I'd never be in that situation again. It was one more reason I had said no to Luc's offer to pay me. So why was I letting his grandfather make me feel small? Why would I allow that man, someone I didn't know or care about, affect me in any way, or keep me from doing what I'd come to do?

I was here for a man who'd become my friend. At this point, insanely, he mattered to me.

A minute later, I returned to the room, more resolved than ever to hold my head high and see this through. The men all stood, and Luc's gaze speared into me, searching my face like he might be able to see exactly what I'd been thinking or what Aurelie had said.

Michele had been speaking and continued once Luc had helped scoot in my chair. His lilting accent was so engaging, it provided a welcome distraction from the swirl of awkwardness slithering around the table whenever a pause in conversation occurred.

After another few minutes, and a few bites of a truly spectacular steak I no longer had much of an appetite for, the waitstaff cleared the tables and set down desserts I didn't recall ordering.

Once everyone had taken a bite, Mr. Devereaux said, "I've been thinking Odette should stay with you."

I blinked, then glanced up to see him looking at Luc.

Luc finished chewing the bite of the double chocolate torte he'd taken. "That's not happening."

"Why would she stay with Luc? Doesn't she have a room at the resort?" Aurelie asked, skepticism ringing loud and clear in her voice.

"Unfortunately no. The resort was full by the time we booked. I looked at booking a little cabin associated with the inn down the road, but I'm not sure the accommodations will suit her needs. Staying with Luc affords them the opportunity to get to know one another."

In a flash, a few things happened.

First, out of my peripheral vision, I saw Luc's entire posture go rigid and his jaw flex.

Second, Aurelie's mouth dropped open enough to show me she was truly shocked by her grandfather's audacity.

And third, I lost my damn patience.

The fantasy that flew across my mind was of me taking a perfectly white glove and swatting it across his face, channeling Dove in all her glory. Since I couldn't do that, I'd take a different tack.

Setting aside my napkin, I turned to the man in question.

"Unfortunately, Luc's home will be full. We'll be there together, and we'd hoped Aurelie and Michele would join us and stay in the guest room. Perhaps, if they're amenable, Odette could take their room at the resort, and then everyone will be comfortable."

Mr. Devereaux's expression hardened.

That's right, sucker. You just got outmaneuvered by a donut maker!

"I hadn't realized you two were living together. It seems a bit hasty considering—"

Luc was on his feet as he spoke. "We're engaged to be married, Grand-père, and with all due respect, it is none of your business who lives where."

He held out a hand to me, which I eagerly accepted and slipped out of my seat.

"We'll see you all tomorrow to get settled at the house?" he asked Aurelie and Michele with expectant eyes.

Michele's grin was so wide, it could've powered the sun as he rose from his seat and pressed kisses to either side of my head. "*Absolutamente.* We'll see you both."

Aurelie repeated the gesture, catching my eye and raising her brows. I returned the look with an "I don't know what happened, it just did," and then we departed.

Hand in hand, Luc led me through the opulent restaurant's main room and down the hallway to the magnificent resort lobby. We exited into the cool night air of spring, a touch of sweetness and the bright tang of green things growing on the breeze. He kept going, his pace measured and a little quick for my taste, though I appreciated his desire to get the heck out of there.

He opened the passenger side door to his car, and I got in. Seconds later, he ducked into the driver's seat and shut the door.

We both stared ahead, my mind running wild with an almost giddy sensation after putting the old man in his place while also edging around some real concern I'd overstepped.

Finally, he shifted in his seat to look at me and our gazes locked.

"So, you're moving in?"

CHAPTER TWENTY-ONE

Luc

Elise had to open the shop early the morning after our dinner with my family, so she hadn't moved in yet. I'd help her load up some basic items she'd need for the next few days to carry out the ruse, and we'd get her set up in my house this evening.

Not just my house, but my room.

My bed.

This was so far from what I'd planned. Between the restlessness plaguing me about the whole setup to this new hurdle, how was I supposed to maintain the distance necessary to manage my family? We were never supposed to be so close for any length of time. This was another level of imposition on her. Knowing I'd promised not to kiss her without her saying the word, I was smart enough to sense distance would be essential. And yet hadn't I been thinking she should get out of that unsecured apartment? Granted, her ex shouldn't be an issue any longer, but still...

Still. We would be very close in the coming days, and the risk had escalated. The odds of me not wanting her even more...

I shook off that thought, but not before Kenny noticed my expression.

"Uh oh, is someone daydreaming about his fake fiancée?" He grinned like the thought of me thinking of Elise made *him* happy.

"Just thinking over some logistics. She's moving in today."

He'd taken a bite right as I started speaking and he nearly spit out his food when he heard me. He chewed frantically, eyes wide and no doubt delighted, before he swallowed and said, "Moving in?"

A breathy laugh tripped out of me as I remembered the blazing fire in her eyes as she told my grandfather in no uncertain terms that Odette wasn't about to stay with me. That *she* was already living with me, and we wanted to have a slumber party with my sister and brother-in-law.

Okay, she didn't phrase it that way, but she'd set us up to all be in quite close quarters, hadn't she? Even if Aurelie and Michele wouldn't be critical of how we acted in the same way my grandfather was, it would be very new territory.

All night, I'd expected a sense of dread to settle in as I came to terms with the plan. Not only were we pretending to be engaged, but to be living together. It was a brilliant plan on the one hand, as it reinforced the idea that my grandfather was too late to effect any change, and yet we hadn't discussed it.

Between the way she reeled me in with her strength and

determination, and this new roommates situation, my plan to stay mostly unaffected and abide by my promise not to kiss her unless she asked was unraveling before my eyes.

"Yeah. My grandfather wanted Odette to stay with me, and Elise stepped in and shut that down right away." Satisfaction burrowed into me at the memory. Whatever damage had been done by the comments about her family, she'd rallied and doubled down. That show of strength stoked my interest and, if I was honest, the care growing in me for her each day.

"Oh, she did, did she? I approve." Kenny held up his hand.

Dutifully, I met it with a smack of my own.

He nodded with a grin. "But now you're going to be cohabitating with Elise? That's..."

"Unexpected," I provided.

"I was gonna say sexy, but sure. Unexpected works, too."

I glared at him, but after a bite of my sandwich, had to acknowledge his point. "It is a little *something*, for sure. She didn't do it as a way to get close to me, but it's going to have that effect since she also invited Aurelie and Michele to stay in the guest bedroom."

Lying to Aurelie didn't sit well, but so far it hadn't felt terrible. I worried being in the same house for several days, even if it was fairly spacious, would exacerbate the guilt.

"Oh, so you're going to be sharing a room." He gasped. "And there's only one bed." His mouth dropped open wide, and he wore the dopiest expression of all time. He was saturated with glee as he whispered, "It's just like *The Proposal*!"

My eyes shut to block him and his expression out, but also to block out the memory of Elise falling asleep on my shoulder as we watched that very movie. I'd liked her leaning on me just like I'd enjoyed every second I got to be near her or touch her.

His enthusiasm was doing nothing to help me keep my feet on the ground, but if I needed a reminder of why I was doing this, I'd have one up close and personal very soon. Apparently, Odette de Valois would be arriving in town tomorrow and my grandfather had arranged for us to all meet for a drink at the cocktail lounge at the resort.

Génial.

"It's not because we're not ending up together. Nor are we staging a fake wedding and duping a wily old woman or feeding small dogs to eagles. We're just..."

With his face cupped in his hands and elbows leaning on the table like a school child, he said, "Spending time getting to know one another? Slowly realizing she's a wonderful person on top of being a total ten? Finding out—"

"Hey, aren't you practically engaged?" I asked, irritation spiking.

"I am very happily imminently engaged as soon as my soon-to-be fiancée will allow me to propose, yes. She would also acknowledge Elise is a ten. I think literally anyone with eyes would, and that's before they taste a donut or have a conversation with her. Don't be an idiot and act like it's a secret." He gave me a disappointed look.

"Sorry. I didn't mean anything by it. I'm just... I don't know. I don't like lying."

No way he didn't recognize the irony of me saying this after just revealing I'd lied to him and all of our closest friends about my past and even my name... but I was turning over a new leaf in that regard.

He snorted. "Well, you sure set yourself up for failure on this one, then."

"Don't remind me." I'd brooded on that enough already, though. Elise had taken the engagement lie and pushed it up a notch, but it all fell within the parameters of what I'd wanted. It only made us more convincing.

So why did it feel like such a step off a cliff?

"What are you going to do about the other woman? And sorry, but why is she coming here? Isn't that weird?" he asked, then took a giant bite of his sandwich.

I exhaled and ran a hand through my hair. "Yes, it is. Supposedly, her family was already coming to the gala, but I doubt that. I suspect it's a ploy to get me to see her and decide I'll give it a chance or something? I'll meet her. I'm with Jenna tomorrow until late so I'll only have a few minutes anyway. I'll play the game to meet the minimum expectations my grandfather has while not letting him elbow in and ruin things between me and Elise."

Somehow, I'd convince him he could move on from his singular focus on me acquiescing to his choice. At some point, I'd find time alone with him and hope that the relationship we had long before my rebellion and his doubling down could reemerge.

"I'm glad Jenna's back. Hope she's doing alright." His brow furrowed, and we ate in silence after I agreed.

Jenna Halter had been an early client of Saint Security. She'd been through the wringer as her celebrity skyrocketed from being a vaguely familiar face to a must-see A-lister in the matter of a year. That fame brought with it opportunity and wealth, but also several forms of unwanted attention. I'd been part of her personal security team when I first left the military and lived in the UK while she worked on a project there and had seen her a few times since. We were good friends, and I was glad I'd get to work her detail again.

We finished our lunch and cleaned up the table in the

break room where we'd been sitting. Kenny liked to post up there so he got to see anyone who came and went from the fridge and microwave. "To maximize social potential," as he said.

"Listen, can I just say something about all of this? I know you know what you're doing and everything's fine, but..." he trailed off as we walked toward our offices.

"Of course. I value your opinion, even if you're obnoxious sharing it at times," I said honestly. He was one of my best friends and there was no denying it.

He grinned. "Good. So, maybe you should consider letting all of this be real."

Real? Was he so deluded with his own happiness he couldn't see that not everyone would end up with a match like his and Elizabeth's? The internal rejection came swiftly, even as something in my gut hitched like some part of me liked the idea.

Didn't matter how much any part of me liked the idea of things being real with Elise. Elise didn't want it, period. There was nothing else to say. So, I raised a brow, which he properly interpreted as my request for more explanation.

"You and Elise are good together. At least, she's good for you, or this situation is, or something. You came clean with us and I feel like I'm seeing more... you. I don't know how to explain it. You're letting us into your life, and it's a beautiful thing."

His expression was so genuine, I couldn't laugh like I might've wanted.

I couldn't deny he had a point, though was it Elise? Or simply the situation forcing me to own up to the truth?

Ironically, even though I was living a lie with my family by birth, I was living the truth with my family of choice, and the unanticipated side effect of that was an incredible sense of freedom. I hadn't realized how liberating it'd feel to have my closest friends know me even more than they already did, but now I was living it, and sure enough, this was me in all my authenticity. They knew the man they'd bonded with during our years in the military, and now they knew my true history, my real family name, and yes, even the wealthy roots that had formed me in key ways.

Whatever came of all of this, I would be thankful for the breath of fresh air this had given me.

Kenny continued. "Granted, I haven't *seen* you together since you actually started successfully stringing whole sentences together in her vicinity, but—"

I shoved him because sometimes he required it.

He chuckled. "My point is, I think you like her. And I don't know how she feels about you, but upping the ante on moving in with you isn't something she would've done if she couldn't stand you."

"An impressively high bar," I said, my insides feeling itchy with the direction of his comments.

Could he be right? No.

Non. Right?

Her display of confidence in our relationship came from the desire to take the agreement we'd made to the fullest extent. Granted, the "agreement" was really just her being kind and willing to help me since she wasn't gaining anything except a jerk-ex deterrent. She hoped to deter Callum further, and maybe it would. That was a small payout for what she'd already had to endure, but I hoped our appearance at the gala together would truly help.

I felt the chemistry between us, the desire to finally kiss her and claim her in some small way, so I knew there was something real there. But she didn't want real, and I wasn't sure I could let myself have it even if she did. I didn't have it in me to hope for such a thing, much less grasp it with both hands and hold on.

"I know you're convinced you're not interested in anything real, but..." He gave me a small, almost reluctant smile. "As a guy who thought the same for a long time, and had really convinced himself he didn't want to risk getting messed up by another woman, I can say with certainty it's worth it."

"What's worth it?" Liz asked as she shot Kenny a smile.

Kenny gasped, then he ran toward her with arms wide open and scooped her up. She wrapped him up, and they twirled around as he pressed kisses all over her face, and she laughed. They were both beaming, though his eyes were closed, and his face conveyed pure bliss.

"You. You're worth it," he said, setting her down gently and sliding his hand into her hair.

And that was where I left them. Liz had been gone for a few weeks, and apparently she'd just gotten back. They deserved to celebrate their reunion without me standing there witnessing it all like a creep.

As I settled back into my seat and tried to focus, my mind kept running back to Elise. Not even Kenny's words about her, but the woman herself.

In the wake of my grandfather's pushing and insults—his machinations to shove her out of my life—she'd stood firm. She truly was the strongest woman I knew, and if I thought she wanted me, I'd...

There was no point in entertaining such thoughts. It wouldn't be fair to either of us. She didn't want a relationship, and I had eschewed the idea for so long, I wasn't sure I could offer much of anything even if she did.

At least, that was what I'd keep reminding myself as I moved her into my house for the next week.

CHAPTER TWENTY-TWO

Elise

The last time I'd been this nervous, I'd been signing my name to the small business loan at Silverton Bank.

It seemed silly to feel so anxious about essentially having a week-long sleepover, but I hadn't spent the night at someone else's house in recent memory, and I hadn't shared space with Luc like this *ever*.

Maybe worst of all, I'd found myself buzzing with a level of anticipation I hadn't dreamed possible. Teasing out what that meant was confusing, and so sometime in the night last night, I'd let myself off the hook.

Luc was a good-looking man who had proven to be thoughtful, gentle, kind, and safe. It was okay that I was excited to spend more time with him and see behind the curtain a little.

In this version of the story, I was the street urchin helping the undercover royal escape the mean streets only to discover he was a prince. And now, the only way to get into the castle was to pretend to be a princess, worthy of him outwardly, but knowing I possessed no wealth and nothing to offer.

Though honestly, that was less a fantasy and a bit more like reality than I cared to admit. So maybe instead, I'd flip the script. Maybe I would play an heiress on the run, and he would take me in for my protection. And while there, maybe there'd be only one bed, and we'd huddle together for warmth...

Ultimately unhelpful, thanks, brain.

I wouldn't mind seeing Luc's place and getting a feel for his life, even if we were still in the Lalaland of a fake relationship. In that sense, it was better than anything real because it was all just for fun. There were no stakes.

Yeah, totally no stakes at all. Suuuuure.

Shoving that unhelpful commentary aside, I refocused on the simple distraction of seeing his home and how he lived. Plus, I really enjoyed Aurelie and Michele, so more time with them was a plus, too.

But as I set my kindle and water bottle on the side of the bed farthest from the door, it hit me.

We'd be sharing a bed. His sister, brother-in-law, and grandfather believed we'd already been living together, so the setup needed to look at least a little like I'd spent a decent amount of time here. Considering I'd never stepped foot inside this home until twenty minutes ago, that would be a feat.

"I'm not sure I'll remember where everything is," I said, turning to find Luc hovering by the door to his bedroom. "I don't want it to be too obvious."

"They won't care. We can blame it on the fact that you've only just moved in. And we could say we spent more time at your place while we were dating since it's closer to town, which is technically true."

His small smile made me reflect the same back at him.

"I guess we'll see."

"They're not going to be here until tomorrow, though. Since Odette doesn't arrive until then, they decided to stay the extra day, so we have tonight to ourselves." He swallowed, then rushed to add, "To get familiar with things, I mean."

"Right, of course." *Ugh.* This was so awkward, it almost hurt. I didn't want this weirdness between us, but it was entirely new territory. I simply didn't know how to get past it. "Mind if I use the restroom?"

I slipped into the primary bathroom as he excused himself. Like everything else in his home, this bathroom was exquisite. Bright white free-standing tub that looked big enough for two, a shower with a rain shower head I was genuinely looking forward to using, and beautiful gray cabinets with what looked like almost iridescent white granite countertops. I wasn't sure what kind of stone it was, but so far, I loved his taste in everything. It tended to be a notch cozier than minimalist. Masculine, yes, but comfortable.

A few minutes later, I found him in the kitchen—another stunning space with beautiful natural stone counters, a deep sink, and stainless steel appliances. Sleek wood cabinets and top of the line equipment wherever I looked.

"Would pizza be okay for dinner? I got groceries today but I'm exhausted and tomorrow will be a long day. I'd love to just sit on the couch and watch a movie with you."

How had he just verbalized what felt like a fantasy?

His hopeful expression could've convinced me to do just about anything, but this? Absolutely.

"That sounds perfect. Yes, please."

Ten minutes later, we'd ordered the pizza and both changed into our lounge clothes. I had bright pink sweatpants, a black T-shirt, and a sweatshirt overtop while he'd chosen some dark gray jogger-style sweatpants and a soft-looking black T-shirt. Inevitably, he looked incredible in his more relaxed clothing, and I had to make a personal choice not to ogle his assets when he walked past me to get the remote.

Extremely difficult. The man was an absolute work of art and between the scruff, the shirt stretching across his biceps and chest, and the style of those somehow slouchy and yet fitted sweats, I was doomed.

His shirt looked so soft, and the way it dropped down from his pecs like there was nothing but brick wall between there and the waistband of his pants had me swiping a hand across the blanket resting on the back of the couch and imagining it being the stretch of territory that lay under his shirt.

"What are you in the mood for?"

My head snapped up and heat exploded on my cheeks.

There's no way he can know what you were just thinking about.

Nope. Couldn't be possible. And yet, what was I in the *mood* for? Yikes. A question I couldn't answer.

He studied me, his head tipped to one side, and added, "I mean to watch—what kind of movie?"

"Right. Yeah. Um, action? Something action-y. With cars."

So that went well.

Totally normal response.

He chuckled softly. "How about a Mission Impossible movie? I heard your friend Winnie's pretty into those."

"Oh, that girl is obsessed. Yes, let's do that."

There was always a female lead and some nice tension between her and Ethan Hunt, but if we stuck to the first movie, it was pretty low-key. I couldn't handle seeing a romance and having any kind of kissing scenes while sitting in a room with this man in that state of dress.

He sat at the other end of his sectional couch and pulled up the movie to stream it. Before long, the pizza arrived, and we chatted along with the movie. He made notes about how realistic some of the spy craft was, and it hit me for the first time since all of this started that Luc was a hard core ex-special ops soldier who actually knew stuff about *spy craft*. What?

"Okay, can we stop for a sec? I'm just realizing I know nothing about what you did in the military and that's a big gaping hole in the story if I'm clueless about that. You were in for more than a decade, right?"

He nodded, his face unreadable. "Fourteen years by the time I got out."

"You didn't think about retiring like some of the guys?"

That'd been what Bruce, Tristan, Adam, and Beast had all done. I thought I'd heard Wilder Saint had started Saint Security right when he got out, and Bruce joined him a while later. Kenny was too young to retire, but he'd been injured so I'd always figured that made the difference for him.

"I got in a bit later than most of them. Wilder joined when he was seventeen, Bruce when he was about that, and I didn't get there until nearly twenty-one."

I laughed. "Practically an old man," I said, marveling at the bravery it would take anyone to dive into military service, let alone someone who'd hardly become an adult.

"Ultimately, I wanted permanence, and I couldn't see myself staying if Beast, Barbie, and Stone were leaving.

When Stone brought it up, Barbie and I were on board. Beast had already planned on leaving since he'd clinched retirement around the same time Bruce did. Plus, I don't need the retirement pension or healthcare that comes with hitting twenty thanks to my mother's life insurance policy and other assets, so that gave me a lot of freedom to leave many don't have."

His eyes dropped to his hands and something about the movement made me ask, "Does that embarrass you?"

He exhaled sharply. "No. I'm not ashamed of the wealth my family has, so much as I feel strongly it is *theirs*. But I have repeatedly and consistently benefited from it, and with the trust, I'd still have more money than most people can imagine managing"—he cringed—"and then I say things like that and I sound like a total ass."

I laughed at the dismay on his face. "You do. You really do."

He smiled and it felt like the temperature went up ten degrees. Goodness, he was handsome, and that self-deprecation paired with acknowledging his privilege... it was deadly.

Couldn't keep focusing on that. I wanted to keep him talking. As willing as he was to tell me facts about his life—his family, his wealth, even the lie he'd told that got us here—I wanted to know him. The hints of humor and softness he let sneak through were basically catnip.

"What did you do? I have no idea what a day-to-day job would be like in the Army, let alone whatever fancy place you Saint guys all worked."

"I was a CMOE which means I'm really good at getting into places even when they're locked."

The half-smile he shot me now was no better than the

full-out one. This one had a boyish quality that made my stomach flip. *Again.*

"Wait so you could break into buildings and stuff?" I hadn't thought about that being an actual job for someone in the Army.

"If there's intel or an asset somewhere that's locked down, I was the guy who figured out the plan to get in and then took lead on making that happen." His gaze dropped to his hands again. "It was really fun."

I giggled then because it was so completely wistful and surprising, though I couldn't say why. "You miss breaking into places?"

He shrugged a shoulder. "Is it bad if I say yes?"

"As long as it doesn't end up leading you into a life of crime, I guess not."

We shared a smile, and all I could think was how much I liked him. He was funny and subtle and a little surprising. Who liked breaking into buildings? I would almost think it didn't fit him except he'd talked about being impulsive as a kid and then rebellious in his early adulthood. Then he'd found an outlet—legal burglary. What a weird thing to enjoy, and yet here he was.

And yeah. Just so appealing.

"No plans for a criminal life. I could go for a Robin Hood situation maybe, but I figured Saint is about as close as I'll get without being active duty and I'll take it." He leaned back and stretched his arms wide. "My grandfather would be horrified to know such a thing."

I laughed at his admission but sobered. We hadn't fully discussed what'd happened last night beyond planning to move me in. I'd added to his lie, and now we were waist deep in it.

"Are you sure you're okay with this? I realize it's a little late to ask, but I feel so bad that I let my temper get the best of me."

He stood and padded toward me with weirdly attractive bare feet, then held out a hand when he reached me. I took it, pulse climbing when our fingers connected, and he tugged me out of my spot on the couch.

"I have never been happier to be fake-engaged to someone than I was when you said what you did. Thank you for thinking so quickly."

He was staring at me so intently, those gray-green eyes pinned on me, and his hand holding mine felt so good. So safe and right and yet thrilling.

Everything I learned about him made me like him more. He had such a noble heart and yet a silly side I never would've imagined existed. No wonder he liked Kenny so much.

All these little pieces added up to someone I found myself caring about more and more. I enjoyed being around him, and I looked forward to seeing him. I *liked* him, even though a huge part of me said that was just about the most foolish thing I could do right now.

It was on the tip of my tongue to tell him to kiss me— just to try it while we were living in this fantasy world— when his phone rang and the moment evaporated with the sound.

For the best. This wasn't a fantasy. This was real life, and kissing Luc wouldn't help me remember that.

CHAPTER TWENTY-THREE

Luc

As I brushed my teeth with a little more vigor than was healthy, I relived the last twenty minutes like a movie in my mind.

Elise taking my hand and standing, her hair in a ponytail that accentuated the delicate curve of her neck and the handful of freckles I'd had the utter need to press my lips to. I'd resisted.

Something had shifted in her gaze, and I could've sworn she was about to tell me to kiss her, when my phone rang. And if it was ringing through, it was someone from work. Anything else would've been silenced.

They needed me two hours early as Jenna's plane was landing at six instead of eight tomorrow morning. I'd need to head in before five to prep. And that meant I had to get to bed since it was already almost eleven.

After finishing up in the bathroom, I slipped into my

bedroom—*our* bedroom—and my heart nearly stopped seeing her sitting up in my bed.

Our bed.

Shaking off that thought, I went to the opposite side and grabbed my book. The weight of Elise's gaze drew my attention—she was watching my every move. Thankfully, I sensed no fear coming from her, but there was something. Nervous energy perhaps, which was certainly what I was feeling, too. And I needed to tell her my plan so she could relax.

"I figured since Aurelie isn't here tonight I'd sleep on the couch. That way, I won't wake you when I go." Why did a dull ache begin as I said that?

"Oh, okay. Are you sure? I could take the couch. You should get some good rest since you're working such a long day." She instantly started moving, gathering her things.

"No, no. It'll be fine. I'll be in here tomorrow." I swallowed hard, the thought of climbing into bed next to her a temptation and fantasy wrapped in one.

"Right," she said, gaze glued to her ereader.

"I can take the floor, Elise. I don't want you to feel uncomfortable. None of this matters that much."

Her head snapped up and her throat worked. "I'll be fine. I'm surprised to say it, but I'm fine."

"I don't want you to dread going to sleep these next few nights," I said, wanting to get this resolved now so we wouldn't have to deal with it when we had an audience in the bedroom next door.

Finally, she looked at me. The fire in her eyes when she let me see it stole my breath, as did her words when she said, "I promise you I won't dread it."

Unable to find the right response, I simply nodded and

left with a quick goodnight. Once settled in on the couch, I realized a stark reality.

The woman had taken over my life. Yes, I'd created this situation, but thoughts of her—how she was feeling about things, how her business was going, if her ex had showed his face again, what she thought about me—had taken over.

And now she was in my house. We'd had dinner together, laughed together. I'd shared what few people knew about my work with her.

It didn't matter where I spent the night. I wouldn't be sleeping much at all.

The day with Jenna had been a good one. She seemed lighter on this visit than she had in the fall. Since Beast and Pop had taken down a famous producer who'd harassed and assaulted a bunch of women including her, I wondered if knowing that man was behind bars had given her some peace. He wasn't the only person who'd caused her pain, but I liked knowing at least one less person who'd hurt her was out there.

The day flew, and before I knew it, I was off shift. Thanks to her generous offer, I changed in one of the spare rooms in Jenna's suite, and right on time, was walking down to the lounge to meet Elise.

A woman hustled in the door, her dark waves rustling around her face and shoulders as she waved at someone behind the lobby Reception desk, then fiddled with a small purse before finally looking up to see me.

"Hello, fiancée," I said, voice a little rough at the sight of all that beauty and energy coming at me.

Her face burst into a grin. "Hello to you." Then she reached out and wrapped an arm around my shoulders, hugging me close.

I drew her in, relishing the heat of her body where my hand pressed in at her lower back and the other on the smooth skin of her upper arm. Tonight, she wore a black cocktail dress with short sleeves and a fitted bodice that tucked in at her waist, then flared out and landed just above the knees. Demure and stylish. Understated.

Mouthwatering.

"You are incredibly beautiful," I said, my lips brushing against the shell of her ear.

"Thank you. You cleaned up nicely," she returned, the apple of her cheek grazing my jaw.

After another moment of connection, we pulled away. Maybe I'd imagined it, but I could've sworn there was as much reluctance in her movements as there was in mine.

She glanced toward the doors of the lounge where we'd be meeting my family and shifted on her feet. I'd avoided any anxiety over the evening until right this moment when I saw her nerves creeping in.

That's when I slipped the small item from its box in my jacket pocket.

"I have a little something for you," I said quietly, taking her left hand in mine and sliding the ring onto her finger. I should've gotten it before the first dinner, but if the question came up, I could say it was being resized at the time.

She searched my face, then looked down to see me settling the ring into place, and her mouth fell open.

"That is... that's too much, Luc. I can't wear this." Her

eyes grew wide, and she was just staring at it like she'd never seen anything more impressive.

Honestly, it was a beautiful ring. Perhaps a bit ostentatious in that it was a three-carat round-cut diamond with smaller rose diamonds surrounding it. It was as much like a donut as I could get, and it reminded me of her.

"You can wear it. I bought it for you."

"No, like, I can't wear this. It's huge. And just like, wow. Like *there it is*." She held it out to me like I hadn't seen it.

"I know, and I hope you'll wear it proudly to let everyone know you're mine."

Her eyes snapped up to meet my gaze, and something shifted in me at either her expression or the feeling of her hand still in mine.

Or maybe it was calling her mine while she stood there looking so beautiful and wearing a ring I'd just put on her finger.

But she's only yours for a few more days.

I heard the voice and instead of running from it and the feeling lacing through me that screamed, "Let's do this for real!" I decided to lean into it. Something had shifted when I bought that ring. I couldn't explain exactly what, but it slackened twine that'd been pulled tight around a part of me and now it was loosening. Easing.

While we were here, we might as well fully play the parts, right?

Dropping my head low so no one could overhear, I spoke softly. "I know it's a lot, but would you wear it for me? It will help them all know you're taken, and I'm taken, and soon, you can take it off and never look at it again if you want."

I wouldn't tell her I hoped she'd keep it. Maybe not wear it as my fiancée because I wasn't fool enough to want let alone hope for such a thing, but certainly keep it for herself. Sell it, even, if she wanted to.

She nodded, glancing at her now-shaking hand, and sighed. "Okay. I mean, yes, of course I will. I—I'll probably have to take it off when I'm at work, though."

"Ah. Of course. I did wonder how cumbersome this might be." As a man who had spent years working with his hands in one way or another, I'd wondered if it would bother her while she shaped her donuts or... whatever that process looked like. From the inside breast pocket of my suit jacket, I pulled out a delicate platinum chain. "I thought maybe you could wear it on this when at work."

"You thought of everything." Her words were slow and surprised.

"I thought of you," I admitted, because I had. Selecting an engagement ring hadn't been something I'd imagined doing, but the process of it had been fun. I'd bought one girlfriend a necklace when I was a teen and still basking in the ease of my identity as a Devereaux, before my mother passed, and having a romantic connection felt like a risk I couldn't bring myself to take.

This was different.

She turned and held her hair off her neck.

"You don't have to wear this if it's not—"

"Please put it on me, Luc."

I wouldn't deny her the request since an odd drive in me wanted to drape her in all kinds of jewelry from me like it made her more mine than if she didn't wear any at all.

I slipped the tiny chain around her neck and fastened it, then rested it against her skin and indulged the impulse to drag my fingers away a little more overtly than I would've if she hadn't captured me so completely tonight.

Right. Just tonight, huh?

She turned back around and her dark gaze found mine again, her expression simultaneously soft and full of need.

My stomach bottomed out and I swallowed, watching her lips as she said, "I think... Before we go in there, I need to say, I think I'd like you to kiss me."

I straightened, the words a bolt of lightning to my system. "Here? Now?"

She huffed out a laugh and smiled. "No, not now standing a few paces away from your family. I don't really want an audience for our first time."

Our first time.

Our first time.

Our first time...

Grasping, clutching, aching need hit me, and a world of possibilities rippled out from her words.

"Maybe after? When you take me home?"

When I took her home. To the house we'd share, and the bed we'd share now that Michele and Aurelie had moved their bags to the house and settled into the guest room while Elise and I had both been working.

There was only one possible answer.

"Alright, Elise. I'll kiss you when we get home."

CHAPTER TWENTY-FOUR

Elise

Mr. Devereaux looked as tanned and severe as ever as we entered the luxurious black and red lounge. Aurelie was glowing, as was Michele, and since they'd had such a happy aura of congeniality every time I'd interacted with them in the last few days, this was no surprise.

With Luc's hand burning a hole in my dress at my lower back and his promise that he'd kiss me when we got home... well, I was basically on fire.

It wasn't just his touch or the impending kiss. It certainly wasn't the highly ostentatious and incredibly gorgeous ring he'd slipped on my finger. It was the little platinum chain he'd fastened around my neck, the brush of his fingers there, and the lingering reminder that he'd thought of me.

He'd considered *me*.

It shouldn't have been revolutionary, but it was. In his

very Luc way, he'd given me a huge gift that might've seemed flashy for the sake of our situation, yet nestled it into thoughtfulness so personal, it made this feel real.

And it just shouldn't feel that way. It couldn't.

And yet you asked him to kiss you? Great way to make it stay totally fake, genius.

Just the thought of the kiss had me igniting again.

I was set aflame right until an absolutely stunning woman stood from a wing-backed leather chair and turned to greet us.

This must've been Odette.

Her long blond hair and giant Disney princess blue eyes fringed with thick, dark lashes and her absolutely ridiculous bone structure gave way to a lithe body with porcelain skin and French manicured nails and a dress so feminine and classy in a blush pink, I could hardly breathe.

Like, really, I could hardly remember how to inhale because it felt like someone had punched me in the gut. *This* was the woman Luc's grandfather had chosen for him?

She's a frozen princess singing at an ice palace and he's a guard who shows up to capture her, then falls for her in the wind-whistling night...

Half of me expected Luc to snatch the ring off my hand and tell me, "Thanks, but no thanks." I honestly couldn't have blamed him if looks were the only factor. But when she smiled as though delighted to see us both and gave prim little air kisses to him, then me, I simply didn't know what to do with myself.

"I'm so happy to meet you both. Mr. Devereaux has told me so much about you," she said, an alarmingly genuine-looking smile on her face. No trace of an accent like Aurelie, so maybe she was actually from New York despite her rather French-sounding name?

But like, she had to secretly be evil or something, right? That was how the stories went. She'd be awful, and then I'd feel happy to have helped Luc escape his dire fate.

If nothing else, she was beholden to her parents, or Mr. Devereaux, in some way. She wouldn't be here otherwise... unless what she wanted was a loveless marriage with a super wealthy, super-hot war hero?

Okay, so maybe her being here isn't that big of a mystery.

"Nice to meet you, too, Mademoiselle de Valois. I hope your travel was uneventful," Luc said, offering her a subdued version of his smile.

A sickly sensation flashed through me—jealousy.

"I heard you own a donut shop, Elise. Are you open tomorrow? I'd love to come try one. I've been in Europe lately and they just don't know donuts like we do," she said, a sweet giggle accompanying her words.

"We are open, yes. Seven to ten-thirty tomorrow." I hoped my smile didn't look as fake as it felt.

Aurelie put her arm around my shoulders, shooing Luc away. "Her donuts are the best I've ever had. I mean that," she said, looking right at me like she needed me to believe her.

"I'm so glad." And I was. I just... couldn't quite care about my donuts right now.

A waiter arrived and set down a tray of drinks including six flutes of champagne and several high ball glasses filled with cocktails. I wasn't one to self-medicate with alcohol but right about now, a glass of bubbly sounded like the perfect distraction from the green monster rearing its head in my chest. Luc wasn't mine, per se, so was I taking this fantasy too far here? No. Let's just say I was invested in my role as his doting fiancée.

"Let's toast." Michele gestured at the tray and everyone took one, Mr. Devereaux the slowest to acquiesce.

"To Luc and Elise and their new engagement," Aurelie said, a sly wink directed at her brother and me.

"And to being open to new opportunities when they present themselves," Luc's grandfather said, then a posh, "Santé."

Well. Okay. Not going for subtle at all then, which wasn't a shock. After all, he'd insisted on the meeting in the first place, so it wasn't like we could pretend he didn't have a motive.

Everyone joined in, echoing his cheers and enjoying a sip. I may have taken a rather hearty drink before setting down my glass and taking the seat Luc helped me into. He'd said nothing, and part of me felt he should've, but he wouldn't poke the bear so overtly, nor would he risk being rude to someone... unless that someone happened to be Callum.

"Odette has just obtained a Master's in Organizational Leadership and will be looking to take the helm of a large non-profit in New York," Mr. Devereaux said, tipping his flute toward her before taking another drink.

"That's exciting," Aurelie said, offering her a smile.

"Si, congratulations, Odette. Do you know which organization?" Michele asked, cheery smile shining over at the woman.

I didn't hear her response because despite the decent preparation Luc had given me, and the warnings he'd shared about how this would go, I hadn't realized just how brutal it would feel to be set up directly next to a woman who was essentially my foil. Her looks were my opposite, her family was no doubt the inverse of mine, and here she was with a world-class education, a master's degree, and heading for a job at what would undoubtedly be an impressive non-profit.

"Are you alright?" Luc asked, his voice so close, I startled slightly, then shut my eyes when he pressed his lips to the side of my head.

Whether the affectionate gesture was rooted in the need to be convincing, or if it'd been in an effort to comfort me, I'd take it either way. I needed to remember who I was. I didn't care about any of the things Odette had. Good for her. So far, she seemed lovely, and her life had nothing to do with mine.

I nodded and patted his thigh to reassure him without drawing any excess attention. Sadly, even the simple gesture did the opposite of what I'd hoped, and Luc's grandfather zeroed in on me.

"Do you hold a professional degree, Elise?" He waited with brows raised as though this were a completely normal question to ask someone.

"I have a bachelor's in communications." I wouldn't mention the half of an online MBA program I'd completed since I'd left that by the wayside almost two years ago. I'd realized I couldn't open the store and complete the degree, neither financially nor with only twenty-four hours in a day. One had to go, and for once, it hadn't been my dream.

I'd spent so long acquiescing to others and, at that time, Callum. He'd talked me into letting him invest, and although it'd made me slightly ill to allow it, he did. He'd even wanted me to continue the master's and he'd cover the difference, but in my heart of hearts, I'd known him helping that much more would make me miserable. I hadn't wanted him to contribute at all, but he'd made a convincing case, and we'd been together for a while at that point, so I'd said yes.

Quitting the MBA had been an important choice for me. Maybe someday, I'd go back and pick up where I'd left off, but it'd been the right move. The more I'd gotten into the nitty gritty of the business, the more I'd seen how some of the MBA programming had been helpful but much of it didn't really apply to my little shop, and that was okay. I'd learned so much by doing and I was proud of that.

Except you're currently failing, which is why Callum is trying to salvage his investment and sell it off.

I blinked away from that cruel reminder right as Mr. Devereaux said, "And this donut shop is... a franchise?"

The disdain with which he said the word made it seem like anything unoriginal would threaten his ability to breathe. One would think he'd never experienced a retail chain in any capacity, but the designer stores with his brands' labels on the doors were, in fact, chains.

"No, it's an original," I said, a little burst of pride hitting with the confession.

"Ah. Well, we can see you and Luc aren't exactly—"

"What made you decide on donuts?" Aurelie asked, quickly cutting through whatever delightful criticism her grandfather would've landed.

I smiled at her stealthy work. "I love them, and I had a period a while back where I experimented with all kinds of baking but kept coming back to donuts after I tasted an amazing one in Salt Lake. It was too far to drive to satisfy the whim of a craving, so I started making them here and sharing them with friends. Soon, people were requesting them, asking if they could order them, and... well, the rest is history."

The community had driven my belief I could have a store here. They'd supported it in peak ski season and in the slim months. I'd never be anything but grateful to the residents of Silverton for the way they'd allowed me to bring my dream to life.

Even if that dream gets sold off to someone I've never met.

"Oh, I love that," Aurelie said.

"É una storia perfetto—a perfect story." Michele smiled.

I beamed at them both, appreciating that they'd taken the time to come to the shop and try a donut, and also that they were clearly trying to help Luc. They were good people, and they were doing right by Luc with every breath tonight.

Odette, too, seemed charmed by my story. I hadn't shared all the details, but I supposed it was nice enough to learn someone had turned a passion or pleasure into a fruitful business.

"It is, however, a clear reason you and my grandson aren't suited to one another. You are tethered here, and he is a member of an international community. You have a... background that has trained you to expect very little from your life and my grandson is in a situation where—"

Luc stood and reached for me, tugging me up from my seat and walking out of the lounge leaving only a murmured "Excuse us," in his wake.

"Are you okay? I'm fine, really. I knew he wasn't approving of us," I said, a little breathless in my efforts to keep up with him as he took giant strides to get us out of the lounge as fast as possible.

He whipped around and his intense gaze was full of stormy emotion. "He has the gall to say such things directly to your face, but he won't speak to me. He tried the other night but I shut it down and I'd foolishly hoped he'd heard me. And now this, this... this vitriol disguised as concern."

He paced away a few steps, then returned a second later. "I don't know how you'll ever forgive me."

His frustration with his grandfather made perfect sense, but I didn't need his outrage on my behalf. I'd felt small at first, but something clicked when he asked about my degree. I didn't need the credentials of a master's degree to give me value and I couldn't manufacture a past with pedigree or old money or links to royalty or whatever it was that man wanted to see in the match for his progeny.

I was fine, and I wanted Luc to know this, so I grabbed his face and pressed our foreheads together, taking a large, deep breath before saying, "I promise you I'm fine."

His gaze searched mine like he thought I might be hiding something from him, but after a few seconds, he shut his eyes and deflated, just a touch. "Thank goodness."

A soft smile grew on my lips because he really was as sweet as I thought, and now I knew all the more what to do.

I was fine. I liked him. And I wanted one thing in this moment. Somehow recognizing how *fine* I was, whatever happened here, gave me the boldness to say, "I need you to do something for me, though."

"Anything," he said instantly, not a millisecond of hesitation.

"Kiss me."

CHAPTER TWENTY-FIVE

Luc

The words chimed through me like they were on a different frequency, or like my body and mind understood them on every plane of existence.

My hands found her waist and something in me yelled, *here's where we live the dream* as I jumped in right as her arms locked around my neck. I pulled back for a moment to make sure I hadn't imagined the words, but when I saw her expression—the desire and request written plain as day—I leaned in.

All worry about the risk fell away. The implications evaporated from my mind. All that was left was the pure desire to do exactly as she asked. No more fake or real. No more putting on a show. Simply her wish as my command.

The first press of our lips was soft, so soft. It held all the care she deserved, every bit of tenderness I feared she'd never experienced. The second was a consolation, a gentle meeting. The third something longer, slightly more. I would take everything she would give but nothing she didn't want me to have, and in as much as *I* wanted to kiss *her*, she had to lead. She had to show me what I could have.

The fourth kiss gave way—it broke past something in me when she opened to me, inviting me into more depth, more warmth, more heaven right here in this dimly lit hallway.

The soft carpet underneath me was what ultimately had me pulling back. I would kiss Elise Cordero until the sun came up, but it just didn't fit. Not here, and not after what we'd just gone through.

Not with this needle of fear reminding me what happened to people who fell in love weaving its way into my side, begging for attention I wouldn't give it.

She seemed to understand as I broke the connection between us, her wonderous dark eyes a little hazy and her focus soft.

"Home?" she asked, as though it was the most natural thing.

As though the two of us going home together was always what came next on nights like these. As though this wasn't all a ruse, as proved by the kiss we'd shared. As though we both belonged there.

And so we went.

It might've seemed a simple thing to take one's fiancée home, but the complexity hit in real time when we walked in the door. The wired energy coursing through my veins in the wake of our kiss had calmed only slightly on the drive home.

Home to where we were not only staying together, but would sleep side by side. Aurelie and Michele would likely take their time before they arrived, managing Grand-père and being as genial to Odette as possible before making their way here. God bless them.

Because we needed time—to more fully discuss what'd happened and to talk about that kiss.

It hadn't been for practice, and it hadn't been platonic or anything but a molten beginning of something I wanted more of. I hoped she felt the same.

And yet, the thought she might was utterly terrifying. Because that would open up a possibility I'd shut down for so, so long. I knew how to navigate this whole thing when it was fake. Not when it became all too real.

Did it mean I'd forgotten all of this was only temporary? A fake solution to a problem?

No. I hadn't forgotten. But I'd start to wonder... what if?

What if we didn't stop everything once my family left? What if we let ourselves linger over each other, take our time and see if, maybe, out of this foolish choice of mine, something good might emerge?

Seeing Aurelie and Michele had a way of reminding me of both what our father had lost and how we'd not only mourned our mother but the loss of *him* because he'd completely unraveled when she passed, but also making me long.

Seeing Beast and Jess did this. Watching Bruce and Nikki, Tristan and Winnie, Jo and Adam, Wilder and Sarah, the Washingtons, and even the glimpses of Liz and Kenny I'd gotten... witnessing their love had needled into me and made me want.

I'd crushed the impulse, having promised myself a long time ago I wasn't going to fall prey to the kind of agony I'd watched ruin my father. Because I knew I was like him, totally his son where matters of the heart were concerned. We Devereaux men fell and fell hard—love was all or nothing, life or death, ecstasy or agony. No in between. We didn't do that, didn't know how to.

Now I'd set myself up with a woman I'd thought was untouchable, but was she? Was she really? The confusing mix of hope and fear mingled in me and spread out to each of my limbs.

There it was again, a pang of something like longing for *more* and yet, a pain knuckling against the bones of my sternum. A harsh, vivid feeling attempting to force my face into the reality that my grandfather not only didn't care for my choices but didn't know me. And neither did my father. And while I was lying to her, neither did my sister.

But I was working toward a place where at least my grandfather would have a chance to, if he wanted to take it. Losing my maternal grandmother had reminded me he was all I had left of that generation. He wouldn't be around forever. I wanted to repair this with him, to have something of a relationship before his time was gone. I hoped he would, but after tonight, it seemed hard to imagine. Aurelie would, for sure, once all this was over.

That maybe, right now, the person who was coming to know me in the purest sense might be Elise.

In fact, it *was* Elise. She'd seen me grapple with my grandfather, my past, my service, and even the parts of me I was working to make peace with. She could laugh with me, then at me when I was being an ass. She was a spring breeze and morning sun and every little wildflower that would soon bloom in the fields at the base of Silver Ridge Peak.

I didn't want to think of that for another second and thankfully, there were more immediate matters to attend to.

Inside, we both went to the bedroom to change clothes, and my pulse quickened the instant we both stood there realizing this was a shared space.

Then I cleared my throat and grabbed some clothes from the dresser. "I'll change in the bathroom—think I'll grab a quick shower. Take your time."

"Could you help?" she asked, turning and lifting her hair.

My throat convulsively swallowed. "Of course."

Tugging at the little zipper, I slid it down over the first ridge of her spine, then the next, down between her shoulder blades and all the way to her lower back. The dress gaped just enough for me to see inches of her smooth skin uninterrupted by anything all the way down to a glimpse of black lace toward the bottom, the fine curves and lines of her bones and skin and a constellation of freckles so beautiful I had to forcibly keep myself from pressing my lips to each one.

"Voilà," I said, clearing my throat and turning instantly toward the door for fear of losing my grip on logic.

Inside the bathroom with the door firmly closed instead of wedged open like I'd momentarily imagined doing, I shrugged out of my suit and made quick work of a shower. No allowing myself any time to think about Elise right outside slipping out of that gorgeous black dress, or what more hid underneath the fabric.

What I'd seen was beautiful, but it was no surprise. Everything about Elise was beautiful, from, yes, her physical appearance, to the way she considered others. Her work ethic, her drive, her passion for her store and the quality of her product but also her friends.

Her kiss. Now that was a beautiful thing, too.

I scrubbed a towel over my hair to dry it and took a moment to focus before I left the bathroom. At some point, Aurelie and Michele would be back. We still needed to have something to eat, and I had another long day tomorrow before the gala. Another evening seated next to my grandfather and Odette since he'd bought a table, and then we'd be free.

"What's wrong?" Elise asked as she opened the fridge and pulled a carton of eggs out.

"I—" My mouth shut as I searched for words. I couldn't tell her how I'd wanted her to join me in the shower, or how I'd wanted to slip my hands into that dress and—no. That would do nothing to help the situation.

"My grandfather only sees me as someone who's failed his checklist. He's got a standard I haven't lived up to, and while I've chosen not to, it hurts. He wasn't always so hard with us—exacting in some ways, yes, but he was... at one point, he was simply *Grand-père*, too. I fear I've only made that version of him disappear faster."

She rinsed her hands and rounded the counter to look me in the eye and revealing fire in her own gaze.

"I know you've not been perfect, but you're not giving yourself enough credit."

I grumbled pathetically. "I've given myself more credit than he ever will."

"I can imagine wanting him to accept you, but please don't diminish what you've done. You could've lived a life of incredible ease but instead, you chose to serve. And not just do a quick tour—you spent years in an elite unit doing... well, aside from breaking and entering, probably some important stuff, right? Getting bad guys and... saving people?"

Bon sang, this woman was adorable. "There were bad guys neutralized and yes, we saved people, too."

That'd always been my favorite, and in some ways, my forte. Getting into a building covertly and saving someone before the bad guys ever knew and *then* eliminating them? Even more fun.

"That matters. That's honorable. And not only that, but you're now part of a community. You've helped and protected some of my friends. You—you've made Jenna Halter feel safe! I mean, I don't know that for sure, but I guess I assume if Bruce keeps assigning you to her, it means she thinks you do a decent job and she trusts you."

Her voice rose and her cheeks were flushed with the impassioned tone, and I could no longer sit with the poor me feelings that'd been trying to surface. I simply slipped a hand around the back of her head and drew her in, taking her lips with mine.

One quick peck, and I backed away, remembering myself. "This okay?"

"Yes," was all breath, but I heard it and took it as law, instantly returning to kiss her again, deepening the pressure with a ravenous kind of hunger I hadn't allowed our earlier kiss to acquire.

Her hands slipped into my hair, and our bodies were flush. I was seconds away from hoisting her up when the front door swung open, and a sharp gasp followed by a low giggle hit my ears and must've met Elise's, too, because we jumped apart.

Only one man giggled quite like that, and turning to glance at the front door, sure enough, there was Michele, Aurelie, and somehow, Kenny and Liz.

CHAPTER TWENTY-SIX

Elise

Kenny dangled a key in his hand and grinned so wide, he looked like he had multiple sets of teeth like a shark.

"Knew having a set of your keys would come in handy," he gloated and sauntered into the living room. "Your sister wasn't sure you'd be home, and she forgot to ask for a key. We ran into each other outside the resort and got to talking. In the name of NATO and our relationship as allies, not to mention my place as your adopted brother, I offered to get them in."

Luc loosed a pent-up laugh and I exhaled out a heap of tension.

Liz's eyes were wide, brow raised, and she had "we have some catching up to do" written all over her face.

Girl, do we.

I owed everyone an update, but Liz had been gone and

super busy with wrapping up her life elsewhere, and we'd only swapped a few texts. The more I got to know her and spend time with her, the more I liked her and wanted her to know me. That thought was novel because I'd only had it with my existing friends, and to feel it so keenly for someone new was unheard of for me.

Granted, I felt that way more and more with Luc.

Liz had let us in either because Jo had sort of forced us on her, or because she'd allowed it—probably both. But I hadn't done the same. I'd kept everything close and deluded myself to think I was doing them all a favor.

I'd kept everything to myself when I was with Callum, and I thought I'd learned the lesson about not leaning on myself when I had friends who genuinely loved and supported me. And yet, the *doing* of it was so hard. Sharing myself and what felt like my massive failures—to see what a jerk Callum was, to successfully fund this business on my own, to handle the pressure from my awful ex, and maybe even to navigate this fake fiancée business without catching feelings... I didn't look forward to it. But at the same time, I would do it because I wanted them.

"You barged into my home for what reason?" Luc asked, his face more than a little perturbed.

"We came to say hi and see how it's going," Kenny said, smacking a piece of gum between his teeth. "See how the happy couple is handling Grandpappy's visit."

The meaningful glance he gave Luc communicated much, not the least of which was that he wasn't about to ruin the whole thing by letting on that he knew we weren't actually engaged.

I went to Liz and opened my arms, eager for a reprieve from the weird tension and genuinely wanting to welcome her home.

"Everything wrap up okay in DC?" I asked, knowing she couldn't tell me much about her past life in the CIA, but hoping she'd settle in and feel more and more at home here.

"All done." She blinked, a smile growing wide. "I worried I'd be kind of heartbroken, and there have been some bittersweet moments for sure, but mostly I just feel happy."

I hugged her tight again, then released her, joining in her smile and feeling the happiness coming off her in waves.

"And how long are you going to make him wait? I heard he's waiting for permission to ask you to marry him?" It was perfectly Kenny that he'd be ready and waiting for her.

What would it be like to have a man like that? Someone so eager to commit to you and delight in you?

My gaze flickered toward Luc and found him already looking back at me. A cork popped and pinged around inside my chest when his eyes seemed to soften and a smile flashed across his face before he focused fully in on whatever Kenny was saying.

"I'm not sure. I think the bigger question is... how's engaged life? You'd know, wouldn't you?" Liz's eyes narrowed on me.

With a deep breath, I brushed the hair out of my eyes and nodded, glancing to make sure the others weren't listening. "Kind of, yes. And I plan to fill everyone in at book club this weekend. We have the gala tomorrow, and I'll see you and most of the guys there, and then I'll be ready to explain everything Saturday."

Nerves whistled through me at the thought of both the gala and laying it all out for my friends.

It'd be a relief to have both events over with.

Liz patted my shoulder. "It's your life, Elise. Just want to make sure you're okay."

She studied me in a way that made my heart prick. She must've known a bit about Callum if she was worried about me—or maybe she'd dealt with women who'd been in bad situations. I loved her for checking on me, even when my supposed fiancé was her almost-fiancé's best friend.

"I really am okay. I promise."

She accepted my vow, and Kenny announced they'd leave us to family time. The phrase had an odd kind of wistfulness winding through me as Liz and Kenny left and we found Aurelie and Michele ready to catch up.

"Grand-père was unspeakably rude, Elise. I am so sorry."

Aurelie clasped my hands and squeezed as though she could imbue me with her sincerity via the touch.

"It's nothing. I'll admit I wavered for a minute, but once he started in on education, it actually helped. I've made peace with my choices in that regard, and I have no regrets." It'd hurt to be reminded of my family's faults, but it'd given me a chance to remind myself I'm not the same woman my mother was. And I was my own person. Whoever couldn't take me as I was could leave it. Their loss, not mine.

Revisiting that part of my history while the business was struggling had been a good thing. It'd reminded me I'd made choices, and I'd stuck to them. Maybe I'd lose the business. Maybe Callum would prove yet again he was determined to be the worst version of himself and finagle a sale of my company to someone I didn't even know just to punish me for not doing what he wanted. But in the end, I'd tried.

Even though I'd had a little help, I *had* tried. And I'd made some freaking awesome donuts.

"Wonderful. You're resilient. That's a wonderful quality to have in a partner," Michele said with a beaming smile at me, then shifted it to Luc.

Uncomfortable with any amount of praise for the situation, I shifted awkwardly and moved to finish scrambling the eggs I'd planned to make for dinner. After another minute or two chatting, Aurelie and Michele went off to bed since they were still adjusting to mountain time, and Luc sat at his bar while I cooked our simple dinner. We ate in silence, both drained and fully aware Aurelie or Michele could come out at any time.

And then it was time to go to bed.

We took turns changing and going through our routines for sleep. It hadn't felt this surreal last night, even before he'd declared he'd sleep on the couch. But now, my heart wouldn't stop pattering around like an amateur tap dancer and I saw my hand visibly shake when I picked up my ereader.

Luc entered not long after I'd settled in with soft-looking shorts and a T-shirt. I averted my eyes from his legs because it felt oddly intimate seeing them after only ever seeing him in pants. They were muscular and covered in dark hair like his arms and just as attractive as everything else on him.

It also made him seem closer to naked. Technically, he was, right? He was missing feet of material covering those shapely calves and the bottom few inches of his ridiculous quads, not to mention his knees. How had no one warned me how sexy knees could be?

Get a hold of yourself!

"This okay?" he asked, standing on his side of the bed with his hand on the duvet.

"Yes. We can handle it."

I can handle this.

By now, I knew him well enough to know he wouldn't try to take advantage of this situation nor would he be upset if I told him I wasn't okay with it. I truly wasn't scared of him, and the nerves rattling around inside me were more on the *thrilled* end of the spectrum. I wasn't about to delineate that thought, so "We can handle it" it was.

He slipped into bed. I couldn't even feel the mattress depress because it was some kind of super luxurious king-sized dream, and once he was settled against the pillows, we were still a solid two feet apart.

But then he did it.

That sneaky Frenchman knocked the wind right out of me with one easy move.

He slipped on a pair of thick-framed reading glasses and pulled out a book.

And all my confidence melted into a steamy little pile of swoon.

CHAPTER TWENTY-SEVEN

Elise

The man sat and read wearing his glasses for a solid twenty minutes before I lost my mind enough and had to speak.

"I like your glasses. Have you had them long?"

Abrupt and absolutely out of nowhere for him, but the only thing I'd been thinking. Well, that and *don't look at the beautiful man with his mussed hair and thick frames and the serious notch between his brows while he holds an honest to goodness book or ye shall perish* plus a dozen little bookish side quests thanks to the current view.

I knew myself and what I could handle. This felt like... more than that.

I'd thought I could handle the bed situation. I mean, I really had myself convinced, what with the king-size of it all.

But this?

No one warned me about the glasses. I had seen him slip them on and off at the shop but somehow it'd never occurred to me he'd wear them at home. Here. All kinds of willy nilly in the bed.

And somehow, the messy hair was killing me, too. He'd tugged at it once or twice while reading in a mindless way I found charming but now that I'd touched said hair, I wanted my hands in it again. I wanted his face pressed to mine, his lips, his hands...

"For just a year or so now, and only for reading. Do they bother you?"

I blinked. Did they bother me? If I hadn't met his grandfather, I might've been more perplexed by his question, but what really informed me was my experience with my ex. Because this was exactly how I would've responded to a statement about some feature or part of an outfit.

My heart twisted in my chest.

"What? No, of course not. They look great on you. They're—honestly, they're really hot." *When in a frantic scramble to make sure someone doesn't feel awkward, make it super awkward by mentioning how ragingly attracted you are to them.*

While in their house.

In their bed.

Both of you in your pajamas.

It's fine!

But it wasn't fine because the half-smile that tugged at one side of his mouth sent a wave of heat crashing over me, and the dark brow rising to punctuate it should've come with a warning label.

"Really hot?" he asked, setting his book aside and leaning over like he might climb toward me, the smile fully notched up now.

Oh, no no no. We couldn't have that. He could not touch me right now, not after the kisses and the reassurances and the walking out on his jerk grandpa and his vulnerability in the kitchen and the glasses... nope.

"No! You—" I laughed, the expression on his face so pleased and boyish. "You cannot come over here." I slapped a pillow down in the space between us like a fence and couldn't hide the embarrassed smile taking over my face. "I mean it. You're—no. You can't cross this line. That's the only way this works. Otherwise, it's the floor for you, sir."

He held my gaze, essentially waving a match right next to a fire, and nodded ever so slowly. "Alright, Elise. Sweet dreams."

"You, too," I scraped out, certain that if I did sleep, my dreams would in fact be very sweet.

Any time with him was, and I could only hope he would show up in my dreams.

I rolled over away from him and shut off the lamp light. A few seconds later, his went out, too, and we were shrouded in darkness. I'd never paused to think about how intimate it was to simply breathe the same air as someone in the dark, to simply *be* with them and not lost in all sorts of self-conscious rabbit holes, but even separated by the space between us, this felt... weighty.

Could I actually hear him thinking? Could he hear me? The room felt full of desires and expectations and unspoken words.

And I knew with certainty I had to stay put. We were getting closer every day and before I knew it, it'd all be over. I couldn't afford to get wrapped up in Luc and suffer the hurt of a breakup when we were done here, when the whole point of this was to convince Callum he had no shot with me no matter what kind of nonsense he pulled. The additional benefit was a chance to think of someone other than myself and enjoy distraction from my own life.

This was never supposed to *become* my own life, but when sleep finally pulled me under, there was no denying it simply was.

Luc was gone when I woke up. I recalled him slipping out of bed and me saying something like, "Have fun," before he was gone. I lazed around enjoying the fact that I didn't have to be at Glazed since Marisol was manning the helm today because of the gala.

I spent the day reading and taking care of some admin work, then signing into my PA job in the afternoon to check that box. I was so sick of this grind but also grateful for the padding.

Luc wouldn't be happy to know I considered texting Callum to make sure he wasn't going to force the sale, but my heart had pounded so loudly in my head when I pulled up his name, I'd taken that as a warning sign. If he was going to do something like that, he'd have to get my permission. I had no intention of giving it. So that meant no news was good news.

Right?

I needed it to be right, and so I embraced it as such. After showering to freshen up, I was slicing an apple in the kitchen for a snack before starting my hair and makeup for the gala when Aurelie burst into the house followed by several people with large black cases and one person with an entire rack of wrapped clothing.

"Uh, hello. What's going on?" I asked, shoving a slice of apple into my mouth before whatever this was exploded all over my snack time.

Aurelie fluttered over to me on tiptoes and held out her hands. Instinctively, I gave her mine.

"This is our gala prep team. We've got hair"— she waved at a tall man with blond hair artfully swirling up like a wave on his head and a wide smile who twiddled his fingers at me, "makeup,"—she grinned at a woman with stunning cat eyes, deep red lips, and a purple Leia bun on one side of her head with the other shaved, "and styling." The final woman offered a nod toward me as she used both hands to unwrap the dresses hanging from the portable clothing rack.

"Wait. I hadn't planned on any of this. Luc said he'd send some dress options, but..." My words faded out as I realized this wasn't Luc's doing. Maybe the dresses were, but more likely, this was all thanks to the maniac smiling so broadly, I could practically feel the elation rolling off her in waves.

I chuckled and accepted my fate, ignoring the twinge of excitement in favor of staying grumpy for one more minute. "You and my friends would get along." If Jo and Dove were here—heck, if *any* of them were here, they'd be delighted.

She pouted, pushing her plush lips out into a ridiculous frown. "Don't tell me you're one of those girls who hates dressing up?"

Her pout might've seemed silly, but her tone and the disappointment in her eyes were clear. I didn't want her to be sad, and I wasn't against dressing up.

"No, not necessarily. It's just intimidating. I don't normally mix with these crowds." Even though I knew many of the people who'd be there tonight, Silverton residents or otherwise, I didn't normally parade around in evening gowns. The two cocktail dresses this last week had been a stretch as it was.

Aurelie's energy perked up again. "You belong there, just as anyone does. But to make sure you look the part, and therefore feel every bit like you own the place, we've got reinforcements." She winked at me, then smiled over at the team. "And when my brother sees you, he's going to want to move the wedding date up. But if you don't want any of it, say the word. Are you in?"

My stomach flipped at the thought of seeing Luc. I'd gotten glimpses of him in tuxes at various events—the film fest in the fall and maybe some other thing the Saint men had to do in their line of duty that entailed looking all badass and also wear a tux like they were our own local James Bonds.

I hadn't fully thought about how powerful it might be to see him up close and personal in a tux. As my date.

As my fiancé.

The ring he'd given me, the absolutely stunning perfection of a ring, warmed my finger. I fiddled with it for a moment, drawing in a long, steadying breath. "I'm in."

No matter that I'd just shared a bed with the man for the first time ever last night. No matter that my heart reacted far too intensely any time I heard his name, thought of him, or actually saw him.

I'd show up looking fabulous and play the part he'd asked me to play. Tonight was essentially our big finale.

Luc

The ballroom bustled with activity in all corners and the opulent room looked even glitzier with gold and black décor like something out of Gatsby. Thank goodness they hadn't made it a themed affair.

My day with Jenna had been fine. I'd been dragging thanks to minimal sleep, but I'd held it together and she'd force-fed me espresso at regular intervals, so I was alert. Maybe too alert based on the way my heart was racing just standing here looking for Elise.

She and Aurelie had taken a car. They'd left my house more than ten—I checked my phone and saw the time stamp—more than twelve minutes ago. They should be here any minute.

"You going to make it?" Kenny asked, chuckling and not even trying to make it under his breath.

"I'm fine," I snapped, then grumbled, "Sorry. I'm edgy. I don't know why."

Kenny slung an arm around my shoulders. "Could it be that you're eager to see your fake fiancée, and that you're also nervous about what kind of nonsense Grandpaps has planned?"

Chuckling, reluctantly it should be noted, I nudged him away. "Yes. All of that. Except the part where you call my grandfather Grandpaps." I laughed saying the word.

"I've gotta go do my job while you luxuriate and be an actual guest at this shindig but enjoy your totally not real, completely fake, definitely not catching feelings date when she arrives." He winked, then scampered off like a coward before I could respond.

But what could I say to the barb? He was an observant guy, and as was so often the case with him, he wasn't wrong.

This fake engagement had turned into something real. There was a closeness building between the two of us, and not simply because we'd kissed or shared a bed.

She may not have wanted a relationship, but she was showing me care and concern in ways no one ever had. She forced me to see the value in my service and encouraged me to be proud in a way I was certain Kenny or Beast or Stone would've, and yet coming from her, who hadn't been with me in the service and didn't necessarily share the same value, it felt rarer. And I was showing her parts of me no woman had ever known, certainly. I'd never been so vulnerable, never showed someone I'd dated the familial wounds or fears. My friends had seen those parts of me in some ways, but she was essentially living them out with me in real time and supporting me every step.

"Che splendore." Michele had sidled up with a drink in hand, but before he said anything to me, his whispered words slipped out and I knew he would only be saying such a thing about his wife.

And with his wife, my beloved sister, would be Elise.

I searched through the crowd and finally found where he'd directed his attention. Aurelie entered in a blood red gown that fluted out around her feet, her hair the same as always and lips matching. Michele would've crawled across the ballroom if she'd so beckoned.

Stepping into the room just behind her came Elise. My breath caught at the sight of her in a shimmering gown that looked like it'd been crafted of liquid gold. The neckline floated just below her collar bone and the cap sleeves draped around her shoulders. Thin straps kept the gown in place. The material flowed over and around her like silk, and my fingers twitched with the need to skate along her waist and touch the fabric warmed by her skin.

Her hair had been pulled up and I couldn't quite see it, but it left the smooth slope of her neck exposed and begging to be kissed. Her makeup was subtle and dramatic at the same time, her lips a soft pink and her eyes dark and as mesmerizing as ever.

"Totally fake, right?" Kenny's whisper came, but didn't pull my attention from Elise. Instead, I moved to her, right behind Michele who'd already been drawn magnet-like to his wife.

"You're stunning," I said the second I reached her, practically breathless from her beauty. It wasn't merely the dress or hairstyle. A glow radiated from her that showed such joy and confidence.

"You are, too. I like your tux," she said, smiling wide and eyes shifting over the fine buttons on my shirt.

"Your dress is beautiful. Good choice." I'd asked Aurelie to find a handful of options the stylist she'd hired could bring for Elise, and fortunately, they must've done their job well. The fit and color were a dream, but the way Elise carried herself, like she belonged here, told me she felt beautiful.

"Thank you for all of the options, and the hair and makeup and all of it." She ducked her head to fiddle with the small strap of the clutch she carried before giving me back her eyes. "I could've been on one of those makeover shows."

"You didn't need it, but it seemed only fair to take care of all those details. Aurelie used to hate the process of getting dressed and hair done—as you can see, she still refuses anything ornate." I glanced at my sister and her husband, who were walking hand in hand toward the dance floor. "Would you like to dance?"

Her eyes lit up. "I haven't danced in a long time, but sure, as long as you can lead."

I may have smirked. "I can lead just fine, Elise."

The way she bit her lip told me she liked the answer. A few seconds later, we were stepping onto the ballroom floor, the live band playing instrumental versions of pop hits, and we came together. She placed a hand on my shoulder, and I settled mine on her shoulder blade. A thrill whipped through me as our other hands clasped and I began moving.

"Am I understanding correctly that the back of this dress is rather... strappy?" I let my fingers splay wide and slide across the material of her dress and patches of bare, warm skin.

"It is rather fancy, yes," she said, her smile so damn charming I wanted to kiss it off her. But I wouldn't do that right now in this crowded ballroom.

Maybe later.

"I'll have to take a look," I said, my voice deeper, my hands urging her closer.

She huffed and shook her head as though to clear it. "Did you have a good day with Jenna? Any chances to break into a bank or something fun?"

I grinned at her reference to our talk about what I'd loved while active duty and searched her face for evidence of jealousy or concern. I'd casually dated a woman while living in Europe and guarding Jenna and when she found out what I did for a living, she hadn't liked it. People always imagined personal security personnel falling in love with their clients, but it just didn't happen that often, and Jenna and I had the chemistry of a cardboard box. On top of that, I had no desire for a future with the woman so I'd been very clear about the expectations, and she'd still attempted to claim me in a bizarre competition with my *client*.

"No breaking and entering, sadly, but otherwise, I did. She was more relaxed today now that the travel is behind her. I'll introduce you tonight if you like," I said, my stomach tightening in anticipation of how she'd respond.

"That'd be fun. I'd love to meet her, as long as that wouldn't be an invasion of privacy for her or anything."

Maybe Kenny was right, and I was already in trouble, but this response made a little piece of my heart lost to her. She wasn't jealous, but maybe that was because this wasn't real. She was, however, concerned for Jenna. And this was one of Elise's qualities I'd never tire of. She was so mindful of others and genuine about it.

Unable to resist, I dipped down and pressed my lips to hers, stealing the kiss. "Sorry. Had to."

One of her dark brows arched. "Had to?"

"Oui. *Tu m'as envouté.* You compelled me."

She laughed softly and we shared another smile. I kept

us moving around the dance floor, and soon, everyone faded away and it was just Elise in my arms and the music.

Until a tap on my left shoulder interrupted us. I glanced over, not sure who I would've expected to see, but certainly not anticipating seeing my grandfather.

"May I cut in?"

CHAPTER TWENTY-NINE

Elise

The fantasy of dancing in Luc's gentle but firm hold evaporated with the sight of his grandfather.

I super did not want to dance with him. What would we talk about? What would I say when the last thing he'd said to me was essentially I wasn't good enough to join his family?

"No, I'm sorry. I'd like a few more minutes with my fiancée."

Luc's expression was neutral, but I could feel the tension in his body that hadn't been there before.

His grandfather said something in French, to which Luc nodded, then Mr. Devereaux walked away.

"He said we should come have a drink before dinner. There's an open bar. I agreed, but if you'd prefer to find friends, I'd be happy for you to do that and not deal with him."

Apology laced every syllable, like he regretted I'd have to interact with his grandfather at all.

"That's why I'm here, though. I can handle him, really."

It wasn't false bravado that had me saying this, either. Gérard Devereaux had caught me off guard these last few nights, no doubt, but I wasn't about to cow to him. I'd spent enough time being degraded by men who thought they were better than me, and in the last twenty-four hours, I'd learned I could handle it. Heck, in the last five years, I'd learned the same.

Anything that man had to say about me, he could say. If he needed to belittle some woman he'd never met, a person his grandson had, to his knowledge, fallen for and proposed to, then he had problems. And they weren't about me.

This odd little adventure with Luc had forced me to confront more than one of my fears—my mother, my past relationships, and even my education and work choices. And tonight, surrounded by the one percent of society in Silverton and beyond, I felt more settled and proud of who I'd become through those trials than ever before. I wasn't done, but I was still growing. Still learning. Not stopping.

"I just don't know how far he's going to take all of this. But if I can speak to him alone, it might help."

The determined glint in his eye clarified it for me. "Okay. Why don't you have a drink with him, and I'll go say hi to Liz and Eddie. Oh, and I see Calla and Jenna over there. Maybe I can just introduce myself?"

He stopped our dancing and gave me a look I couldn't decipher, then kissed my forehead.

The action was so soft and slow, it shouldn't have startled me the way it did. It was just that I wasn't sure anyone had done anything so purely sweet, and it made me feel a little bit like my heart was breaking.

"She'll love it. I'll come find you in a few minutes," he said, that... *something* still there.

I cleared my throat of the emotion that'd suddenly jumped there and pressed a hand to his perfectly close-trimmed beard. "Perfect. And, hey—"

He gave me his full attention, right here in the middle of the bustling room with glitz and glamour and his grandfather's expectations crowding around us.

"Be honest with him like you've been with your friends and me. Help him understand you. He'll have no choice but to be proud of you."

I hoped my suggestion wouldn't be off base. I didn't mean to tell him things between us were fake, of course, but more that he wanted his grandfather's approval so much. He even seemed to miss the man in some capacity. I wanted him to have some healing in all of this, if possible.

His eyes glittered in the low light, and he dropped a kiss to my temple, then squeezed my hand. "Merci."

We parted ways, a stupid longing clogging up my chest as I moved to the side of the dance floor and finally registered just how busy it'd gotten. The ambient noise levels had ratcheted louder and there were bodies everywhere. Mercifully, I caught Liz's eye where she stood a few feet behind a group of people.

She was working even though she'd just gotten back into town, but that was Liz. She might've changed her whole career path, but the woman loved work. So many of the Saint people did. I wondered if Luc felt the same, though I had to believe he did, too, since it seemed he probably didn't have to work a day in his life to pay the bills.

"Psst. Is it illegal for me to talk to you?" I asked, sidling up next to her and bumping her shoulder.

She laughed. "No. It's not illegal. But I shouldn't chat

long." Her gaze cut to meet mine, then dropped to take in the dress. "You look absolutely fabulous."

I beamed. "Thanks. I *feel* it. I thought I'd feel like a joke walking in here, but I actually feel great."

She'd been surveying the room while I spoke, but her eyes came back to mine. "You belong here if you want to. There's no other qualification."

She might not have known my whole story, but Liz was smart and observant. And she'd recently fought a battle within herself trying to decide whether she belonged in Silverton or if she had to stay the course and do what she'd always planned to do, even if her dreams had changed. I was so proud of her, and I understood she wasn't just throwing out a trite statement.

"Thank you. And on that note, I'm going to go be bold and meet the woman my fiancé is spending all day every day with." I flared my eyes a little, both at the *fiancé* and the other part.

She winked. "I can promise you it's possible to guard an extremely attractive, charismatic person and still want to go home to the one you love."

Our gazes turned right as her person tonight, Jack McKean, threw his head back and laughed at something Julian Grenier and his wife Quinn Darling-Grenier were saying.

I patted her arm. "Strong woman."

We both laughed knowing she didn't need strength to resist Jack. She was completely gone for Kenny, and he for her, and they were both good friends with Jack, who was apparently a really good guy.

I wove my way toward where I'd seen Calla Saint and Jenna Halter, nerves amping up a little bit, when someone stepped in front of me.

"Hi, oh, sorry. I don't mean to waylay you, but just wondered if we could talk?"

Odette smiled apologetically but all this meant was that her beautiful, perfect face was both pretty and sincere and... wow. The ice blue gown she wore accentuated her eyes and she looked like a Norse goddess. Honestly, the woman needed to chill out because the rest of us mere mortals didn't stand a chance.

"Uh, sure. Yeah. What did you want to talk about?" I asked as I stepped closer to a bistro table and fiddled with the edge of the tablecloth draped over it.

She set down a champagne glass she'd been holding, then startled. "Wait, you need one of these. Do you want a drink?"

"Sure. Yeah, I'd love one, actually, but it's no—"

She looked around, her hair swishing in golden curls around her, and a waiter literally came jogging over from one of the bars nestled against the wall a few feet away.

"Could she have a glass of champagne?" she asked, smiling prettily.

"Yes, of course. One moment," he said, breathless to do her bidding.

She turned back to me. "Okay, so I know you want to get back to Luc, but I just wanted to clear the air between us."

My face likely spelled out the confusion without me having to say anything, but I still said, "The air?"

"Mr. Devereaux suggested Luc and I marry years ago, mostly thanks to our family's heritage and maybe some business connections. It's always been something my parents had planned on—*banked* on, if you get my meaning."

She'd lowered her voice conspiratorially and spoke like we were in on to something together. *Odd.* I didn't know where this was going, but I'd certainly stick around and find out.

"I hadn't met Luc or seen him in real life, and frankly, I didn't need to. Everything I know is from his family, and I barely know them."

She didn't want this any more than he did. *Interesting.*

The waiter returned with a glass of champagne for me and one to replace hers which was still half-full. We both offered him thanks before he stepped away and we continued.

"So, if you don't mind my asking, why are you here?"

She sighed and a sadness shadowed her face. "My family doesn't approve of the person I would choose. I've tried to convince them, but they have their motives and don't seem concerned with me or what I want."

"That's so... medieval. They think you'll just get married to someone you barely know and then *stay* married for their sakes? Is there a dowry young Luc would get for taking you off their hands?" Fury on this woman's behalf pumped into my bloodstream.

She grimaced. "They have their reasons for believing I would, but it's actually the opposite." Her expression turned cagey for a moment, and she glanced away. When she turned back, that pleasant, placid expression had taken its place. "So here I am, going through the motions, but I have no intention of doing anything to undermine you and Luc. The way he looks at you... that man has no interest, even if I had a heart to give away."

A flashbulb of joy burst in my chest, and I bit my lip, but a laugh still jumped out. "I don't mean to laugh, I just..."

"You don't mind hearing your fiancé's in love with you? I can't imagine it's a bad thing." She held up her champagne flute. "To true love. May it prevail."

There was a hope shining out of her, like maybe if she toasted to true love enough times, she'd get to have a happy ending for herself and the one she loved.

Could Luc love me? Could I love him? She seemed so certain, and she was so kind with her words. I had no idea where reality fell—maybe he'd taken notes from Jenna and Jack McKean and any other famous actor he'd worked with. He'd certainly managed to keep me in the dark as to how he really felt—or maybe he'd simply convinced everyone else he was in love.

I touched the edge of my glass with hers, smiling at her in full agreement with her toast. I wished for her sake, it would.

And though she wouldn't recognize it or realize what it meant, I feared the hope in her eyes was echoed in mine.

CHAPTER THIRTY

Luc

My grandfather sipped his cabernet with the usual imperious expression, though I could've sworn I saw a little crack in the façade of stoicism.

"You have to accept that I'm marrying Elise. I'm sure Odette is lovely, but she's not interested in me, and you know it."

If he couldn't see that, I pitied him. She was cordial and animated enough, but she made no effort to speak to me alone nor had she seemed interested in allowing him to put down Elise. This gave her points in my book, no doubt, but also spoke to her ambivalence.

"Of course she is. She may not be interested in *you*, per se, but she's interested in keeping her parents happy for whatever reason." He sipped his wine, the liquid darkening his teeth when he continued. "And this is an agreement set up without reference to her opinions or yours, however much you might want to resist that truth."

My teeth ground together. "I can't do that for you. I won't."

He whirled on me, grasping one side of my suit jacket, and hissed his next words. "You will do as you're told after spending decades wasting my time. There's only so much I will take before I am forced to—"

"To what? Disown me? Isn't that what you've essentially done until you decided you needed this from me? What do you have to gain here? Why go through with this when it's clear I don't want it? I thought we could fix things—I thought maybe seeing each other face to face might give us a fighting chance."

Elise's encouragement to be honest—to show him who I was—echoed through me. This wasn't likely what she meant, but right now, it was the most immediate truth he needed to comprehend.

He released me, setting me away and swiping a hand over the wrinkled material of my tux jacket. "If you were more like your sister, you'd comply."

Wasn't that always where we landed?

"I wish I could be that for you, but I can't. And I won't pretend I want anyone but Elise. If being with her means I'm disowned, then so be it. The money has never motivated me, as you know, and it still won't." Not enough for me to cow to him, if he was still going to refuse it. Saint Security would thrive with or without me financing it. I'd hoped an alternative—the idea that I'd already found love and made a commitment—might convince him to drop this.

What a fool I'd been.

He hummed a low, unamused sound. "Ah, but it motivates her, doesn't it?"

My jaw hardened. "Not in the slightest. Just like it didn't motivate my mom, and you still never accepted her, not even in the bitter end."

He glanced away like he didn't have time for me, but now that I'd finally said what I wanted, I wasn't going to stop. "I don't know how you can stand to look yourself in the mirror after the way you treated her. And now your own son can't stand to be present because he's so broken."

His nostrils flared. "He's broken because of her. Because she twisted herself around him so tightly he doesn't know who he is without her." He blinked rapidly, the movement betraying his rising emotion wasn't all anger.

"He *loved* her. There was no twisting, nothing wrong. They just loved each other, Grand-père, and the idea that such a thing is bad is what's wrong. Ignoring his grief, isolating her in her illness because you saw her as a money-hungry poor waitress from the US even after twenty years in the family—I don't want that for my life. I choose this."

I gestured to the room, my eye catching on Kenny, then Bruce in the far corner by the back doors, Beast standing sentry just inside the main exit, and Tristan a few feet away from Jenna. My friends—the men and women who'd become my family when I'd felt abandoned. The family I'd chosen.

My gaze found Elise, who was chatting with Jenna, smiling brightly as Jenna gesticulated and no doubt cracked jokes that would have Elise beaming the rest of the night.

"I choose love and kindness and offering the benefit of the doubt. I choose family, but not if that family insists on valuing money and connection over everything else." I held out my hand to him, hoping he'd accept. "I love you, Grand-père, and I wish you well."

His throat worked as he swallowed while eyeing my hand, then turned and walked away.

My heart sank. It wasn't a shock, but I'd hoped for more.

"He'll come around. Even if it's months from now, he'll accept it. He does love you, and I know he'll come around."

Aurelie's words were cold comfort in the wake of his storming off, but I wouldn't give up, even if it seemed like a long shot.

And in truth, wasn't it better if he did disown me? He wouldn't be around to see me and Elise dissolve back into what we'd been. Into essentially nothing.

The thought weighed in my head, tipped one way then the other as though being evaluated for truth, then clattered to the floor.

I couldn't imagine a time when we'd be nothing. I couldn't imagine moving backward. *All I want is to move ahead.*

But she didn't. And I had to respect that.

I grimaced at the thought and Aurelie squeezed my shoulder. "It'll be okay. I promise."

She likely thought I was worried about our grandfather and didn't like where we stood—or didn't stand—but it wasn't him causing my heart to twist. My gaze found Elise and after a second, she turned slowly until her eyes locked with mine.

The sensation of loss doubled until she smiled. Her beautiful lips tipped up and spread wide and she looked so genuinely happy and at ease, my heart nearly burst in my chest for an entirely different reason.

I loved her. Somehow in all of this pretending, all of this certainty that I wouldn't end up feeling more than simple attraction and admiration for her, I'd fallen.

Hard.

Instead of guarding myself against the thing I feared most—the thing that was ultimately at the root of what drove me and my grandfather apart, even—I'd let it come for me. And it had, without mercy. She'd encouraged me to be myself, and though I felt crushed with my grandfather's dismissal, I also felt the inklings of freedom.

Instead of fear and dread and anger like I almost wished for, I felt... joy. Like I wanted to scoop it into my mouth and fill myself up with this love for someone who wanted the best for me, who cared for me. A woman I admired and yes, astoundingly, loved.

Even if she couldn't, or wouldn't, return the sentiment.

"Thanks. I—I've got to go," I said, still entranced by the woman across the ballroom.

"Yes, you do. Love beckons and you must answer!" Michele said, and even as Elise drew me to her, I couldn't hold back the laugh at his cheesy lovesick little heart.

When I reached Elise, I didn't say anything. She took the hand I offered, and we whisked out onto the dance floor. The perfect excuse to hold her close, especially when I wasn't sure how much longer I'd get to.

"How'd it go?" she asked after a minute or two of twirling around the dance floor.

"I won't be shocked if he isn't at dinner." I also wouldn't be surprised if he was and simply didn't acknowledge my existence, but we'd see. There were only about ten minutes left before they'd ask us to be seated for the dinner portion of the evening.

She inched closer and brushed her hand over my neck, the contact sending a shiver of pleasure through me.

"I'm sorry."

With slight pressure at her back, I urged her closer. I wanted her plastered to me, but that wouldn't be appropriate, though a glance around would show a handful of couples getting as close as they could while still managing to stay on tempo—impressive.

"I'm not. I regret that he seems unwilling to listen to me or accept anyone's opinion but his own, but I don't regret being honest. I'm sorry dinner will be awkward if he does attend." It wasn't fair to subject her to any more of this, so maybe we'd just leave. I could see what Aurelie thought.

"It'll be—" Elise's words halted, and her attention was pinned over my shoulder.

I turned to look and saw what'd snagged her focus. *Callum.*

He stood by one of the bars with a scowl so exaggerated it would've been comical if it weren't upsetting Elise. Before I could twirl her away, he shoved off the bar and sauntered over with a sneer on his lips.

"Well, well, well," he said, like he'd found us in a compromising position and not dancing in a ballroom at a formal event.

"What do you want, Callum?" Elise said, all impatience.

"Oh, nothing. Just taking a minute to give my best to the happy couple. But you know people who get together by cheating don't last, right?"

Elise sighed, and I clutched her close.

"No one cheated, Callum. You and me? We weren't together. We haven't been for a long time." Energy coursed through her, but her breathing stayed calm.

He muttered something under his breath, and I nearly lunged for him, but Elise's hand on my chest held me steady while he stalked away.

"He needs to get a life and move on from you. This should help him figure out you're really not going back to him." The grit in my voice might've betrayed my repudiation of the man. I almost wished he'd given me an excuse to make good on my promise.

"He's lost it if he's been thinking we were together. He must've decided his scheme to sell out from under me wouldn't work, but it makes me nervous that he's planning something bigger." She'd directed her attention in the opposite direction, straining away from even the vicinity of where the man had gone.

Leading us to the far side of the dance floor, I used the moment to ask a few questions I'd wanted to but hadn't wanted to upset her with. "Have you spoken to him recently?"

"No."

"Good." It was simple. He shouldn't have been contacting her at all, especially now. More importantly, "Are you alright?"

Her dark eyes found mine, and she seemed to understand I meant more than generally. I meant was she okay about Callum—with him talking to her and now glaring. She needed only say the word and I'd find a way to haul him out of here.

Her gaze flickered between my eyes as though searching for something, or maybe deciding, and then she pressed up on her toes and brushed her lips over mine. "Yes. I'm alright."

It wasn't a declaration of anything, but peace settled between us—around us—new and weighty.

It almost felt like a promise.

CHAPTER THIRTY-ONE

Elise

Dancing in Luc's arms? Lovely. Dreamy. A magical experience on a night that ended up feeling less like an obligation and more like a fairytale.

His grandfather had simply ignored him at dinner, but he hadn't been overtly aggressive. Michele and Aurelie had kept conversation flowing and they'd done it flawlessly. I could listen to them talk all day between their accents and storytelling and Michele's silly romanticism.

We'd all gone home together, back to Luc's beautiful house, and just like the night before, we'd gotten ready one at a time, taking turns in the bathroom and sliding into bed.

But I didn't place the pillow barrier between us because I didn't need to. More and more, I had to admit I'd never felt safer with anyone.

My little fantasies and movies I made up were safe. They'd been a diversion from the total lack of desire for real romance for a while now. But Luc... Luc was safe, too, and not because he was fiction.

He was real.

He was considerate of me in every possible instance, protective but not in a way that made me feel crowded or weak, and he seemed to... well, sometimes I caught this look in his eyes I swear meant he wanted me.

Like I very much wanted him.

What did all of this mean? How did I handle the fact that this fake relationship had sneakily shifted into something more real than anything I'd ever had? I had no idea.

I'd shifted from watching little stories in my head to living one out in my life, too, now, possibly embodying the role of female lead in a dream that felt more and more like I was awake. And I simply didn't know how to process that.

But waking up in Luc's arms?

Heaven.

Yeah. We'd ended up nested together, finding each other in the night and holding each other. Waking up cocooned in his warmth had been a dream. An absolutely comforting, safe dream.

Right until I zeroed in on his hand splayed over the bare skin of my stomach and how our bodies were cradled together rather intimately. His steady breathing told me he was still asleep, but it would be wrong to stay here, wouldn't it? I shouldn't let myself snooze in the wondrous warmth of his arms while I was conscious and he likely had no idea we were spooning like professionals, should I?

A contented sigh slipped out, and his warm breath on my neck sent a shiver through me. Then he said something in French, his arms tightened around me, and I died.

Fine, I didn't die, but I was very nearly going to expire from... feelings. Lots of feelings in all directions and all of them rather delicious and all of them... mine. Not a character. Not a princess or a maiden or an enamored heroine, but *me*.

But one thought flared out over the dark messy sea of my desire and longing—caution. I needed to proceed with caution.

All of this was supposed to be for appearances, and there was no one in here checking to make sure we were behaving like almost married people did. No, this was all behind the scenes.

When I agreed to this, it wasn't like I couldn't see how gorgeous Luc was. I'd thought he was too handsome to be real the first time I'd seen him and that hadn't changed much. Now I knew about his small scar and the miniscule imperfections that made him less like an AI fancast of himself, sure, but I hadn't thought my desire to be with someone would change.

I hadn't thought I could meet someone I'd feel like trying again with. But here I was, not only savoring his physical closeness, but wishing I could burrow into his heart, too. Wishing he felt a little of what I had because my bruised little walled-off heart had softened to him. I'd become... open.

That thought had me moving and, strangely, tears pricking my eyes as I went, grabbing clothes and slipping into the bathroom to get ready.

Clearly, all the cuddling had gone to my head.

Because this was fake. Maybe I'd opened up to the idea of something real... maybe someday. But all of this was fake, and I needed to keep that in the forefront of my mind, or I'd drive myself crazy.

Last night, Callum saw us together. He got the message that, whether he liked it or not, he was *not* the man for me. I'd gotten exactly what I needed from the bargain.

I needed to talk this out and thank goodness it just so happened to be book club again tonight.

We'd discussed our book, chatting and laughing and so happy to have Liz back with us. I'd also managed to not talk about myself at all, but when Dove leveled her gaze at me and raised those blond brows, I couldn't pretend I didn't know what she was talking about.

"So, you may have heard that Luc and I are fake-engaged right now." Why not just put it all right out there?

Dove grinned and rubbed her hands together. Jo, Nikki, Winnie, and Catherine all nodded and murmured their awareness. Liz raised one brow ready for more, and Jess crossed her arms.

"Yeah, let's get into it. Jude said you guys were glued together on the dance floor and even kissed, so sounds like the deception is going really well." There was accusation in her tone, but it wasn't mean-spirited. Jess liked honesty and I didn't blame her.

"Sorry, but why is this happening? I think maybe I missed that," Nikki admitted.

With a big sigh, I launched in. "You didn't miss anything. I didn't share anything because I was chicken." I made a face, and they all chuckled, bless them. "Luc asked me to pose as his fiancée because his family is pressuring him to marry someone, which sounds insane and kind of is. That said, he comes from a very prestigious family and his sister did marry the man chosen for her, so there is a precedent."

Everyone absorbed that while Dove clapped gleefully. "It's the perfect set up for a marriage of convenience, right? He marries the woman his grandfather chose for him despite his wishes..." She swoons back into her seat on the sofa.

"Except for the part where he gets fake-engaged to me because he refuses to go along with it. So." I held my arms wide. "Here I am, Mrs. Jean-Luc Devereaux to be."

Jess squinted. "Devereaux? I thought his last name was Doux?"

"Apparently, he legally changed it? Or something? I don't know. But his family name is Devereaux as in..."

"The conglomerate that owns multiple billion-dollar companies?" Nikki asked, right as Liz said, "I knew his clothes were fancy."

"Yeah. He has money, to say the least." I shifted, the reminder sending a swipe of discomfort through me. He didn't seem to think his grandfather would release the trust to him now that things had soured so completely, but I hoped it would turn around. Even without it, he was set up very well financially.

"So you're his fake fiancée for this deal, but you're also dating?" Winnie asked, curiosity ringing through her words more than any shades of judgment.

"He doesn't want anything serious, and I certainly don't either." Dove gave me a look and after swallowing hard, I added, "Didn't."

I couldn't have anticipated the way saying those words —*doesn't want anything serious*—pained me now. I'd felt sure it was the best possible scenario when he'd proposed it.

I'd doubled down on it, reminding him I didn't date and didn't want to. Now...

Jess clapped once, Liz, Catherine, and Nikki grinned, Dove raised her glass high in celebration, and Jo and Winnie shared knowing glances.

"But that's what I need to talk about. What am I doing? I mean, I'm barely done disentangling myself from Callum." At the heart of my worry was exactly that—what if Luc really was too good to be true?

"When did you and Callum break up?" Nikki asked, usually the first to focus on tangible things, God bless her.

"It's been almost eighteen months since our main break up, and over eight months since I finally stopped being reeled back in." We'd been together almost three years by that point, and I cringed thinking about all that time wasted.

"Are you still tangled up in feelings for him?" Winnie asked, her words gentle.

"Callum? Gosh, no. I feel frustrated I ever let myself get wrapped up in him, and I don't want to repeat that, or my mom's pattern."

They knew a little about my mom and most of them aside from Liz had witnessed me working through some of the process of distancing myself from him. I hadn't wanted them to see—hadn't even willingly *let* them, but from this point of view, it seemed so foolish. Like I'd lost out on their support and love, and now all I wanted was to tell them everything.

Or, if not everything, then most of it. Definitely about Luc, because I didn't know how to handle this.

"A relationship like that is bound to have some fallout. If you're not ready, you're not ready, but only you can say whether you are or not." Catherine tended to be quiet, but when she spoke, we all listened.

"Agreed. If you feel ready for something, then you're ready," Jess confirmed.

Dove leaned over and reached for my hand, grasping it when I set mine in hers. "And if you're not sure you're ready, but you're feeling like you *want* to be... that you want anything with him, that's a huge sign."

Her sparkly blue eyes were seconds away from getting teary. I could hear it in her voice. My sweet best friend who'd supported me as much as I'd let her and was holding so much up herself. I hugged her, holding her tight and whispering my thanks.

No one else knew the true extent of my disinterest in anything romantic. I'd made jokes about not wanting to date, even declarations at times, but I hadn't told anyone but Dove how unappealing even the possibility of romance sounded... except that little inkling Luc had always sparked in me.

Some of it made no sense, and some was linked directly to how crappy Callum had been. But the point was, it'd all happened so seamlessly with Luc.

Maybe it was because he'd been eating in front of me for months? Maybe because he'd proven to be protective but not bossy, careful but not coddling, and this might've made me pathetic but I felt it down to my toes... he seemed to want me. I didn't know to what extent, but he seemed to genuinely enjoy being around me, choose to be around me, and not have a list of things he'd like me to change. Maybe it could simply be what it was—the distraction I'd set out for it to be, the fantasy come to life, for now. The first mission had been accomplished—Callum had seen us very clearly together. And the rest...

Luc and I didn't make sense on paper any more than we did in real life, but in this little fairytale I'd gotten caught up in? Maybe I could let myself enjoy it. Since I already knew we had an ending, it wouldn't be a surprise. I also wouldn't —literally *couldn't*—get swept up in something that turned rotten.

A practically perfect plan.

"Luc's a great guy. I say that confidently," Jess said, and her knowledge of him both as a Saint employee now and a former EMU member meant a lot.

"He really is," Jo agreed.

"He's one of Kenny's favorite people on Earth, so that speaks well of him," Liz said, her smile fond.

"I don't know exactly how this will play out. But maybe I just... enjoy it."

They all cheered, and I laughed, joy filling me to the brim as I embraced their excitement and, maybe even better, my own.

Now to find out what Luc had to say about it.

CHAPTER THIRTY-TWO

Luc

Two days after the gala, Jenna left. Most of the celebrities who'd flown in were gone and the Saint workload eased.

I'd hardly seen Elise. She'd been at her book club last night and I'd stayed up chatting with Aurelie and Michele, but by the time she got home, I'd passed out in the bed.

Our bed.

I also woke up in that bed. Yesterday, she'd slipped out before I'd roused—I'd gotten to report into my shift a bit later in the morning, so I'd taken advantage of that freedom after the last night at the gala. This morning?

The minty-sweet scent of her hair was the first thing I sensed. Then the warmth of her body pressed to mine— warmer than I was used to, and yet I didn't want her to move. She could sleep with her leg rucked up over my hips any old time.

Might be a touch problematic in some ways, but for the moment, I let myself enjoy breathing her in, the faint sounds of her own breath, and the pleasure of her contact and pressure against me.

Once my mind got creative, I forced myself out of bed and prepared for the day. Grand-père, Aurelie, and Michele would leave tomorrow, and I'd need to at least attempt to initiate contact, but I didn't particularly want to.

What I wanted most was to talk with Elise. After tomorrow, there would be no reason for her to stay here, would there?

Of course not. And that was why I couldn't let us get through the whole day without talking about what happened when we didn't need to pretend anymore.

Right as I'd gotten dressed, my doorbell rang. Could be another ambush from Kenny, but since I had plans to meet him and Stone—and for once Beast now that Jess was back on her own two feet—for afternoon tea, I doubted it.

Opening the door proved me right—on the welcome mat stood my grandfather.

His silver-gray eyes and unreadable face peered at me.

"Please. Come in." I stepped back to give him space and he took it, still not speaking.

"Coffee?" I asked, knowing he'd likely been up for several hours.

"Non, merci."

His gaze traveled around the kitchen, then the living room, the weight of his judgment heavy whenever he paused or jutted out his chin when he noticed something particularly American, no doubt.

"Why are you here, Grand-père?"

If he heard the exhaustion in my voice, he didn't point it

out. "I've extended my trip. I don't fly back until Thursday, and neither do Aurelie and Michele."

Why was I surprised? He did what he wanted without consulting me. Perhaps more surprising was that I didn't mind. In fact, it gave me more time with Elise, more time I absolutely wanted, and perhaps more time for me to help him see my perspective.

"Alright. Anything I should know?" Who knew what he had planned.

"I'd like for you to meet with Odette once more. Her family arrived for the gala, but I don't believe you were introduced." He turned his head away from a stack of thrillers sitting on a built-in shelf and waited for my reaction.

My gut response was to say it wasn't happening. I had no need to meet Odette's family because I wasn't getting engaged to her. She had no interest and it made no sense to plow ahead as though either of us wanted this.

At the same time, he was bound and determined to see this through. Maybe I needed to jump through a few more of his hoops so he could see I wasn't simply being stubborn. Of course, I *was* being stubborn, but for a justified reason. Add to this the reality that I had no plans to return to France or move to New York, I wasn't certain how anyone thought this would work.

Maybe seeing me in this town would help. Meeting some friends and seeing me with Elise a bit more... maybe all of it would help him understand how far from his version of life the one I was living was.

"I'd be happy to meet them. As long as there's no confusion about who I'm engaged to."

He craned his neck away as though barely interested.

"There is no confusion about your current engagement, trust me. They simply need to see for themselves there's nothing more I could've done. It should help the girl's case."

This piqued my concern. "The girl? Odette?"

"Yes. Her parents aren't convinced she did her part. So perhaps you can convince them she couldn't have done anything to persuade you to walk away from your... Elise." He strolled to the front door, unhurried and completely at ease with the fact that he'd pointedly put down my fiancée without actually voicing an insult.

"Alright, Grand-père. Just let me know when."

Before I shut the door behind him, he turned.

"I don't want to lose you to her." He held my gaze another second before leaving.

My cheeks burning with frustration and no small amount of shame, a part of me that I hated to examine collapsed in on itself. Why did these interactions make me feel like such a child? Perhaps because I was still lying to him when I should've been honest from the start, and worse, now I had actual feelings for Elise that'd confused every aspect of this.

Was it the simple act of engagement to someone he hadn't chosen that made him want to make sure I wasn't lost? Or was it—I swallowed against the thought.

No. No. I might love Elise, but we weren't like my parents. Were we? He didn't see that in me, didn't see my father's volatility or a future where, when I lost her, I'd disintegrate.

I didn't feel that much already. Maybe some of this had turned real—the feelings had come, unbidden—but that didn't mean I would drown in them. We Devereaux men loved with all we had, but I was also made of sterner stuff. I'd done fourteen years in the military, for starters.

I breathed deep, shoving away all those concerns and centering myself. Then I checked on Elise before I went out for a run, and the tenderness that filled my chest while I watched her sleep for those fleeting seconds was like a serving of wine in a too small cup. It ran over the edges and spilled out underneath me, unwieldy and messy and unfamiliar.

So visceral and powerful, like liquid emotion pumped through my veins, it terrified me.

I pushed myself on the run. Then I pushed harder. At some point, I saw the workout for what it was—my effort to figuratively outrun the mess with my family and the messy feelings I'd developed for Elise. But there was no evading them.

Elise had sent a text while I was out saying she would be checking on a few things at the bakery and then dropping by her house for a while. She had plants to water and mail to pick up. I would've liked to see her, but maybe this was better—some space for both of us.

When Bear greeted me at Stone's door, I sank down to pet him and give him his due.

"Bonjour, Monseigneur Bear. Comment allez-vous?" I pet his head, and he leaned in, all those protective instincts utterly disarmed thanks to the contact.

"Stop whispering sweet nothings to His Highness and get in here. We need to talk about your love life."

Kenny's voice came from the living room and punched me right where it already hurt.

Love life. I could pretend and say I didn't have one or I didn't even want one, but in my heart of hearts, I always had. I'd wanted what my parents had. I'd wanted to be so in love with someone I never wanted to be parted from them.

What I'd never been able to stomach was the thought of

such loss and grief that I ended up losing myself like my father had.

"Sit. Drink tea. Have a snack. Then talk."

Stone's face brooked no arguments behind his bushy beard. It'd gotten wilder lately, and I wondered if we should gently suggest a trim. Last time he'd looked this untamed, he'd been in a far different place. He hadn't been taking care of himself. The signs had been everywhere—no house-keeping efforts, hardly any clean clothes, no regular show-ers, and absolutely no self-care.

My stomach clenched at the memory, but as I looked at his tidy living room and the small plates of delicate, inevitably delicious creations, it eased. He was not in that place. He'd set his single-minded focus on baking and didn't seem to care about his appearance at all.

I sat without a word and did as told, taking the tea cup Kenny gave me and eyeing the snack selection. Beast grum-bled at me like he was seconding both Kenny's demand and Stone's order.

"Glad to have you back," I said, relieved I'd stolen a moment to update him on everything so I didn't have to lay it out now... not that whatever was coming would be fun.

Happily, every little bite I took was delicious, as always, and I realized I probably should've had lunch instead of coming here after a run and no recovery food and gorging myself on all of Stone's hard work.

"Have as much as you like. There's plenty."

Bear settled at Stone's feet and tucked his head over his paws.

I nodded in thanks as I chewed a bite and Kenny grinned.

"You know, you're such a gruff, quiet guy on the outside,

but I feel like your hospitality skills are top notch. The world out there's missing out on you."

Beast hummed, his mouth full, apparently echoing Kenny.

Stone shifted and frowned, not looking at any of us. Kenny recovered it immediately by gently setting a hand on his shoulder. "No pressure, big guy. Just saying you're doing great."

This was why I'd come. These were my brothers, and whenever I feared the hollow dread of being disowned, which might indeed happen, I needed to remember I wouldn't lose these men. I wouldn't lose Aurelie and Michele either, though I didn't know how complicated my grandfather might make their lives if he did want to disavow me completely.

"Okay, it's time, man. Let me cut to it." Kenny waited for me to signal and when I raised my teacup to him, he bowed. "You asked Elise to be your fake fiancée thinking she would be unattainable as someone who's pretty public about not wanting to date. But, since you are a sensitive soul who doesn't actually want to be single until he dies at a hundred and two, you ended up opening up, and now?"

The teacup bobbled in the saucer as I set it down, hand shaking ever so slightly. "And now?"

Stone and Kenny had nearly identical expressions.

"And now you've fallen." Beast's words cut to the quick.

Scrubbing my hands through my hair, I flopped back against the sofa and stared at the ceiling while they waited, two of them far more patiently than the other.

Finally, I admitted, "Yeah. I've fallen."

Kenny let out a whoop and a low, quick laugh came from Stone. Beast's low, satisfied chuckle topped it all off.

"This is great news," Kenny said, holding a hand up for me, which I slapped.

"It feels good for the most part, though she has no interest in anything beyond this. She made it clear she doesn't date and doesn't want to before we ever started this." I reached for one of the snacks, a little sandwich I didn't look too closely at because whatever it was, it'd be delicious.

"After seeing you guys at the gala, I am not concerned."

Beast's matter of fact delivery sent a bolt of longing through me while Kenny winked as though he had insider information.

I wished they were right. And yet I dreaded the same, because then we would both end up hurt, wouldn't we?

"I hope you're right. And I also..." I hated admitting this, but I had to be honest with them. "I also don't."

"Because you're scared." Stone's words were not a question.

"Yes. This feels big and I've never even approached this level of feeling for someone. Some of it was already there if I'm honest but I thought I could contain it. But the more I get to know her, the more I see her be herself, the more I think I was always doomed."

Kenny clasped his hand over his heart and sighed dramatically. "Doomed to love!"

I rolled my eyes, and the jerks next to me chuckled. Well, Beast rolled his, too.

Kenny sobered and held my gaze.

"Your dad lost it and that was scary for you to watch—traumatic in some ways, even. So this fear makes sense. But you're not your dad, nor is Elise your mom. If I could implore you for one thing, it'd be to let yourself take a chance. Elise is a good woman who deserves a good man and that's you."

I swallowed hard, hope and fear warring in my chest. But I wanted what he challenged me to. I wanted to take the chance. I could at least... confirm she felt the same as she did in the beginning.

I just didn't know if I could.

CHAPTER THIRTY-THREE

Elise

Luc arrived home right as I finished measuring the dry ingredients.

"Hey. I'm glad you're home. I feel like I haven't seen you in days."

Granted, we'd slept together and had ended up snuggled close this morning. He'd been the one to slip out of bed first, and since I'd been wiped out from a late night with my friends, I'd indulged in another lazy morning.

But I'd spent the afternoon doing my VA work and now I'd prepped a little project for us.

"What's all this?" he asked, entering the kitchen and going immediately to wash his hands.

This was something I really liked about him. He didn't automatically linger outside the kitchen. He'd clearly spent hours inside it and enjoyed cooking.

"I decided we need cookies." I had to do something for

him, and I couldn't figure out what. So my old reliable default I'd funneled into my business came out to play. I wanted to leave him with something, if this was about to be over. Leave myself with a memory we'd made together, too. Something real.

Interest flared in his eyes. "Is that so?"

I turned on his mixer to cream the butter and sugar, as much to deflect from the swoop of my heart at this last realization as a need to get on with it. "It is. I need to bake them, and you need to eat them."

The half-smile gracing his mouth was enough to make me blush. The man was just so handsome, and it felt like I'd hardly seen him, even though we'd been next to each other all night long. The key there was that we weren't talking, or even touching, on purpose.

We ended up that way but never acknowledged it. I'd decided I didn't want to mention it in case it made him think I didn't want him close.

"What kind of cookies are these?" he asked, then set a hand on the counter on either side of the mix, effectively caging me in.

My pulse started on the stair master, climbing bit by bit without stopping, especially when his stubble grazed against my cheek as he said, "Don't tell me they're chocolate chip?"

"Is that a problem?" I asked, dropping in the shelled eggs one at a time.

His breath coasted along my jaw, and he seemed to almost nuzzle me behind my ear. Was he... was he snuggling me? Seducing me?

Was this what happened when you made a man nicknamed Cookie chocolate chip cookies? *Note to self: cookies every day.*

I'd greet him at the door with a cookie and a kiss on the cheek. I'd leave work hours earlier and spend time doing something fun or volunteering, then I'd come home and make fresh cookies and wait for that little smile he just gave me that made my heart flutter.

And maybe he would seduce me then, and I'd let him, because—

"Not a problem at all. A gift, I think."

His hands slid closer to where I worked measuring out a teaspoon of vanilla and dipping it into the mixer, almost like he was trying to resist touching. Like if he nipped at my jaw and inhaled my scent, it didn't count, but if his hands got involved...

"I hope you'll like them, but I should caveat this recipe is nothing special. It's straight from the back of the bag of chocolate chips. I have another one I like but it takes a few days and I haven't—"

My words cut off when one of his large, warm hands pressed against my belly, urging me to lean against him.

Don't mind if I do.

Maybe we wouldn't have that everyday scene, but this, like much of it had already been, could be the indulgence.

"I love this recipe. I'm certain I'll enjoy the cookies, and all the more since you had a hand in making them."

His face was tucked into my neck, one hand against my body, the heat of him radiating across my back. The temptation to drop my head back on his shoulder and forget all about the cookies nearly overpowered me, but then he nudged the bowl of dry ingredients toward the mixer with his free hand.

"Don't overmix, non?"

I huffed an exhale, releasing a bit of the pent-up tension

building in me, and nodded. "Wise. Though less important with cookies. But still, wise."

"Less important? Than donuts?" he asked, his tone sounding almost casual, though the way his fingers splayed out along my abdomen, the tips of his index and middle finger brushing along the top of my jeans, and his voice low and rich in my ear were anything but casual.

Dear sweet Nestlé, the man was melted chocolate itself. He was decadent and delicious and more tempting than, well, melted chocolate.

The thing was, I didn't want to be *consumed* by melted chocolate. And right now, with his perfectly trimmed stubble and his graveled voice and what I could swear was a more intense accented lilt to his words, I wanted to drown in him.

"Elise, *mon ange?*"

His prompt came low and sensuous, but the use of French, for once, didn't lull me into a melty daze. It spurred me into action.

I fed the dry ingredients into the slow-moving mixer and explained. "Certainly less important than cake. Over-mixing cake batter can ruin its ability to rise completely—it wipes out the leavening agent due to eliminating the—" I breathed out heavily as his lips brushed against the sensitive skin of my neck. "The air. And, uh, donuts vary, but since most of mine at Glazed are yeast donuts, they have that leavening power."

And was I really going to keep talking about leavening agents while he was... doing what he was doing?

"Fascinating."

Both of his hands explored me now—nothing more than a slow slide of his thumb arcing over the fabric of my shirt to the left of my navel, or the soft, almost ghosting of his palm along my forearm.

Never had I imagined this simple contact could set me on fire. He was a double boiler, and I was the unsuspecting chocolate chips helplessly losing shape against the heat of him. Or... something. I couldn't describe it.

As soon as the dry ingredients were combined into the mixer, I turned, took his face in my hands, and pulled his lips to mine.

The press of our mouths was like lighter paper, one edge singeing and the burn racing to unravel the rest of the surface. One press, then he took over, his mouth as hungry for me as I was for him. But just as we got going, he pulled back, his fingers pinching my chin lightly to keep me in place.

I blinked, coming to the moment with surprise at the sudden halt and frustration. "Why?"

He knew the question. "Because. I shouldn't be distracting you. And you—" His gaze flickered away, his jaw flexed, and then his eyes came back to meet mine. "You didn't ask me to."

A rough exhale preceded my next words. "I would think me kissing you supersedes you needing to be asked. It's asking without words, isn't it?"

Those eyes bore into mine, digging into me in the most delicious, intense way. My gaze fell to his lips again, and he dropped his forehead to mine.

"*Oui. T'as raison.* But I—I can't think when you touch me, and—"

I leaned back, shooting him all the skepticism fizzing through me.

"*You* can't think when *I* touch *you*?" My laugh had never been more incredulous.

This man only smirked, though it wasn't irritating. It was alluring.

Okay, so we've entered the phase of finding every darn thing he does attractive. Noted.

"I may have gotten carried away. But when my…" Something flickered over his face but disappeared before I could figure it out. "When I find you here making cookies you intend to share, am I supposed to keep my hands to myself?"

I burst out laughing. "I see how it is. It's really the cookies." I didn't even feel bad he was essentially saying it wasn't *me* who had drawn him in, but the classic chocolate chip cookie ingredients.

"Exactly. Not at all you."

But his eyes seared a path so laden with desire from my eyes to my lips, I reached up to touch my mouth as though it might've been burned, not merely kissed. Interest flared in his gaze yet again.

"So if it'd been Michele here, you would've done the same thing?" I asked, moving to the sink to wash my hands and give me space.

His low laugh sent a shiver through me. "*Mais oui.* Though maybe not exactly since I don't think Aurelie would appreciate it. An abbreviated version, let's say. *Peut-être seulement* a high five."

I shook my head, surprisingly charmed by his refusal to tell me the truth. Normally, it would bother me, but what he said with his words directly contradicted everything else. It certainly contradicted this sense that he was holding himself by a very thin leash.

Where was this coming from? And why now, right as we were about to part ways?

He watched as I moved through the motions of adding the chocolate chips, then joined me as I scooped spoonsful of dough onto two pristine cookie sheets I'd found in his glorious kitchen.

Once I slid the first tray into the oven, I turned to find him watching me. His eyes hadn't left me save for when he'd been scooping dough.

"You have to be the most extraordinary woman I've ever met."

The slight smile gracing his lips dropped and everything about him became more intense, almost severe. He stepped forward and suddenly, instantly, the change in his entire bearing sent me on alert.

I swallowed hard and tried to find words to respond. "I —where did that come from?"

"From every interaction I've had with you since I moved here. Seeing you for what felt like the first time at Oak's wedding, so beautiful it hurt to look at you, to the mornings at your shop over the last year where you were endlessly kind to your customers. Every time we've talked, everything about you..." His jaw flexed again, and his chest rose and fell betraying how hard he was breathing.

And me? I was stunned. Standing there with one hand on the counter to anchor me to Earth and the other pressed against my chest, I could hardly comprehend his words.

He moved toward me, plucking my hand from my chest and bringing it to press against his, over his heart, then covering it with his own. "I have heard you every time you've said you don't want a relationship. If you still feel that way, I will respect it."

"We're pretending." My voice came out stilted and unsure. What did he mean?

"We've been pretending, yes. At least in part. But every bit of what I've said to you, the things I feel for you... those are real. And I want to know if, perhaps, you would consider allowing this to be more."

"More," I repeated, almost numbly, pulse ticking up.

His eyes narrowed, sweeping over my face. "Oui, *more*. More than a fake engagement. Maybe we let it ride a few more days, we let it run a bit."

Under my hand and the fabric of his shirt, his heart thudded wildly. I stood there staring at my hand over the sculpture of his chest and marveled at the raging muscle underneath betraying so much.

Revealing this wasn't an act.

This was real. Or... closer to it, though temporary.

And though I'd worried maybe my ability to desire someone, or even care for them beyond friendship, had died with my relationship with Callum, Luc had revived all of that.

From the first time I saw him, I'd recognized attraction. But these last few weeks together had grown friendship as well as something more...

A longing for more.

And this way, I could indulge a little longer, but still within those guardrails of our agreement.

He didn't put a fine point on this being for life or lasting or whatever, but that, too, was safer. It was better, wasn't it? And if nothing else, accepting this small concession to our deal was a sign of progress—a show to myself that I'd moved past all the mess Callum had made of my heart and mind.

Tipping my head up, I rose to my toes and pressed my lips to his. "Let's be more, for now."

He pulled me into his arms and lifted me up, kissing me as he moved, and I wrapped my legs around his waist. I was ready to give whatever he wanted to take and likely would have if the oven hadn't beeped obnoxiously and our beloved houseguests arrived home at the very same time.

CHAPTER THIRTY-FOUR

Luc

Waking up to an empty bed felt like a cruel joke after the night Elise and I had.

And no, it wasn't the one I would've liked to have. At least, not all of it.

Her cookies were delicious and her response to my question a dream. My sister and brother-in-law arriving exactly when we were coming together on the same page felt more than a little cruel, and yet, it'd likely saved us from rushing things.

Not that we wouldn't have savored every second.

But the time with Aurelie and Michele had been nothing short of beautiful. Elise and Aurelie had clicked at some point and seemed to genuinely enjoy each other. Michele was, as always, charming and fun. Spending time with the three of them made my whole house full and vibrant. Sitting there with two of my favorite people, and a woman who was rapidly becoming another one—maybe my very favorite—*I* felt full.

We talked and laughed and paired the chocolate chip cookies with a nice Banyuls wine my sister smuggled into the country on their private plane, the red wine and perfect dessert heightening everything—the laughter, the bliss, the satisfaction in the company.

Could I have more of that? I'd asked Elise if she wanted more with me—more than a charade. And she'd said yes.

We'd get a little more time, enjoy this a bit more. It'd be beautiful while it lasted.

Then last night... the way we all meshed; it gave me a glimpse.

She knew Kenny and Beast already, loved most of my friends' partners, and if she got to know Stone, she'd love him, too. The vision of having this family I'd made for myself here paired with my sister, and adding Elise?

It was nearly more than I could bear, particularly paired with the overwhelming longing I felt as I woke up and didn't get to see her next to me. A cruel hallucination of a life I couldn't allow for myself, though I'd let myself fantasize about it a while longer. Until we were really done.

Yes, I wanted Elise. I wanted to worship her body and show her how much I cared for her. I wanted to explore everything together. But I also simply wanted to be near her. I'd wanted that for far longer than I'd been willing to admit to myself until just recently, but Kenny and Dorian had seen right through me. They'd known. Even Jude had taken one long look and huffed, like it had been a predetermined conclusion.

Yes. I loved donuts. But not *that* much.

Since I'd been deprived of seeing her and I didn't have to be at work for another hour, I arrived at Glazed a little after eight. Elise typically opened at seven on weekdays so she caught the breakfast crowd, and when I wandered in at five after eight, her line was nearly to the door.

One look at her face as she spoke to the customer she was helping, and I knew something was wrong. Catching her attention as I moved inside and stood to the side of the line, my heart squeezed when I saw the way her eyes glistened with tears.

"What is it?" I asked as she ducked to get donuts, low enough so others wouldn't overhear.

She sniffed and didn't look at me again as she loaded a box full of a dozen beautiful-looking donuts.

"One of my fridges went down so I lost a bunch of ingredients and Marisol called in sick. She was supposed to be working out here while I filled a special order, and I don't know how I'm going to do it since all of a sudden there are tons of people coming in." She blinked down into the box for a second, then summoned a smile. "Great problem to have but... crap day for it."

I wanted to hug her so much, but instead, I slipped past the counter and into the kitchen toward the sink. I scrubbed my hands and found a spare apron, emerging just in time to see her holding another box made for a dozen.

"Let me take that. Give me the run down on the register when the crowd dies down and then I'll deal with this while you get to the special order."

Her mouth dropped open, then pressed closed, lips disappearing like she might burst. She nodded, then turned and beamed at the customer. "Luc will help you with that if you'll step right over and tell him what you'd like."

And so went the next fifteen minutes. When the crowd dissipated, she showed me the computer system but only after I promised her I could be late to work. Her store would only be open for another hour and a half, and I could be that late.

"I don't know how I'll thank you for this," she said, wrapping her arms around me for a quick hug.

Before she pulled away, I dropped a kiss to her temple. "No need."

She raised an unimpressed brow. "Pretty sure calling into work warrants thanks, at the very least."

Unable to resist additional contact but knowing I shouldn't kiss her at work, I nudged her chin up and brushed my nose against hers. "How about it's a small form of repayment for dealing with my family?"

She chuckled and patted her hand against my chest over the logo embroidered on the apron I now wore. The sincerity in her eyes and voice rang loud and clear when she said, "Thank you."

Slipping past me into the back, she gave me one last soft look so full of gratitude, it almost made me angry. This was simple, this helping her. Was having a supportive partner so foreign to her?

Everything I'd done in the context of that rat's tail Callum felt even more fitting.

The bell above the door rang as Kenny pushed through the door and, to my surprise, Dorian followed.

"Well, well, well, look at the new sexy donut man! Had I known they hired former model Euro-princes, I would've been in here sooner!" Kenny winked in his obnoxious way.

Behind him, Dorian's face held mild amusement and almost none of the nerves I'd come to expect from him when he came to town. He'd made his home a little farther out than the rest of us and worked part-part-time for Saint Security, primarily consulting and occasionally surveilling. He tended to exclude himself from any of the large gatherings or events, though once or twice he'd participated. I'd never figured out if it was because he'd offered or because Bruce and Wilder had begged, but we all knew they wouldn't ask him if he wasn't doing well.

Him wandering in so casually, even if it was with Kenny, meant good things. It didn't exactly shock me because he'd seemed good, but it was just so… normal.

"Are we going to keep on with the prince thing?"

Kenny smirked. "Only as long as you are one."

I rolled my eyes, then looked to Stone for help.

He shrugged, clearly enjoying the harassment.

"Fine. What can I get you two?"

Kenny leaned an elbow on the glass case and stared down. I wouldn't have been surprised if he'd pressed his whole cheeseball face into it like a sad puppy, but before I could say as much, he grinned. "Plain glazed for me and I'll take another for m'lady."

Valiantly, I didn't roll my eyes, and instead took a waxed paper sack and retrieved the donuts.

"One of the specials. Maybe a glazed, too." Stone squinted at the menu, then eyed the case. There were still five or six flavors left, but normally, she offered upwards of twelve options on weekdays and often more on weekends. I wondered whether we'd start seeing donuts at our afternoon teas soon.

I retrieved his donuts and passed them over, then rang them each up. Kenny chattered on about the absolute nothing happening at work now that most of the celebrities had left in the wake of the gala, and Stone observed in that quiet but alert way he had.

Foolishly, I thought maybe we'd make it out of the exchange without addressing the glaring situation, but no such luck. After eating his donut in three large bites, Kenny brushed off his fingers on a little napkin and tilted his head in a way that said I was in for it.

"So..."

I glanced at the doorway to the kitchen, then widened my eyes in warning. "So."

Kenny's Cheshire grin had my stomach tightening with dread. Would he draw attention to the fact that I'd called out of work in a rather uncharacteristic way and that I was clearly in deep with this woman while she stood not twenty feet away and could likely hear him?

Granted, I'd told her I cared about her and made it quite clear I wanted anything she'd give me for the time being, so maybe it wasn't that bad?

But Kenny, like he sometimes did and didn't get nearly enough credit for, took the high road. His smile softened into something still joyous but also deeply genuine. "You talked?"

The smile pulling at my own lips was unavoidable. I couldn't pretend the way things had gone were anything less than better than I'd hoped. "We did."

It wasn't the happily ever after Kenny would want for us, sure, but it'd gone well. I'd seen the way her breath had hitched and how she'd frozen when I asked if she still didn't want anything. I'd seen the signs. She didn't want to tell me no, and so I'd adjusted on the fly. No more a suggestion of forever—a suggestion of real-while-it-lasts. She'd said she wanted more for now and that was... perfect. Exactly what I'd wanted, in a way.

The sliver of something sharp that jimmied its way between my ribs meant nothing.

Inconceivably, his smile grew to meme-like proportions. "Good."

I nodded, praying that'd be the end of it. Because while

Elise had said she wanted more, I didn't want her feeling like I'd been gabbing to my friends about her or me or us... I just didn't want any pressure on her.

Stone nodded, the closest thing to a smile on his face, too, and the familiar glow of their friendship warmed me.

"Thanks." They knew I meant for their support and for not making it a big thing.

Kenny winked as Stone exited, then turned to me but spoke far too loudly and said, "Now go see if your new girlfriend needs help frosting her donuts, if that's what the kids are calling it these days..." And with a childish little waggle of his brows, he left.

I turned to see Elise standing there wide-eyed, and then we both burst out laughing.

CHAPTER THIRTY-FIVE

Elise

The last time I'd had fun at work like I had this morning was before I ever officially opened Glazed.

Before I'd allowed Callum to invest. Before I'd realized how hard I'd have to work to make ends meet in the off-season. Before I'd discovered how desperately I wanted to quit my day job and just run the shop and yet had to accept it wasn't about to happen any time soon.

Today, with Luc, I'd felt... happy.

Honestly, truly, happy. And it wasn't because he magically swooped in and solved all the problems. His showing up had been a godsend for sure, but he messed up ringing up Chief Whitacker and forgot how to void something... in short, he was human. And it was completely perfect.

Because instead of complaining or getting mad at me when he made a mistake, he asked for help. He apologized, but not so much that it made me feel bad for needing to correct him. He just... functioned like a human being who was learning something new. He admitted when he'd messed up and he did his best to fix it.

He stepped in when it felt like my whole day was melting down and proved my choice to admit I wanted more with him the night before had been right. Because a man like this? A man who'd show up for me and even call out of his own work, potentially at the risk of his bosses getting mad at him?

That was a good man. I'd known Luc was, but he kept proving it.

And sure, Bruce and Wilder were unlikely to be mad at him—from what I understood, Saint Security didn't function that way. And yes, my bar had been programmed to be set at the lowest possible rung thanks to my past relationship.

Still.

Luc was good to me, and I dared say, *for* me. Instead of letting me get spun up and sob all over his shirt, he dove in. He steadied me in a stressful time. He refused to let me creep out and help him when a rush popped up right before closing, insisting he could handle it and that I needed to focus.

He was right. And while I was back there, sure that if he ran into a problem he'd holler and I could decorate the special order just the way I'd envisioned, there it was. That joy I hadn't felt in far too long. A pleasure at creating delicious things for someone, a delight in the simplicity of the work.

Closing came and he appeared in the kitchen, set a soft kiss to my lips, gave me a heated look that made my toes curl, and left for work.

Liz waved outside the door as I moved to lock it behind him, so I yanked it open. "Hey, what are you doing here?"

"Got any leftovers?" she asked, face alarmingly blank.

I narrowed my eyes. "Three options. All yours if you want. But... why the spy face?"

A small smile broke through then. "Spy face? I feel like that's an insult."

She followed me behind the counter and into the back, washing her hands at the sink after I did. As we dried, I explained. "It's just that look you have when you're keeping everything close to the vest."

One brow raised. "One could also call that *donut maker face.*"

"Touché. But I've been working on that." Her awareness of my cagey tendencies, even after only a few months of knowing me, should've caused me the usual combination of hurtful pride and shame, but instead I just felt grateful she got it.

"I'm just here to check in. The fake engagement thing is coming to an end and I'm wondering what's next."

I held out a tray of three donuts and she picked one, promptly taking a large bite.

"Are you the emissary for everyone?" I asked, strongly suspecting she somehow got put up to this. Not that she wouldn't come on her own, but Dove was running around working three jobs, cleaning out her house, managing her grandmother, and probably six other things I had no idea about.

She shoved another portion into her mouth and chomped down, once again giving me spy face.

"Okay. Well. I'm good. I feel..." I looked around at the sparkling industrial kitchen where I'd just spent the morning working on the special order boxed on one of the steel worktables. My heart felt peaceful and hopeful and all kinds of things I hadn't felt at work in so long, let alone about someone else. Especially a man. "I feel hopeful."

She chewed her last bite and raised a brow.

"I just mean, I'm enjoying time with him. And that's progress for me. So even if this thing crashes and burns, it's been good for me. A good experiment." There'd be fallout, but I would handle it. I'd gotten stronger, hadn't I?

She brushed off her fingers and dabbed the napkin I handed her to her lips. "That's fantastic. Can I completely overstep and say something weird?"

"Uh, sure?" She was pretty straightforward, so I couldn't deny her. Plus... what on earth would she say?

"I've taken a chance on being with someone for... a time. I convinced myself it'd be fun while it lasted. That I'd walk away unscathed and grateful when the time came."

Her eyes zeroed in on mine and I swallowed hard when she said, "That man, as you know, was Kenny."

I nodded, not sure what to say. She praised the glorious donut and accepted the other two to hand out at work when she returned. We hugged, and I locked the door behind her.

And I didn't cry. Because she and Kenny weren't me and Luc, and that was okay. They were something magic, something meant to be like a romance novel, and our little trial had been a fleeting thing. A shooting star compared to a constellation.

I'd made huge strides in several ways during this bizarre period with Luc, and I didn't want to feel bad about that. I didn't want to dread how horrible it'd feel when that "for now" ended. I couldn't.

And so I decided not to.

Now I paced his living room having thought of him obsessively all day and wished we'd had a few more minutes before we had to rush out the door to yet another Devereaux family dinner.

We needed a moment to ourselves and yet we wouldn't have it until after dinner at the soonest. Michele and Aurelie would ride with us, and he'd walked in from work ten minutes ago, delivered a devastating smile, and jumped in the shower with a, "I'll be ready in ten."

Right on time, he exited the bathroom in yet another gorgeous suit, this time with a deep navy hue. I shifted in my heels, restless and almost aching for time with him. We needed to talk—about this morning, about last night, about... everything. Liz's caution, or testimony, or whatever it had been was ringing in my ears. And yet, I also just wanted to rip his suit off and have my way with him.

So. Yeah.

"Elise, you look incredible." He leaned down and brushed his lips against my cheek.

"You do, too."

Our gazes caught, and like I'd come to expect, awareness sizzled through me. He swallowed, his thick throat bobbing.

"I enjoyed working for you today."

For some stupid reason, the *for* gave me a thrill. "Are you considering a career change? I hear donuts are a typical career path for veterans."

A half-smile creased his left cheek. "Maybe. Or perhaps

I'm now even more keenly aware how lucky I am to be yours."

To be yours.

Air rushed out of me and my stomach swooped. *To be yours.* Not a claiming, but an offering. Not ownership of me but this alternate willingness to be mine.

At least for now.

A longing so fierce and unfamiliar gripped me hard enough I had to breathe through it.

His brow furrowed. "What is it?"

How could I explain what his words meant? What his entire approach to being with me meant? How much I wanted this to extend past this moment, this evening, this agreement, and into the future?

"Nothing, I just—"

"*Allons-y!* Grand-père will be a bear if we're late to dinner with his fancy friends." Aurelie slipped a small clutch over her wrist and held out a hand, which Michele clasped without stopping and then rushed to the door.

"What were you saying?" Luc asked quietly, apparently entirely unaffected by his family's arrival.

"Luc! Let's go!" Aurelie hustled out the door with Michele, who made a "what can you do?" face as he went, hollering something to us in Italian.

Luc responded with a quick few words I didn't know and were, I was fairly certain, also in Italian.

Because of course this man spoke more than just English and French. Two languages would be practically *lazy* and here he was, tossing out a third like it was an old penny he'd forgotten about in a pocket.

"Elise, if what I said upset you, I'm sorry."

He stood rigid in front of me, and the concern in his face and voice finally registered.

I reached for him, grasping his hand and savoring how warm he always was. "No. I'm not upset."

Come on. Woman up! Be bold! You don't have to be a coward. Let yourself be brave!

"You're certain? I don't want to make you uncomfortable. I thought we were on the same page, but we've hardly spoken since last night and not about anything—"

He blinked down at me while my hand covered his mouth.

"I promise you I'm not uncomfortable. I was thinking how much I liked you saying you're mine." I huffed, nerves lighting up my belly, but excitement, too, as I admitted, "I loved it."

There. I wouldn't caveat it. I simply did. And I didn't feel like shutting it down, all these good feelings, with the harsh reality of an ending. So I wouldn't say "mine for now."

The muscles in his face moved, and I could sense his smile blooming. Right as I removed my hand so I could see it, too, he caught it and pressed a kiss to my palm.

"That's good news."

"I thought so. Hoped so." Why did I feel shy? How did he manage to say he was *mine* but then make me feel so... so giddy and shy?

Outside, we heard Aurelie calling both our names.

He shook his head. "We should go. But could we plan to go to bed early tonight? Take some time before we're too tired to talk and..."

Oh, the things my mind wanted to fill into the blank were many. I knew what he meant, though, and it wasn't anything as sexy as I might've liked. Instead, it was exactly what we *needed*, and that fit.

"Yes. Please," I said, and we walked hand in hand out to the car while my mind sifted through a cascade of thoughts.

I hadn't wanted anyone. It'd been a long time since I'd let myself need anyone, especially a man. But what settled into my heart as we drove to dinner was the simple realization that Luc had been giving me what I needed *and* what I wanted.

And without knowing it, it was quickly feeling like I needed and wanted *him*.

CHAPTER THIRTY-SIX

Luc

Bernard and Cynthia de Valois were as politely judgmental as I'd expected.

What I hadn't anticipated was how pleasant my grandfather had been thus far. Kind greetings to me, an air kiss near Elise's cheek and a show of admiring her dress. She did look incredible tonight, but the gesture put me on alert more than anything else.

Because when Odette and her parents walked in, he fawned over all of them in the most French way possible. Subtle smiles, glittering eyes, a sly compliment to Odette and the suggestion Cynthia looked like she might be her sister... even in his late seventies, he had charm many couldn't resist.

He trotted out all the tricks to accomplish his goal, which I supposed was convincing them their daughter had been given a warm welcome and every consideration. For their part, when introduced to my fiancée Elise, they both smeared smiles into place and nodded, murmuring congratulations which were so disingenuous, I might've laughed if I hadn't seen the embarrassed set of Odette's mouth.

We made it through dinner unscathed and generally focusing on polite talk of business and travel, but my grandfather had insisted on dessert, and something about his affect had changed in a way that set me on edge. Whether from decades of knowing him or years spent observing people in operational settings, I sensed something was coming.

"So, Luc, do tell us how you and lovely Elise met," my grandfather asked, as though he cared.

"Yes. We'd love to hear the story, wouldn't we, Odette?" Cynthia said, brows raised high on her pretty but un-wrinkling forehead.

Odette offered a thin smile, but her demeanor had been subdued tonight. It made me want to send her away from the table to free her rather than endure her brightness dimmed so much she seemed like a bird with clipped wings.

"Technically, I met her at a bar, though it was through mutual friends." I glanced at Elise sitting on my other side, anticipation and a crush of desire flooding me at the sight of her beautiful face.

Have I ever wanted anyone more?

"What did you think when you first saw her?" Michele asked, ever the romantic voice in the crowd.

Elise huffed, fingers knitting together in her lap like the question made her uncomfortable. She must not have realized how distinctly I remembered our first meeting.

I caught her eye, waiting for her to stop glancing away and hold my gaze. When she finally did, I spoke to her. "I thought she was the most beautiful person I'd ever seen."

She exhaled sharply, so I settled my hand over hers, needing the contact, and continued. "I'd heard about her from our friends, knew she was impressive. But then there she stood with this expression like she didn't care a bit about meeting me after I'd interrupted her conversation with her friend, and I... I could hardly breathe for looking at her."

Her lips parted and I drew closer. What would I give for a few minutes alone with her? Maybe she could excuse herself to the bathroom and I could slip out, too. It wouldn't be much, but I could kiss her, taste her, have her to myself for a moment and confirm every word of this was true. It wasn't a show for the de Valois family or my grandfather.

It wasn't a fact meant to fade sometime in the future.

Let's not think about that right now.

"Una storia perfetta, fratello," Michele said, satisfaction lacing his words exclaiming our perfect history.

"And did she know who *you* were? It's hard to imagine anyone not recognizing you, let alone your name," Bernard asked, severing the moment.

"No. Actually, she only recently learned, as did most of my friends and colleagues." Of course, Bruce and Wilder had been privy to my full background check and legal name. I'd wanted them to know the full reality and also to understand why I was so comfortable overseas when I'd initially signed on to work the overseas position after active duty. But everyone else who'd just found out? They'd all given me incredible amounts of grace for having lied to them for years.

"Stunning. I'm sure she was rather pleased to be marrying into such a family," Cynthia said, a perturbed expression on her face.

Elise shifted, and I laughed as though it wasn't a deeply awkward thing to say. I'd owe her more apologies after tonight, though she must've known there'd be some of this considering the context.

"I for one am certainly delighted to be a part of the Devereaux family," Michele said, beaming a smile at all of us before setting a smacking kiss on Aurelie's lips.

God bless the man for his valiant attempt to distract from the weird but not entirely unexpected turn.

"And I'm so glad you are, my love," Aurelie said, giving him a showy, adoring look.

"Yes, we had hoped to see our families connected. The Devereaux name is storied, and joining with les de Valois would be a wonderful, historic event."

Cynthia's words silenced the low bustle around the table. For some reason, I hadn't expected such an overt statement.

"Ah, yes. But sometimes, we must follow our hearts." Michele linked his pinky with Aurelie's like they'd followed their hearts to each other. One would think so by looking at them.

"It's a bit old-fashioned, isn't it? This idea that we marry for love and pretend the rest of it doesn't exist?" Cynthia pressed.

"The rest of it?" Odette asked, a crystal-clear hollowness to her words.

Her mother flicked a manicured hand in my direction but spoke to my grandfather. "How will he fulfill obligations as a member of the family? Will he live in this ridiculous ink smear of a town as though it fits? Will he wear his shop girl on his arm at international events while he represents you, Devereaux?"

As a man who moved to anger rather slowly, I found myself at an immediate ten. "I am not the only representation of the family, Madame de Valois, nor do I plan to participate in the family business. And Elise isn't looking to benefit from any of it, nor does she want any part of this."

Not my most eloquent, but at least I'd gotten something out through my clenched teeth.

Aurelie and Michele spoke but Bernard's voice rose above them. "You may think she doesn't want any part of it but just look at her. She's hungry for it—maybe *you* while you're young and look like you do, but no doubt she's after what's in that trust of yours for the long haul."

The self-satisfied look on his face had me clenching my fist to anchor it to my side in lieu of swinging across the table at him.

Odette gasped. "Dad, that's not okay."

Michele grumbled, and Aurelie's eyes grew wide.

It was my grandfather who spoke and quieted everyone.

"Indeed. Though it's my understanding she's already benefited, has she not?"

Elise, who'd been utterly still and silent, said, "What do you mean?"

It hit me far too late, what this all was. The plan he'd spun, the web he'd weaved that I'd walked right into like a rube.

"Why, he's invested in your company. He owns nearly half, doesn't he? Bought it from that pathetic partner of yours and is single-handedly keeping you afloat?"

The words settled around us like ash. What had burned? Any trust I'd built with Elise. Because she was putting it all together—why Callum was still casting her furious, longing gazes and approaching us like he'd somehow been betrayed. Why she hadn't heard from him about selling the shop. Why she'd been so free lately.

How I'd done what I wanted, even when she told me she didn't want my help.

Just like my grandfather had always done to me.

Her throat worked as she turned to me, devastation in her gaze when she finally spoke and everything inside of me hollowed out.

"Is it true?"

Frozen in my seat, my mouth worked without sound. I wanted to drag her away from here and tell her what I'd done—how I'd done it for her. For her *good* and not to control her or harm her. But she read my silence as the answer it was.

"How could you?" she breathed out, gaze on her plate, then stood slowly and set down her napkin, facing Aurelie and Michele. "It was lovely to meet you."

I was out of my seat following her, wanting to reach for her but sensing my touch wouldn't be welcome and I didn't want to do anything to make this worse.

"Please, Elise. Let me explain."

She didn't turn, just kept walking toward the main building, toward the exit, head down looking at her phone periodically. Was she texting someone?

"Elise," I tried again right as she stepped out into the cool spring evening.

Arms crossed and tucked close to her body, she shook her head. Without looking at me, she said, "I'm sorry. I can't do this right now."

Then a car pulled up and she got in without another word.

CHAPTER THIRTY-SEVEN

Elise

Dove pulled up in front of my apartment ten minutes after I did. Thank goodness for the ride share being available or Luc probably would've convinced me to talk to him.

No idea what I would've said. I couldn't even identify what I thought except that something delicate and tentatively brave had crumbled inside me when Luc's grandfather revealed what Luc had done.

I swung the door open to find her sweet face wrinkled with worry, hair up in a ponytail and wearing... sweats. I rarely saw her in anything other than scrubs and her favored pretty dresses, the presence of something else stole my attention.

"What's wrong? What did he do?" Dove asked, hands clasped together and nearly white-knuckling herself into submission so she wouldn't reach for me until I raised my arms for a hug.

She launched into them, holding me tight. Even while I felt crushed, attacking me with her affection made me nearly glow with love for her.

When we pulled back, I still felt locked up. Like I couldn't make sense of it.

"Elise, you've got to tell me. Do I need to call the police? Did he hurt you? Should I call Nikki and have her get Bruce? What?"

"He didn't touch me. You don't need to call anyone." My face crumpled right along with my heart. "But he lied to me."

The sob that came out was filled with so much grief, it should've been ridiculous. Could I even explain why I felt so upset?

But Dove didn't demand that. She held me close and let me sob into her sweatshirt. She petted the back of my head and practically cradled me until I came up for air, my face undoubtedly a blotchy mess of sadness.

"You go get out of this beautiful dress and take a minute, and then we'll talk." Her bright blue eyes were wet and she made no attempt to hide she'd been crying sympathy tears. My sweet, tender-hearted friend was just precious.

"Thank you."

A few minutes later, I returned to find her nestled into a spot on my tiny couch with a mug of tea steaming in her hand, and one for me sitting on the coffee table. She had a sleeve of cookies and a bag of popcorn, too.

"Where did you find snacks?" I had no memory of bringing them, and since I hadn't been home in days, I didn't think I had much in the cabinets anyway.

"I brought them. Emergencies always require snacks." She picked up the mug. "Take your tea and start talking. Or... you know, sit in silence, too. We can do whatever you want."

I suspected that if I sat here in silence, she'd internally combust. She was a verbal processor, and she loved so deeply, this whole situation would be ripping her heart out. That was part of why I'd reached for her—because she wouldn't let me spiral into an awful state and let my mind take over with my worst fears.

And a big part of me desperately wanted her to talk me out of feeling so hurt.

I needed her to tell me this wasn't real. Because hearing Gérard Devereaux tell me the truth, when a man I'd felt safe with—someone I'd trusted more and more—had so blatantly chosen not to be honest, signaled the end of a fantasy.

And silly me, I hadn't realized it was one I'd been spinning since that first day he talked to me about something more than donuts.

With a long sigh as I cupped the mug of tea in my hands and absorbed its warmth, I started talking. "My ex invested in the business. It was about forty-five percent. I had a small business loan, but a few things happened in the beginning and the store needed repairs I hadn't budgeted for. In the end, Callum gave me the money as an investment."

Dove's eyes were big, but she nodded. I almost wished she'd interrupt, but she didn't give me the excuse to clam up again.

"About six months ago, Callum started talking about wanting his money back. I told him we could work out a payment plan but that I wasn't sure I could get him the full amount within the year." I closed my eyes against the onslaught of self-recrimination coming. "I hate that I ever took money from him and believed he'd be reasonable about it. I hate even more that I didn't have paperwork in place to define repayment or what any of this would look like past him just giving me the money and making it seem like..." I shook my head.

"Hey. None of that. I'm fully aware that guy was a jerk and you still have to grapple with how some of it happened. But you're not going to sink into that right now. You made the best decision you could at the time, and I have no doubt you've attempted to deal with it as best you could considering the human garbage on the other end of the deal."

Dove's fierce words unearthed a watery chuckle from me. "Thank you."

She sipped her tea, waiting a moment before she said, "So how does this connect with Luc?"

Clearing away the tightness in my throat, I willed myself not to cry again.

"Uh, long story short, he figured out Callum was pressuring me about either selling the business to a donut chain out of Salt Lake, or getting back together with him? And he offered to help. I told him no. Without telling me, he did it anyway—he bought out Callum and now owns part of the business."

Dove's mouth opened, then snapped shut.

"I know it seems silly not to just accept his help, but that's exactly how I got in this situation. I trusted someone—I let him in and he crushed me, Dove." My voice whittled down into a whisper. "I couldn't let Luc do that. Even though Luc is ten times—a hundred times the man Callum is. I can't do it again. I can't be under someone's thumb financially."

Dove nodded, her face full of compassion. "That makes

perfect sense. It's just... do you think that's why he did it? Why Luc did?"

This was where things got twisted up in my gut. Because in my heart of hearts, the easy answer was no. Thinking of just Luc and how little he seemed to care about money or how much he appeared to be cautious of being like Callum, the answer rang out a clear and resounding no.

But... he'd lied. And the reason we'd gotten together for a fake engagement was all built on a lie to begin with. So why would I look at that evidence and pretend he was someone else?

Wasn't that exactly what I'd done with Callum? Hadn't I worked myself into the ground to convince myself he wasn't being mean and controlling? That he wasn't holding me a little too tight, being a little too clingy and aggressive?

Luc isn't like that.

The words echoed through my mind, and I wanted to believe them. I wanted to reach out and grab them and stuff them into my chest and make them true.

"I don't think it was the whole point for him, no. But I'm not sure if maybe it was part of it." I hated those words, but I couldn't look away from them. If I did, then I hadn't changed a bit.

"Oh, my friend. I'm so sorry."

"Thanks. I just feel..." I started to say I felt like I'd taken a step backward, but was that true? Was this like anything I'd been through with Callum? Luc had lied, and that wasn't okay, but did it have to mean I couldn't trust myself? Did it suddenly mean I'd become my mother, throwing myself at any wealthy man who gave me a second look, because a man who'd asked me to be his fake fiancée had lied and bought out my sole investor?

No. It didn't mean that.

"You just feel?" Dove asked, gently, but not giving up on me either.

"I mean... heartbroken. Angry with him. But... I don't think I'm angry with myself." Tears welled in my eyes. "And I'm proud that I tried. That I let myself be with him like this, even if this moment feels crappy."

"Yes. *Yes.* You've made huge strides, and he needs to make this right somehow, but it takes nothing away from what you've gained through the experience," Dove said, right as the doorbell rang. Her gaze jumped to the door, and she held out a hand to me. "I'll get it. You stay put."

Since the entryway was basically a straight line down the hallway to the couch, I could see Luc's dark eyes and hair when the much shorter Dove swung the door open. My heart leapt and everything in me wanted to talk to him.

"She's here. She's fine. But no, you can't talk to her," Dove said, raising her chin and setting one hand on her waist in a defiant pose right as I walked up and put a hand on her shoulder.

"It's okay. Just give me a minute?"

She narrowed her eyes like I might be making a secret distress signal, then stepped back. I pulled the door closed behind me and crossed my arms, needing the reminder that no, I wasn't going to go to him or hug him, even though insanely, that was what I most wanted right now.

"I'm sorry I didn't tell you. I didn't want him having any leverage to hurt you."

His voice was rough, like he'd lived a week without sleep between this moment and the hour or less since I'd last seen him. His hair was askew and somehow he looked sallow and more worried than I'd ever seen him.

"I told you I didn't want your help. I know it might not make sense to you, but I didn't want anyone else having leverage over me either." He didn't know the full extent of how my mom had looked for men to prop her up and how much I hated that was the legacy I had in her, but he knew a little.

His jaw ticked. "I'm sorry I lied to you. I wanted to help and it wasn't right, but I just kept wondering, what would you have done? What was your alternative? Giving into him and selling the shop? Or letting him start dating you and hurting you again?"

The words came out harsh and his lips formed the closest thing to disgust I'd ever seen on his face.

"No. I wouldn't ever be with him again. Believe it or not, I've been researching other options. An additional small business loan, and even a program through the convention and visitor's bureau for local small shops. I—honestly, it doesn't matter what I was going to do because it wasn't up to you."

He exhaled slowly as though to calm himself down. "I know it wasn't. I'm sorry I did this without telling you. I didn't keep it a secret to deceive you. I just... I didn't want you to worry. I didn't want one more thing for you to manage."

"But it's my business! It's my life and my livelihood. It is exactly my problem and one hundred percent *not* yours!" My voice had notched up, and I pressed the back of my hand over my lips to calm myself. The last thing I needed was a neighbor calling the cops on me for a domestic disturbance to put the cherry on top of the day.

And yet... had I ever verbalized myself so clearly to Callum when we were together? Had I done anything but cower those first few times he'd lied or hurt me? Even this, this heartbreaking disappointment and anger with him was... progress.

He ran a hand through his hair and looked away, that sharp jaw visibly clenched beneath the trimmed stubble. When he looked back at me, desperation bled from his eyes.

"I want it to be my problem, Elise. I want *you* and anything to do with you to be my problem." He shook his head, forehead scrunching up like his words were all wrong. "Actually, no. Not my problem. My *joy*. Everything about you would be my joy, if you'd let it."

He took a step toward me, then stopped himself. "There is no part of me that wants to take anything from you. I don't want to coerce you or convince you of anything other than my sincerest regret that I hid this from you. My arrogance drove on this one and I have no excuse—I won't try to make it better."

He... he wouldn't?

"More than anything, I need you to know I will do whatever you want me to with it, but for now, here's this." He handed me an envelope.

I eyed it, my brain not fully functioning. "What is it?"

"Just open it. And if that's not what you want, you tell me and I'll do exactly as you say. *Exactly*. No strings, no expectations. *S'il te plaît, mon cœur*, please look at it."

I sucked in a halting breath. "Okay. I will."

I wouldn't tell him no. I could. But I wouldn't.

More progress.

He nodded, hesitating for a moment before turning and descending the stairs. I watched him as he walked with long strides toward the parking lot and my heart skipped when his dark gaze caught mine before he ducked into his car.

I didn't know what to think, but that was like no other apology I'd ever received. And the words ringing in my ears as I went back inside were the ones that stayed with me all night.

Everything about you would be my joy.

CHAPTER THIRTY-EIGHT

Luc

Kenny and Stone offered to come over, but I refused. I didn't need them piling into the house that already felt too full.

Too full and yet empty. Bereft of the person I most wanted here with me.

Aurelie had tried to console me when I walked back in from my feeble attempt to convince Elise I didn't want to control her or her business. I only wanted to be with her.

Aurelie had promised that Elise would see the truth. That if she knew me at all, she'd know. But would she? Would she know I wasn't like her ex? That I was trustworthy?

How could she know such a thing when our relationship began as a lie? Granted, it was a lie she was in on, but that didn't matter at this point.

Did I deserve her trust?

More and more, with every hour that ticked by with the speed of a month, I worried the answer was no.

At seven the next morning, I showered and dressed. Without waking my sister and Michele, I left to meet with my grandfather. He'd summoned me late last night via text, and though I had nothing left to say to him, some part of me yearned for him to make this right. I didn't know how he could, but the Luc who'd grown up with him as a loving if sometimes distant grandfather longed to repair at least one thing in my life right now.

After I'd followed Elise out last night, I'd run back inside to get my phone. Everyone had been arguing, Odette with her parents and Aurelie with Grand-père. When I entered, they stopped, and I looked him in his face and said the only thing I could think of.

"I don't understand you."

He only stared back. I paid no mind to anyone else, leaving Aurelie and Michele to their own devices to get home. They'd handle it. And in the meantime, I went to print off the documentation I had about her business so I could at least give her that proof.

This morning when I walked in, a twinge of relief swept in at seeing only my grandfather. In fact, he answered his hotel suite door in a robe, his pajamas still on underneath and his feet bare.

I blinked and grabbed the door frame. "Are you ill?"

He'd already walked away from the door and spoke only in French when he replied. "No. I didn't sleep last night."

I entered, completely disarmed by his unkempt appearance and the way he seemed to be moving slowly. Maybe he was coming down with something?

He lowered himself into a chair in the sitting area of his suite and gestured to a vacant seat next to him. I complied, unsure of how to behave on this alien planet where my grandfather was visibly human.

"I've wronged you."

My breath caught and I stilled, the small cup full of black coffee only partway to my mouth.

"I thought it was all a ruse. Thought your Elise was a smoke screen. Thought you were just acting out, another version of Japan or the Army or that time you pretended you broke your arm so you wouldn't have to attend the cotillion classes."

I huffed a surprised laugh and set the cup back down. He would've been right before. And I had every right to refuse him. But now, saying Elise was anything but everything I wanted would be the lie.

"I'd made promises to Bernard and Cynthia, but I have no loyalty to them. I've spent my life attempting to instill devotion to family and here, I've abandoned it." His forehead furrowed and he looked at me from under his silver brows. "When I saw her face, her devastation, and it hit me what I'd done... when I saw you and your regret... I knew how deeply I've failed you, Jean-Luc, and for that I am sorry."

Emotion cinched my throat closed as I processed words I'd never dreamed of hearing. In all the back and forth conversations, all my resignations to him mentally and even in real life, I'd never imagined he'd admit wrong, let alone apologize. And yet here he was, truly saying it. And it seemed, truly meaning it.

"Thank you. I'm sorry I couldn't do what you wanted me to."

He shook his head, regret fully bloomed on his face. "I'm sorry I didn't listen."

I huffed at nearly the same time he did, both of us

holding any further outward show of emotion at bay. I didn't know what this meant going forward, but it gave me hope I hadn't had for years regarding this man who'd been here all my life in the only way he knew how.

His eyes met mine. "Please. Forgive me."

"Of course."

He leaned in, and we embraced for a few seconds before releasing one another.

"Will she forgive you after what I did?" he asked, what looked like genuine worry threaded in his tone.

"After what *I* did, ultimately. And... I don't know. I hope." I couldn't stop hoping, even if I wasn't sure I deserved the forgiveness.

"I've gotten everything wrong here, and I fear your father has wronged you, too, though I don't know if we'll ever see him long enough for him to admit it." He frowned, deep regret etched into the lines of his weathered face. "But you're right about me on that count, as well. I didn't let your mother in. I didn't allow for how she loved him. I didn't see how losing her was destroying him, and now that I do, I so feared it happening to you. I didn't want you to love because love hurts. A marriage that's a business deal... you can protect your heart in it."

I nodded, my heart aching. "I thought I could protect myself. Keep myself from that full-force love we Devereaux men seem to fall into."

He laughed softly and shook his head. "Ah, you always were a stubborn child."

I laughed, too. "I didn't mean to put you through everything I did. But I didn't know who I was. And when you called weeks ago, it felt like when Mom died all over again. Like you were ready to tell me who I was. But I know now." I swallowed hard, the clarity utterly crystalline. "I'm Jean-

Luc Devereaux. I love my family, and I love the people who've adopted me into theirs."

Eyes shining, he nodded.

"And I love Elise."

"*Très bien*," he whispered, and I rose, eager to get back home, or maybe stop by and see if I could talk to Elise at her shop.

"Me, too, then. Of course you don't need it, but you have my blessing. And the trust is also yours. I'll have it released once I'm back on French soil, *chez le notaire*."

We hugged again, and I left feeling confusingly lighter, but heavier at the same time. One major part of my life had just improved—it'd broken open in a pivotal way. But the part that'd rapidly become the most precious thing to me... that was still broken. And I might've been a patient man, but I couldn't wait.

I went to Glazed and found Marisol at the register.

"Sorry, Luc. She called me last night and asked me to open." Her wide smile was kind, if a bit perplexed.

Yeah. Logically, I would know. I'd been with her nonstop lately. Everyone knew we were together and only the people closest to us knew it was fake—or that it'd started that way.

"Thanks, Mari. Have a good day."

I shouldn't have been surprised she'd called out. In fact, I was glad she had. She needed rest and I'd placed extra demand on her life this last while with all the dinners and familial obligations. Hopefully, she'd been able to sleep last night and had slept in.

By the time I arrived at her apartment complex, I'd promised myself I'd text her and wait a few minutes. Sitting in my car and feeling more restless than I had all night, I sent a message. After three minutes, I got out of the car and paced on the sidewalk.

After another three, I sent another text. I didn't want to crowd her, but my gut told me something was wrong. Could be I felt the distance between us was the problem, and every instinct in me wanted to solve the problem, but the low hum of dread had me on edge.

Finally, I couldn't stand waiting any longer. I'd been here ten minutes and hadn't heard from her. There was every possibility I'd knock on her door, and she'd come open it and shoot daggers from her eyes at me for waking her up on a day when she could've slept in. I'd accept the title of selfish jackass and it'd be one more thing I needed to grovel for.

At first a quick knock. Then a full minute and a half later, a more forceful one.

Nothing.

"Elise. Please, open up," I spoke to the door to no avail.

The temptation to bang on the panel separating us grew rapidly, but I didn't want to wake the neighbors and start drama. I texted Adam to request Jo give him Dove's number.

After a quick call with Doc to reassure him everything was fine, I called Dove.

"Hello?"

"Hey, Dove. This is Luc. I know Elise is upset, but I'm wondering if you could just..." I tugged at the wild ends of my hair, no doubt leaving them sticking up. "Can you tell me she's okay?"

"Aw, you'll be okay. And she will, too. I left late last night because I have work this morning. She had planned to sleep in a bit and then go for a jog."

The red flag started waving.

"What time?"

"Uh, not sure exactly when. But we joke all the time how we're early birds. She once told me seven was like a whole lifetime of sleep after waking up at four most days. Do you—"

"Thanks, Dove." I hung up, not staying on the line long enough for her to finish her question, forgoing the concern over the neighbors and leaning into the very real worry I had now.

"Elise. Please. Please open up." I knocked again, then tried the door handle.

When it inched open, my blood ran cold.

Out for a run or still in bed, either way, this door would be locked. She was careful, especially after Callum had showed up at her place weeks ago. She wouldn't have left this unlocked for any reason.

No hesitation. I entered, eyes clocking the entryway bench and the three sets of shoes tucked neatly under it, including the sneakers she used for running. It all piled up, leading to what I knew I'd find—an empty bed, and worse, her phone still plugged in next to it.

In seconds, I searched the rest of the apartment, then called the police. First things first. After that, with shaking hands as reality settled in, my next call was to Bruce.

"I think Elise—" I sucked in a breath, the adrenaline making me short of breath, and pushed out the words hammering through my mind. "I think she's been taken."

CHAPTER THIRTY-NINE

Elise

Waking up this morning, a forgotten item on a list dangled just out of my mind's reach before I ever opened my eyes. Fuzzy-headed despite not having more than a few sips of wine last night, my brain felt bleary and almost cotton-stuffed.

What had I gone to bed thinking about? What was this *thing* I was trying to remember?

I lay with my eyes closed, filtering through what I remembered.

The realization that Luc had bought out Callum's investment. Going home and crying all over Dove after she came over. Telling Luc I'd look at the papers he gave me, then sitting in stunned silence as I saw he'd put the investment in my name from the very beginning based on the date of the notarized signature.

Dove had stayed a while longer and I'd asked Marisol to

open for me today. I'd fallen asleep on the couch a while after Dove left and dragged myself to bed sometime in the two-o'clock hour.

And then—

I gasped as my eyes popped open, then moved to sit up in a scramble of legs and arms. These weren't my walls. This wasn't my bed. And my arm...

There was a cold metal handcuff around my wrist anchoring me to a radiator. I was on a mattress next to it on the floor, and the room appeared to be empty otherwise. Beige walls and dirty cream floorboards lined the small square space, and only one frosted glass window above me on the wall was letting in watery, weak light. The door was closed, and for some reason, that detail was the one to pull a sob out of me.

"Hello?" I asked at a far too reasonable volume considering the absolute panic raining down on me, pulling on the cuff around my hand with absolutely no success. *"Hello?!"*

I leaned away from the heater, bracing the cuff around my wrist so it wouldn't bite into my skin so hard, and prayed the other side would give.

No luck.

My hand ached. I couldn't slide it out of the cuff, which was essentially a given, but I had to try. The metal ripped into my skin, and I could already see a dark bruise forming around my wrist. I couldn't really afford to break my hand to get it out though, could I? I wouldn't be able to do my job —either of my jobs—if I did that.

Yeah but if you're about to get murdered, the broken hand won't matter much!

I shut my eyes and tried to calm myself for a second, brain scrambling for anything that might help.

Wasn't there some trick about forcing your hands

down... wait, no. That was for zip-ties if both of your hands were together.

Helplessness and panic welled up again and I screamed. "Help! Help me! Heeeeelp!!!"

The door banged open, and I scrambled back in fear, then swallowed hard at the sight of Callum.

Callum?

"You need to shut your mouth, or I'll have to tape it shut, okay, Leesy?"

Bile crawled up my throat at the hard, satisfied look in his eyes as he used his old pet name for me.

"What is this? Why am I here and what are you doing?"

My voice sounded scared and small. I hated it, but I couldn't pretend I had the wherewithal to face down a man I knew was violent from a mattress on the floor of an empty room with one hand cuffed to a radiator.

He dropped to a crouch and his face took on a sympathetic expression. "Oh, Leesy. You're going to be fine. We're going to get through this and everything will go back to the way it was."

"The way it was?" I asked, horror filling me.

He nodded. "Yep. As it should be. You being mine and us living happily ever after."

The horror ebbed ever so slightly in favor of resounding disbelief and anger. I yanked at the handcuff, pain slicing through my wrist, and only barely resisted flinging out my free hand to try to push him further away from me.

"We're not going to be together. Ever again. I've told you that before, and if it hadn't been clear to me before, which it was, it absolutely is now."

He squinted at me, his handsome face looking as put together as ever. He wore a medium blue shirt and khaki slacks like he'd come from, or maybe was going to, the office. What the heck was happening?

"I'm sorry you feel that way. This rich Euro-trash boyfriend of yours has made things confused, but I've got a way to solve that problem, and when this is all over, we'll both be happy." He tilted his face and got this soft, affectionate look I couldn't stand.

He'd never been soft or sweet with me. At one point, he'd been charming and flattering, playing on my need for attention maybe, and any other vanities he could detect. In retrospect, I could hardly remember how he'd gotten so deep under my skin I didn't know how to get out.

"I'll never be happy with you. I'll never forgive you for this, and you're going to jail when this is over, not anywhere with me—"

The pain in my cheek bloomed hot and loud with the contact of his hand. For a second, I could hardly breathe— like somehow my face getting hit had knocked the wind out of me. Tears pricked my eyes instantly, and I ducked away from him, instinctively putting as much distance between us as I could.

"You'll learn. And until then, you'll be here."

His formerly calm façade had broken and here was the man I'd seen peeking out more and more toward the end of our relationship.

"They'll get their money, I'll get a little bonus, and you'll be back where you belong. It's all just a matter of time."

He stood and marched toward the door, turning back right before he exited with one hand resting on the knob. "We don't want the duct tape, do we?"

I shook my head, tucking down again. I definitely didn't

want my mouth taped. Just the thought sent a bolt of panic down my spine.

He smirked. "That's what I thought."

The door slammed, and I was alone again. My thoughts were muddled, my cheekbone throbbed, and my wrist ached. I didn't know what to do. If I screamed loud enough, could I get someone's attention before he got here to silence me? Were we anywhere near someone who could help?

My energy flagged, and I slumped down against the mattress and let the tears flow freely. Who was he talking about? Did he really believe I'd be with him again? This time, he was the one living in the fantasy and I was grounded to the here and now in the stark reality he'd forced me to see.

All of this had been real. Every moment with Luc I'd managed to trick myself into accepting as fiction so I didn't have to fear the potential pain. But it *had* been real, and yes, it'd been painful, but also so clearly worth it.

His face when I'd talked with him last night... my heart clutched at the memory. He'd been wrecked, and even though I'd been justifiably angry, I should've made sure he knew I just needed time.

Callum? He'd been an awful partner, and I'd learned hard, horrible lessons no one should have to learn. But that didn't mean I was my mother, and it didn't mean I was doomed to do it again.

And this man looking at me like kidnapping me would somehow bring me back to him?

He was deranged. That much was clear. And he wasn't working alone.

Luc will find me.

The thought echoed through my mind, and my heart grabbed onto it with both greedy hands. Gosh, I hoped so.

Then I realized... he probably would. If anyone in the world was equipped to find me, it was Luc and the Saint Security team.

My friends.

He wouldn't rest until I was found, regardless of our fight and my inability to speak to him last night. He wouldn't let a mood deter him from helping me.

He'd been the kindest, gentlest, loveliest man to me. His buying out Callum had been *for me*, not to control me. I'd seen it late last night and I'd wanted to tell him I understood this morning. I'd been ready to explain I couldn't have him do stuff like that, but that I could see how he'd thought he was doing something good.

I'd planned to accept his apology.

I still will.

People made mistakes, and in a relationship, it wouldn't be all billowing pirate shirts and fairytale settings. There would be real pain, and no amount of wishing it away could prevent that. But as I sat here in this dingy room missing the chance to apologize and accept Luc's apology, the pain of missing that part hit me like a blow.

I wouldn't hope for fights, but when they came, I would look for ways to repair instead of run. Based on the way he'd handled owning his choice and sincerely apologizing, it sure looked like I could trust Luc to do the same.

We'd work together, be together. Equals. Partners. I'd be his just as much as he'd be mine. And that was no fantasy. He'd shown me this was what it would be like.

I shut my eyes against the beige room and mattress of unknown origin, and I promised myself I wouldn't give up hope. I wouldn't lose it and beg Callum to let me go or cave to whatever sick demands he had coming for me.

No.

I'd stay strong and keep the faith in a man I knew. Maybe we hadn't been close all that long, but I believed he'd come for me. He'd find me.

And when he did, we had some things to discuss.

CHAPTER FORTY

Luc

Two officers combed through her apartment while I stood outside, stock-still, and waited. Everything in me wanted to bust in there and do it myself, but I didn't have specific training in collecting evidence of an abduction.

This part wasn't our forte.

The recovery?

Literally part of the job description from over a decade of service.

Yes, we hunted down terrorist organizations and disposed of their leaders. But we also recovered kidnapped Americans all over the globe.

We wouldn't have to go far, I hoped. The fact there was a regional airport ten minutes from Elise's apartment made me twitchy, but we hadn't confirmed she had been taken. Not yet. Maybe she'd gone for a run and accidentally left her phone and forgot to lock the door since she wasn't going to be home? Maybe she'd gone with a different friend and—

"You okay?" Bruce asked, hauling me into a hug I readily accepted, right as Kenny walked up and did the same thing right when Bruce released me. Stone stood stalwart behind him, eyes sliding over the stairwell and propped open door like they might provide answers.

"I don't know. I keep thinking maybe she's out with someone but... I don't think so."

Bruce's hand patted my shoulder. "If your gut says something's off, we don't ignore it."

Everyone agreed. How often had one of us had a feeling that proved to be mission-saving or even life-saving? More than occasionally, that was certain.

"Thanks. I hope I'm wrong. Maybe she's—"

"Found a smart watch, and we've got her phone here. No clear evidence of foul play, but the bed's unmade and seems like enough people are concerned, we can start some paperwork," an officer from Silver Ridge PD said, holding out Elise's watch.

The sight of her watch confirmed it in my mind. She wouldn't have run without it, nor would she have left without her phone. I couldn't be certain about the unmade bed, but so far as I'd noticed, she tended to make the one we shared at my house if I was already up and out.

A sharp ache flared in my chest.

Bruce patted my back again but spoke to the officer, holding out his hand and flashing his toothpaste commercial smile, as we'd all come to call it.

"Mind if we get started?"

The officer accepted his handshake, and after one aggressive pump up and down, agreed. "Chief says you guys are good to go. Just keep us looped in if you find anything."

"Will do, Officer. Thanks for getting here so quickly." Bruce smiled again, then turned back to our small group as the two men left Elise's apartment.

Left alone, he whipped out his phone but started talking to us. "We need to set up a CP. We'll get Beast in, and I want you to—"

My phone rang obnoxiously loudly with an unknown number. I'd taken it off silent so I wouldn't risk missing Elise if she called, but this... this raised the hair on the back of my neck.

Bruce's eyes narrowed, and Kenny stiffened. Stone's energy crested and he huffed, then stepped up to the balcony of the open floor to look out at the parking lot.

"Go ahead," Bruce said, already hanging up his call.

Kenny popped his phone up and hit record, then I answered the call on speaker.

"Who is this?" I asked, knowing this wasn't another spam call.

"We have her. If you want her back, you follow our instructions." The voice came out distorted so of course we couldn't ID the person that way—at least not yet.

"What do you want?"

Despite the heartbeat rushing in my ears, I kept calm. The years of training, despite never touching me this close, had clicked into place.

"Twenty million dollars transferred to an account of our choice by the end of the day, or she's dead."

I grit my teeth, but Bruce gripped my shoulder to steady me, and I pressed on, knowing what we needed. "I need proof of life first. Put her on the phone."

"Not about to do that, sorry."

"How do I know she's not already dead? I don't know you."

But clearly, they knew me well enough to know I could pay twenty million dollars' worth of ransom without much struggle—at least if I had my trust. Maybe they assumed I'd simply ask my grandfather for it. Logistically, I wasn't sure I could move that kind of money on such short notice even if Grand-père immediately released the trust to me, but them asking for it so far gave us the hint they likely didn't know either.

"She's not. Why would we kill her before we get what we want?"

Some swearing in the background had my ears perking up. Was it a group of kidnappers?

"I'll need proof before this goes any further."

We waited, all staring at the phone, my heart pounding out of my chest. We needed more from these fools, and this might be the way we got it.

"Fine. You'll have your proof in the next hour. After that, all communication will come by text. If all goes well, you'll have her back as soon as you get us the money." The line disconnected.

We were all moving now, hustling down the stairs and to our respective vehicles, all heading toward the Saint offices. I called Aurelie on the way, letting her know she and Michele should get over to the resort and stay with my grandfather, and I'd update them when I could. She was freaked, but she'd almost been taken more than once over the years and understood the importance of staying calm and doing what needed to be done in a crisis. She'd also probably freak out when she ended the call with me, but I couldn't think of that right now.

She would be safer with my grandfather, who'd traveled with his personal security team of three. When you were a billionaire, security wasn't negotiable. Plus, I'd made sure he understood Saint was tapped out and couldn't offer him security since we'd been booked for other people, though I doubted he would've deigned to use our services anyway. Well, maybe he would now, but prior to our reconciliation just hours ago, not a chance. He had a faithful crew, and I didn't blame him for keeping them with him. I was grateful he had them tonight.

Within minutes, I pulled into the Saint parking lot to see Bruce jogging up the front steps, Stone close behind, and Kenny waiting for me.

"You okay?" he asked, concern etched in his brow.

"No." It was all I could say.

"We'll find her. We'll get her back safe." He hauled me into a hug, roughly slapping my back before releasing me. "We will."

My phone buzzed, and once the image came through, Kenny and I bolted up the stairs, through the front door, and into the tech room we'd use as a command post.

"We've got a photo."

My heart squeezed in a vise grip of worry as I finally stopped and looked at the image. Elise sat with red, tired eyes and dry lips, one wrist in a metal cuff, the skin around it bruised. Her left cheek was bright red, and the same eye looked like it might be starting to bruise. She wore a short-sleeved T-shirt and shorts that made me swear under my breath. "They took her from her bed, I'd bank on it."

No way would she have been dressed like that unless she was in bed. She had sweatpants she'd change into the minute she got up, and it hadn't only been when Aurelie and Michele were at the house.

Beast walked in and came straight at me, snatching the phone with one hand but resting a big paw on the back of my neck for a second before continuing farther into the room. In seconds, he had the photo sent to the Saint servers and was milling around for whatever information he could find.

"Amateurs for sure. I've got meta data." He typed away, clicking and tapping through different screens. "They took it ten minutes ago. Can't see the geo-tags but I bet we know someone who might. Can almost guarantee they didn't know to scrub 'em."

"On it," Bruce said, pulling up the hardline phone we kept in the secure room and dialing.

More experienced kidnappers would've scrubbed any data associated with the photo. The fact that Beast could see a time stamp or anything else at all gave us good information. First, it told us whoever had called was likely in the same location as Elise was. Second, the presence of data meant we were dealing with, if not novices, at least not professionals. This should work in our favor, though it also could mean more danger for Elise.

My stomach clutched at the realization.

"East, my man. Hoping you can hook us up, or maybe Clover can if you're not free. Cookie's woman was taken. Need you to see what the kids left on the image."

Bruce's voice sounded deceptively calm, but that was his forte. In moments of crisis, he became utterly calm and capable. We all did, but right now, I could only appreciate his leadership and the casual way he called in a favor. Was it technically illegal for someone in the EMU to assist a civilian with information like this?

I wouldn't worry about legalities. And if Bruce wasn't concerned, if East or Clover were willing to do it, I'd take it.

All these details, all this training and resources, and they had to mean something. They had to give us the tools because if we didn't get her back—

I sucked in a gasping breath, the thought of losing her was worse than last night when I thought I'd been the cause. Because then, there'd been hope. I'd held out a sliver of possibility that she might just see my intentions. And more, that she might see through all our bandying of "for now" and she'd want forever. At least a shot at it.

This? This not knowing if I'd see her again, let alone get to love her the way I wanted?

Utter agony.

Would I have been better off never loving her and not knowing this fear? Damn, but it didn't seem like it. Removing all worry and fear would also take away that unimaginable fount of love that just kept growing, and I didn't think I'd want to.

There was no going back and smacking myself in the face to skip the denial I'd just conned myself into accepting for too long. Time to get her back, and then we'd deal with whatever came next.

Training kicked in when my heartrate spiked with anxiety and I calmed myself, grounding into the floor underneath me, the sights and scents and sounds around me.

"Send it. He'll be ready." Bruce set his phone down, and Beast tapped away, apparently sending the image to East.

This was good. More information there would help, plus any minute now, these idiots should be sending along how and where they expected me to drop twenty million dollars, which would give us more information.

We didn't have much, but we'd get more. Everyone available was here or on the way in. This was what we did.

This is what we do.

I shut my eyes and breathed through the panic clawing at my ribs.

This is what we do.

This felt different than any K and R job we'd ever done, though. I'd cared when Jo had been taken—it'd felt personal then. But this?

This was a waking nightmare.

What if I didn't get another chance to tell her I was so sorry for betraying her trust? That she deserved someone who respected her no matter what, whose actions reflected this even when they disagreed.

That I wanted more with her than I'd ever wanted with anyone. That I was terrified of loving her and losing her but that the possibility of never really having her to love in the first place hurt like hell anyway.

Or more to the larger, more unimaginable point, that I loved her so much I could hardly breathe without her knowing it?

CHAPTER FORTY-ONE

Elise

I'd seen Callum once in the last... some amount of time when he came in without a word, took a photo, and left.

It felt like hours, but I couldn't be sure. The sun had shifted along the wall enough for me to know it'd been minutes, but how often did I hang around a room watching the sun move? And it was muted through the frosted glass so I couldn't be sure.

My body ached from sitting. I couldn't stand without slumping thanks to where he'd attached the cuffs, and I couldn't believe how thirsty I was. I leaned into obsessively thinking about how dry my mouth felt instead of letting my mind wander to the worries clawing at me—that maybe Luc had no idea I was even gone. They circled my brain like vultures, and after I couldn't stand it anymore, I started yelling.

"Callum! Callum, please. I need to talk to you!" If this resulted in my mouth being duct-taped, so be it.

Granted, easy to say now while my mouth wasn't covered, but I convinced myself I could talk him into leaving me tape-free since I wasn't screaming my guts out for no reason.

He opened the door with an irritated snarl. "Didn't I tell you to keep quiet?"

"You did. I don't have any other way to get your attention, and I..." I swallowed, realizing he wasn't about to give me anything and the thought of sitting here for who knew how much longer without contact, without any information, made me feel like a caged rabbit. "I really need to use the bathroom."

His jaw hardened, then his chin jutted out in this mean-mug look he'd given me a dozen times at least. "Fine."

He approached with zero caution and pulled out a small silver key, then fiddled with the lock until the side attached to the radiator released. With a yank on my left arm, he turned me and connected the cuff to my right wrist, then hauled me up to standing.

My knees ached, but I happily stepped forward, eager to exit the room. As subtly as possible, I took in the space as Callum lead me to the bathroom. Sadly, I didn't see much. White walls, a few other doors, all closed, and the bathroom. Clean and stocked only with toilet paper and hand soap—no towels I could see.

He shoved me in and shut the door.

"Uh, I can't uh... I need at least one hand." I ground my teeth against the urge to cry. How humiliating to have to ask someone to uncuff me so I could use the bathroom?

He shouldered back in and without a word undid the right cuff, then grabbed my chin and held it *hard*.

"Don't do anything stupid, Leesy."

Fury rose up in my chest and I was a heartbeat away from spitting in his face when he whipped around and shut the door after himself. I wanted to sink to the floor and cry or manifest a window and climb out of it. But, I moved through the motions quickly, too afraid to have him burst back in and find me moving too slowly. Then he'd think he had excuse to hit me again.

Something inside crumbled with that thought. I'd tried to stay away from it being him, but here he was. A man I'd once thought I loved. Who I'd been convinced loved me, in spite of some of his behavior. But here, he'd just shown clear as day that he'd just been waiting for an excuse to hit me.

At the same time, I'd been right. Not that I'd ever felt unjustified in leaving him, but now I knew. All those rough grips and harsh statements had been leading to more abuse.

Banging on the door jolted me into finishing rinsing my hands. With one last look in the mirror, I took a deep breath.

You can do this. You'll make it through this.

As Callum marched me back to the room, I thought of my friends. I thought of Jo, who'd been held at gunpoint by a crazy person. Winnie had been abducted and had to be rescued, too. I thought of Jess, who'd saved so many people, and Liz who'd saved Jack McKean and his friend, not to mention all the spy stuff she'd done overseas to stop terrorists. I thought of Nikki, who'd fiercely protected Kiley and supported Bruce. They'd survived, and so would I.

Maybe we'd start a club.

Isn't that what Silver Ridge Romance Readers is?

As though I wasn't currently handcuffed and being led to a practically windowless room by my abusive ex, I laughed.

He pushed me forward and I only narrowly missed catching the doorframe with my face.

"I don't know what you're laughing about. Your little boyfriend is about to be out twenty mil, and then you're mine."

I could hear the smirk in his voice—that self-satisfied grin he'd give when he thought he knew more than me. It was the only thing keeping my mouth from dropping open because *twenty million dollars?*

Callum's obnoxious, blustering laugh rang out. "Did you really not know he had that kind of money?"

Focusing on breathing through my nose and not letting him see my face, I gave myself a moment to process the information. Of course I'd known his family was hugely wealthy, but I'd gotten the impression he'd been cut off financially, at least while he was in the military. Twenty million dollars was an insane amount of money, but maybe that was what was in his trust? Also, it was way more than Callum would dare ask for on his own.

"Who are you working for? Who's getting the bulk of that money?" I asked, right as he affixed one of the cuffs to the radiator again. I tried not to let my hopes sink. Why would it matter if I was right back where I'd been a few minutes ago? I'd known that would happen, hadn't I?

And hey, all my fake fiancé has to do is pay my horrible ex a cool twenty mil and then I'm out of here. A wave of hopelessness washed over me.

Did he even have that much? His grandfather did, most likely, but just... sitting around?

Maybe, but the bigger point was, he shouldn't need it. Luc didn't, either. He and the Saint guys would find me before they ever sent that kind of money anywhere, right? Of course.

Calming breath out. Slow breath in.

I could handle this. Callum would leave soon, and I could organize my thoughts and figure out how I'd ever make all this up to Luc.

"Never thought I'd take anyone's charity," he spat, as though not needing help made him superior to everyone else. "I view this as an opportunity. And you know I'll never waste one of those."

His grin made my stomach roil. He'd always been entrepreneurial and that was his line—never miss an opportunity. He'd made decent money, and of course he'd talked me into his investment in Glazed like not taking it would be missing an opportunity.

Somehow, I managed not to cringe as the memories assaulted me.

"I'll get a nice little pay day, and of course—" he grabbed my chin again, forcing my face up to look at his despite him standing and my place on the mattress. "I get you."

I jerked back, out of his grasp, but this time, he grabbed me by the hair.

"You seem to be missing it, Leesy, so let me spell it out for you. He loses the money, and once that's gone because of you, he's not gonna want you anyway. I get you, and no one around here is the wiser because you're not going to say a word." His voice dropped into a steely whisper, words slipping out between sneering teeth, and my heart shuddered.

He really thought he'd "get" me after all this?

It should've been a blow to hear him speak so confidently, but it showed me he didn't know me. Certainly not anymore, though I didn't think he ever really did. But what he certainly didn't know now was I had a support system. It was the one I'd used to mentally and physically pry myself away from him more than once, and it'd only grown stronger. Dove and I were closer than ever now that she knew the truth about Callum, and Liz... Liz was my badass spy friend who was the most observant person I'd ever encountered with the possible exception of Luc.

Luc.

The thought of his name brought tears to my eyes, but I held them at bay, averting my gaze even though Callum held my head fast. Just a few more minutes and he would get tired of his monologuing and I could cry for a while. I wouldn't sink into the worry that what Callum said was true because he didn't know Luc either. He couldn't possibly understand someone so unlike him.

I just wanted him. I wanted to apologize and let him do the same. I wanted to be wrapped up in his arms and smell his warm, clean scent, and watch him eat one of my donuts. Or cookies. Or anything he wanted, because I wanted him happy.

I wanted *us* happy. But could we be after this? Could we be for real?

Callum's voice softened. "You'll see. It'll all work out."

He dropped my hair, and I slumped back down when a shrill sound burst from his phone.

He fumbled to get to his pocket, then pulled out the device, and a huge grin spread across his face.

"Looks like Mr. Moneybags is ready to make the payment." His eyes were wild when they centered back on me. "Pretty soon, this'll all be over."

He slammed the door behind him, and I let myself sink down on the mattress. Tears slipped out as hope and fear warred in me.

This'll all be over.

I just hoped when it was, I'd be in one piece, and Luc wouldn't hate me.

CHAPTER FORTY-TWO

Luc

Our connection with EMU and the genius work of East—Shane Easton—paid off.

"I've got the general geolocation. It's about a quarter-mile radius," Beast said as he read through what East had sent.

"We need to get their instructions for Elise before we send the cash," Bruce said, reiterating something I'd emphasized one too many times.

I paced over to check the phone where it was plugged into the network of computers at Beast's station, driving my focus into the small steps to keep the spiraling worry at bay.

"I'll text again."

I'd sent a message confirming we'd send the money, but we needed bank account information and the location where I could find Elise. The account details could give us more clues about who was behind this mess, and as soon as we had any information about getting Elise, I'd be out of here.

A quarter-mile radius wasn't terrible. I could comb that alone in an hour, maybe less, depending on how many properties were there. If I had help?

I'll find you. I'm coming for you. These words kept cycling through my mind as though she might sense them somehow.

Maybe it was the Frenchman in me, but I hoped her soul would know I was doing everything possible to get to her. She was it for me—I saw that now so clearly and I could slap myself for not acknowledging it before this nightmare started.

"Grandpappy's doing just fine," Kenny said as he and Liz entered the room. He tossed his hat onto a chair and hooked an arm around my shoulders, squeezed, then released me. "For real, they're fine. They can make cash available as needed." He gave me a wide-eyed look like that was mind-blowing. *Yeah.* We'd deal with that later. "Security looks good and they all willingly let me check their phones—no trace of ransoms there. Looks like you're the special boy."

"What an honor." I didn't mind being the target except that it'd resulted in Elise being dragged into this. When I found out who'd done it, there'd be hell to pay.

"Your grandfather offered his 'resources' beyond the ransom money, but I assured him we had it in hand," Kenny added, brows rising on *resources*.

Yes, billions of dollars probably could help if we needed it, but we didn't. At this point, it was a matter of time. I wasn't overly confident—I just knew what we could do. Since we'd had a little help from the dark side, we had a basic location and in a few minutes, we'd likely have more.

I'd be holding Elise within an hour, or very close. If she could hold on a little longer, I'd get to her.

I'm coming, mon cœur.

"He also asked us to convey his sincere apologies. And for what it's worth, I do think he feels genuinely awful."

Liz's addition to Kenny's update was helpful. Or, if not helpful, good to know. He apologized this morning, and I believed he was contrite. It wasn't a hard leap to make to think he felt that something had happened to Elise, even as much as he disliked me with her.

We'd deal with that at a later date, though I suspected it had very little to do with her in particular. It was his fear, as he'd explained... just like it'd been mine that'd kept me from begging her to be with me for real, for *good*.

My phone pinged, and everyone shuffled close, but Beast switched the screen taking up the wall to the text field. The message included routing and account information, and then, "Once we have the money, you get the girl."

I swore and immediately tapped back. "No. I make a small deposit in the account and only at the point you surrender her do you get the remainder."

Bruce's low chuckle was almost sinister. "They're not going to like that. But you're being more generous than we normally would."

Kidnapping and ransom recovery went one of two ways. First, don't negotiate at all if you have enough information to find the hostage. Just recover them. Second, if you're blind and have to, pay them knowing it's a loss, but not before you get the hostage. With professional entities, you still never counted on them making good on their word. You had to have eyes on the person and swap the cash. But twenty million dollars was not about to be a cash transaction, so there was no scenario in which we'd stand twenty feet apart with bags full of money and Elise would walk to me. Maybe in the movies.

Or maybe for less money.

Someone knew who I was, and they likely had time to prove it.

Adam hung up the phone. "Police just got a tip from someone who works the first shift at the hospital saying they saw a black sedan pulling out of her complex around five this morning. Apparently, they don't usually see that car at that time and wanted to mention it just in case."

It clicked instantly. "Her ex. Callum Davis. He drives a black sedan."

We'd considered him, but he wouldn't have the balls, frankly. Everything I knew about him told me he functioned out of fear, selfishness, and cowardice, and this was no different. Someone else had to be driving the plan here.

"He's the grunt, but not the brains."

Everyone murmured their agreement. No way was he behind this by himself. He likely wouldn't have known I had that kind of money, but he had seen me at the gala, so maybe he'd put together who my grandfather was and assumed. Still, asking for twenty million would be extravagant unless they knew I could pay it and then some.

The timing was too coincidental, too. It had to be linked to my grandfather's visit, though no ransom demands made to him told me whoever this was thought they could get more out of me. Maybe someone had been watching the gala, waiting for the right mark. Maybe it was someone Callum had teamed up with, someone smarter and greedier than he was, and he saw it as a way to hurt Elise, me, and get cash.

I exhaled through my nose, willing myself to calm.

Another text came through. *"Make the first deposit."*

"Sounds like they're playing ball. Here we go." Kenny clapped his hands together like he couldn't wait.

He wasn't alone. Everyone moved then, working on their tasks like the well-oiled machine we were. Twenty minutes later, the money landed in the foreign account and the text with an address came.

"It's not in the radius," Beast said, showing us where the geotag from the original proof of life image was located and where this house was. It was out of town, not far from Stone's place.

"That's an empty cabin, last I checked," Stone said, eyeing the satellite image of the location. "Sego Lily Commune folk mill around there sometimes but it hasn't been occupied since I've been here. I'll get ahold of their leadership and check in."

"Could be a good place to stash someone," Kenny said, but the way he was squinting at the screen told me he didn't buy it either.

"Stone, Liz, and Doc, head there to check the box. Cookie, Barbie, Ed, Oak, and I will head to the neighborhood. Beast, Pop, and Saint, you're CP." Bruce held my gaze. "We're almost there."

I nodded. We were.

In minutes, we were all kitted up and wore firearms. We weren't law enforcement or military anymore, so these were weapons we all held permits for and didn't ever plan to use unless forced to. Bruce made the courtesy call to the local PD, and we all rolled out. It'd take fifteen minutes or more for Kenny and Stone to reach the place these fools were claiming she was, but in my gut, I knew it wasn't this simple.

If Callum was involved, he wasn't going to hand Elise over. Not without a fight, or potentially harming her first. The sooner we could get to her, the better, and even more ideal if we could do it before he realized we'd solved his little puzzle.

Tristan drove, his stalwart, steady energy stabilizing the whole vehicle. Next to us, Bruce drove the other. Always good to have options and be able to split up, and in this case, we wanted flexibility.

Beast came in through the comms system. "Found his car. Pretty sure it's tucked into the garage of the house at eight-oh-five Wasatch Lane."

Tristan accelerated and we confirmed receipt of the information.

"You good?" Kenny asked, adjusting the Velcro at the wrist of his left glove. It'd been adjusted to fit his three fingers, and he liked it snug.

Was I good?

Was I ready to find Elise? Yes. Was I low-key terrified she might be hurt, or worse?

Also yes.

But I wasn't going to give in to those fears. I'd find her, we'd get Callum put away for a nice long time, and she'd be safe. Since I planned to spend the rest of my life with her if things worked out, I'd refrain from delivering on my promise to kill him in favor of him spending a nice long time in prison.

"Good as I can be." It was an honest answer, and that was what I owed myself and him. Honesty had to come first now, no matter if it was ugly or messy.

"Tap out if it gets too much. You know what you can handle."

Tristan's words were calm but confident. He had a few years on me in the military, in life, and certainly in love. His faith that I knew myself gave me a needed boost.

"Will do."

We parked at the end of a street and slipped out of the vehicle after reviewing the approach plan. In some ways, it felt like I'd done this a hundred times—approach a structure, breach it covertly, recover whatever asset or hostage or *insert important thing here* and get out safe.

But this was different. The woman I loved had been taken, and it was time to get her back.

Tristan used hand and arm signals to lead us forward. Soon, we saw Bruce and Ed approaching from the other direction on foot. They folded in with us, and we moved around the house. It appeared to be a basic residential home at the end of a cul-de-sac where the neighboring homes had For Sale signs up.

All the windows around the sides and back had shades pulled or were a kind of frosted glass that prevented seeing in. No telling where she would be inside, if she was even here. Stone, Liz, and Doc hadn't gotten to the cabin yet to confirm that location.

Bruce approached the door, then nodded for me. I approached, picked the lock and slid the deadbolt back with ease, then stepped back. Now Kenny rounded the corner, ready to pull it open for the breach.

We stepped inside, and chaos erupted.

CHAPTER FORTY-THREE

Elise

The house went from virtually silent to a cacophony I couldn't make sense of. Yelling, screaming, and the sound of what my terrified mind processed as gunshots.

I ducked, covering my head on instinct, when the door flew open. Callum ran for me, dragging me up and holding me in front of him as best he could, though my wrist was still cuffed to the bottom of the radiator, so he had to crouch instead of stand.

"What's going on? What—"

"Shut up. Shut. Up."

His hand slapped over my mouth, but my adrenaline-fueled brain finally caught up and I started fighting.

I sent an elbow into his chest and stomped on one of his feet. He pulled my hair hard, and my eyes watered. His hand slipped off my lips and I screamed, "Luc! I'm here! I'm here! Help!" before he clamped his hand over my mouth again.

I kept screaming, futile though it seemed, and thrashed around until something sharp angled up into my neck. My cries for help stopped with a sharp gasp as I realized he had a knife to my neck.

Two dark figures appeared in the doorway. My heart leaped and my pulse skyrocketed. *Luc!* And Kenny. The good guys were here!

"Don't come any closer," Callum yelled, angling the knife a touch closer to my trachea. "You're going to send that money and I'm going to walk out of here."

Without a word, something popped, and Callum jerked backward. At the same time, both men rushed inside the room, Luc straight to me, and Kenny directly to Callum, whom he jabbed in the throat and forced to the ground.

"I'm here. I'm here," he said, his face lined with what looked like agony as he clipped the cuff from the chain, then unlocked it and freed my poor, mangled wrist. "I'm so sorry it took so long."

I launched into his arms, so relieved to see him and feel him wrapping around me.

"It's alright. You're alright," he said, rubbing soothing circles into my back with his gloved hands. "You're okay."

I'd hardly registered how hard I was crying, but wow. I was full-on sobbing into his shoulder, and I'd never felt so heartbroken and so relieved. Shouldn't I just be happy?

He eased back and cupped my face in his hands. "You're going to be alright, Elise. I promise you, *mon amour,* you'll be okay."

Inhaling a deep breath, I tried to steady myself enough to speak. "I know. I just... I wasn't sure."

I wasn't sure you'd find me. I wasn't sure I'd see you again. I wasn't sure you'd still want me.

"Oh, *mon cœur, je t'aime. Je t'aime.*" He pressed a kiss to my forehead, my temple. "I'm so sorry this happened. It's all my fault."

Amidst everything, I hadn't dreamt of his soft, sweet words. Maybe I'd hoped for them, but I couldn't have guessed how beautiful they sounded, his accent rolling over the consonants and bringing me a kind of comfort. I had to tell him what I'd feared I wouldn't get a chance to. "Luc, I love—"

"You'll never have her the way I had her, you idiot. You'll never—" Callum's words cut off when a sharp ripping sound cut through the space.

"That's enough of that, sweetie pie." Kenny slapped a piece of duct tape over Callum's mouth, then pulled him to his feet. "I'll take out the trash. You two take a minute." He winked and hauled a stumbling Callum behind him.

"Catch your breath and then let's get Doc to take a look at you. He'll be here any minute. You might need to head to the hospital," he said, his dark brows furrowed as he rotated my wrist one way, then the other. "I'm so sorry."

"It's not your fault. He did this. Him and whoever *they* are," I said, settling my palm against the curve of his stubbled jaw.

His gaze sharpened even as he pressed his face into my hand, nuzzling slightly. "What else did he say? Who else was he working with?"

"I didn't see anyone but him." I moved to stand, and he jumped to his feet, then held my hand and arm to guide me to standing. "He only referred to how 'they'd get their money,' and I guess he'd get a small payout and..." I swallowed. "Me."

He swore under his breath. "Not happening."

It probably didn't bode well for my mental state, but I laughed at the lethal edge to his voice.

"I think it's safe to say you're right about that." My head shook as I added, "I can't understand what he thought would make me be with him again ever, much less after this."

With his arm around my back, he walked me slowly out of the room, the living room, and into the breezy spring afternoon. I blinked against the light and inhaled the fresh air.

"Sounds silly, but I really hated being locked up in that room. It made me realize I need to get out more."

He scowled at me. "It doesn't sound silly. You were kidnapped and detained in a room with nothing but a mattress." He wrapped me in another hug.

Two grumbling men were being loaded into a police cruiser, and behind them, Callum was already seated and stewing in the back of another one. Funnily enough, the police hadn't removed the piece of tape on his mouth. The old me would've wanted a big show down with him—a moment to put him in his place and help him understand I'd never be with him again.

But the man was lost. Somewhere along the line, that mean streak had turned into a sickness, or maybe it always had been. He wouldn't be able to hear me now if he didn't understand that kidnapping me wasn't going to get me back any more than threatening my business would.

He'd understand when he was in jail. That would hopefully get the message through to him, and I didn't need to be the one to send it.

Acknowledging this had me slumping against Luc. My

eyes fluttered shut and a wave of exhaustion hit. "I'm so tired."

His arm steadied me against him, and he pressed a kiss into my hair. "Adrenaline crash, not to mention the whole ordeal in itself. Let's get you checked out."

Hours later, he drove me home and paced my living room while I showered. Or at least I assumed he did since I emerged to find him burning a hole in my carpet, his gaze on his phone as he wore a path around my couch.

"Luc? Everything okay?" I asked, running a towel through my hair.

His gaze tracked over my slouchy T-shirt and sleep shorts—a clean set—then hooked into my eyes as his throat bobbed. "Everything's fine."

The rough texture of his voice grabbed at me, luring me close with the gruff, used sound of it. "You sure?"

"I'm sure. I just..." His brow wrinkled, and he took my hand and guided me to sit on the couch, then slipped to his knees in front of me and pressed my palm over his pounding heart. "I'm so sorry. I'm so sorry for this. Please forgive me for buying him out to begin with, and please know I never meant to hurt you. It's not enough, but I've learned why it was wrong, and I will not do anything like it again."

I curled my fingers in to grip his shirt and pulled him to me, wrapping my arms around him.

"I forgive you. I'm so sorry I didn't just call you and tell you. I don't want to be someone who punishes the people they love when they're angry or even when there's something wrong." I pulled back to make sure he could see I meant it. "Next time something goes wrong, I won't shut you out. I was mad but I wasn't about to walk away because of it, especially after you explained and apologized."

His eyes shut slowly, and he exhaled. "Part of me has feared maybe we were done. That your willingness to let me comfort you was a kindness, and not because you still want—"

"You. Luc, I still want you." The truth made me smile, but it was nothing compared to his beaming, glorious grin. "I needed some time, that's all. I was processing it and would've called you this morning."

"I love you, Elise. I love you so much."

His words set off fireworks in my heart and I laughed, the words tripping out before I could stop them. "I love you, too."

We stayed like that for a beat before he leaned in and devoured me with his kiss. His lips found mine and he didn't hold back. He wasn't tentative or unsure, and he wasn't treading with caution like he might hurt or break me. Every press and taste were laced with pleasure for both of us, and it quickly unraveled into so much heat and desire, I could hardly think straight when he pulled back and pushed off the ground to find a seat next to me.

"Better stop that before we can't anymore," he said, his kiss-swollen lips making me feel like I'd conquered something.

"Mm, but do we care?"

He chuckled, the small smile on his handsome face injecting liquid wanting into my veins. But when he laced our fingers together and kissed the back of my hand, that inferno banked into a steady flame.

"You need rest, and I need to go speak with my grandfather for a moment and then come back here with whatever food your heart desires."

My heart sank. "Okay."

He cupped my face in his hands. "He owes you an apology, too, but he has admitted how wrong he was."

"He'll let you fake-marry me, even without a dowry?" I asked, the sting of everything that'd happened last night—had it really been last night?—niggling at me.

He kissed my cheek, then my jaw, then just behind my ear. "No dowry needed. Odette didn't have one and—"

He froze, then sat up slowly, a few French words slipping out in a whisper.

"What is it?" I asked, anxious to know what'd shifted his focus so drastically.

"I know who did this."

CHAPTER FORTY-FOUR

Luc

My grandfather did exactly as I asked without question when I sent him my suspicions.

With Elise by my side, we walked into the Silver Ridge Resort restaurant's private meeting room to find Odette, her parents, my sister and Michele, and my grandfather all waiting.

The de Valois' smiles remained stapled in place, even after Elise took her seat next to me.

"We've had an interesting day. Anyone have a guess what we've been up to?" I said, casual as could be despite the simmering anger just under my skin.

"Did you two sleep in and make love until you were forced to exit the bed and face your obligations?"

Michele's innocent expression almost made me laugh. He knew very well but would never miss an opportunity to live in a romantic fantasy land.

Someone grumbled something under their breath, but Cynthia asked, "Why don't you enlighten us?"

I took Elise's hand and kissed it, cradling it to me. She was okay, and now that we'd narrowed down the perpetrators, I felt better, but I wanted to get this over with.

Then we'd see about Michele's suggestion.

"I'd rather know what *you* were doing this morning, *Monsieur et Madame de Valois.*"

The pointed way I spoke alerted Odette. Her shoulders stiffened, and she turned to her parents. "What did you do?"

Cynthia waved her away like her question mattered not. "Nothing of importance."

"I suppose not. You had Callum Davis doing your dirty work for you, no?" I accused, though I remained seated, holding Elise's hand.

"How dare you!" Bernard and Cynthia said in unison, somehow both equally outraged despite my vague statement.

"Mom? Dad? What did you do?" Odette asked, leaning away from them and turning to me. "What happened?"

It was then her gaze snagged on Elise's face where a bruise had bloomed and purpled along her cheekbone and below her eye. The abrasions at her wrist were obvious, too.

"I was kidnapped," Elise said, then turned to the de Valois. "And I think we know who was behind it."

The gasps from Cynthia should've won an award, but Bernard de Valois stood up and nearly knocked his chair over when he did.

"I'll accept no more of these baseless accusations. Kidnapping?" He scrambled behind his chair, and I could swear he was inching toward an exit.

Did he really think he was going to slip out of the room and get away with this?

My grandfather stood, buttoning his jacket as he did with the habitual grace he innately possessed, and spoke the final blow. "I should've known you were so desperate. My largest regret is that I didn't see you for what you are."

Another gasp, and then Cynthia started in. "We agreed the children would marry. It was to benefit us both. And then he trots in here with his donut-peddling fiancée like she's a valid replacement for Odette? *Odette de Valois?*"

Odette's head dropped into her hands. She was visibly crumbling as her parents' bad behavior came to light.

"We did discuss it years ago, and I'd accepted it as a good idea back then. What I failed to do..." My grandfather set his eyes on me and Elise, a tender contrition there I'd never seen, "was consider what my grandson wanted. He never wanted Odette, not because she isn't lovely, of course. But because he's in love with his Elise, and no amount of familial pressure will change that."

Whispered expletives tripped out of Cynthia while her husband rather foolishly fumbled around in his pocket. I jumped up, raced around the table, and caught his arm right as he pulled out a handgun. Since he didn't expect me, I hammered my fist against his forearm to force his hand to open, then pulled the gun from his grip.

"Don't think so," I said, shoving him back into his seat as his wife screamed and Grand-père yelled in French.

"What is the meaning of this? You kidnap my grandson's fiancée and attempt to get money? Now you brandish a weapon? Are you mad?"

The ridiculous antique revolver didn't have a safety, so I stepped back, aimed the barrel at the floor, and emptied the chambers to make sure no one's excitement resulted in injury or worse.

Apparently, the two de Valois parents were mad, because Bernard ran out of the room as though he could outrun his many imbecilic choices, and Cynthia launched herself around her daughter, right at Elise.

Before I could get to her, Elise and Cynthia had fallen to the ground. Odette wailed at her mother, begging her to stop. Aurelie and Michele were grabbing at the woman's arms trying to pull her off Elise, and right when I finally reached them, Elise shoved her off and scrambled away, into my arms.

Arriving just in time, the officers who'd first responded to the call about Elise being gone stepped into the room and took charge.

"Cynthia de Valois. You're under arrest for conspiracy to kidnap, extortion, and coercion. You have the right to remain silent. Anything you say..."

They led her out of the room, giving me a nod as they passed. I held Elise tight, not wanting to be even an inch apart from her, until she pulled back.

"You okay?" she asked, her dark eyes tired but alert.

"I'm fine. You?" I brushed some hair out of her face and indulged in kissing her forehead.

"I am. I can't believe they were convinced they were owed that money. Did they think they could've shot one of us and gotten it?"

Her disbelief echoed my own. What had been the plan with the weapon?

My grandfather stood nearby, weight shifting from one foot to the other. I'd never known the man to display his anxieties, but it was scrawled in perfect script across his whole being now.

"May I have a moment?" he asked, stepping forward as we turned to face him.

Elise nodded. "Of course. I'll meet you out—"

"Non, Elise. I'd like a moment with you," he said, reaching out and taking her hand in both of his.

She blinked. "Um, sure."

"I'd like to stay," I said, sensing Elise didn't want to be left and supremely curious what he wanted to say.

"Bien sûr. I need to apologize to both of you. I was so very wrong. I've been looking out for this family's enterprises for so long, I prioritized them over you." His gaze shifted between the both of us. "Aurelie admitted to me last night that you were not actually engaged..."

Elise's eyes snapped to mine, and I found Aurelie, who approached with Michele.

"How did you know? Why didn't you talk to me?" I asked, worry stitching along my chest.

My sister gave me a soft smile. "It was Michele. He figured it out. But just as soon as he did, we had the gala and I decided not to ask. I thought, 'what if I let my little brother learn something for himself?' And here you are."

I rolled my eyes but hooked my arm around Elise's waist and pulled her close while Michele beamed.

"You lied to me, but I'm the reason why. I'm sorry I pushed you. I can't promise it won't happen again, but I hope you'll accept my apology—both of you." His face had softened more than I'd seen in recent memory.

"Of course," Elise said, with all the grace and goodness I'd come to associate with her.

"Thank you." It was really the best thing to say because it meant the most. No lofty promises he'd change his whole personality, but an intention to do better. That meant something here.

"And perhaps you'll come visit me in France sometime?" He ducked his head and whispered, "It's a lovely place for a honeymoon."

Elise laughed softly and offered him a smile as he pulled me into a hug. I couldn't pay attention to his show of affection, though, because I was looking at her.

She didn't seem horrified at the idea of a honeymoon. Not even totally surprised by it. Of course, maybe she was still pretending—maintaining some level of the façade we'd created, even if we'd been found out.

Into my ear in whispered French, my grandfather said, "*Ne la laisse pas filer, cette fille.*" *Don't let her get away.*

Our eyes met as we separated, and I nodded.

I had no intention of letting her.

CHAPTER FORTY-FIVE

Elise

After the ordeal at the hotel and another round of statements to the police, Luc drove me home and I passed out in my own bed.

When I woke, I was cocooned in his warmth, his arms wrapped around me with one big hand cradling my hip over the sleep shorts I'd slipped back into before dropping into the loving embrace of my mattress. Then he pulled me closer, effectively plastering me to his hard chest and hitching one leg over his hips so we were just about as close as two clothed people could be.

"You're not asleep?" I'd sort of thought he was since he'd been completely still as I woke.

"No."

A thrill zipped from my brain all the way to my toes. "Aren't you tired?"

He made a sound not unlike a hum of satisfaction, but it

almost felt like it came from his very firm, and now that I was more fully awake, very bare chest.

Instantly, I leaned back. "You can't be like that right now."

Confusion shadowed his gray-green eyes as he searched my face. "Like what?"

"All sexy and alluring. We have things to discuss and…" I inched back, separating us a touch because his nearness and that possessive grip on my thigh was doing things to me. Not the productive, clear thoughts kind.

The slow slide of his smile might as well have been a match lit an inch from a bowl full of lighter fluid.

Who's leaving lighter fluid sitting around in a bowl? Great question.

I blamed the man with artwork for a face and body who had literally rescued me and was now using me as his own personal blanket.

"And? Elise, *mon cœur*, won't you tell me what you need? Is it really talking?"

His words were grit and fire, and I absolutely wanted to melt. "I—no. I mean, I might need more than one thing."

He pressed a kiss to my jaw, then my neck.

"Luc, please, talk to me for a minute."

There was a pathetic little whine to my voice he had to hear, but he backed away and maneuvered both of us so we were now sitting and tragically no longer smashed together in delicious ways.

But this is better. For now. Focus!

"I'm sorry. We do need to talk. But I…" His gaze slipped from my eyes to my lips, then he shook his head as though to clear it. "Let's talk."

Ho. Ly. Fire.

We would circle back to all of this. But for now, I took a steadying breath.

"I need to give you this." I slipped the ring off my finger—the one I'd worn faithfully for what was, in the scheme of things, a heartbeat in time.

He held up his hand, and I dropped it in his palm. His fingers closed over it, and his gray-green eyes pierced me with their intensity.

Nervous energy rolled around in my belly, but I pressed on. "If you're interested, I think we should keep dating."

His face split into a charmed smile. "I'm in love with you, so yes, I'm interested."

A relieved laugh tripped out of me. "Good. Me, too." I swallowed, then clarified. "I'm in love with you, too. And I want to keep going."

He reached for me, sliding a hand into my hair. "Good. Because I'm only holding this ring for safekeeping. Unless you'd prefer something else, but otherwise, barring a major change, I intend to give it back to you."

I bit my lip, but my smile broke through anyway. "You have another fake engagement up your sleeve?"

He moved so quickly, I hardly realized what was happening until I was on my back, and he was leaning over me, his lips brushing mine before he said, "Not fake."

"I guess we'll see," I said, grinning like a madwoman.

Did I want to be engaged to Luc? Right now, no. Honestly, no, because we'd hardly dated. But we'd also been through a kind of trial by fire, and he was the man I wanted. I knew this. He was obviously open to dating, and eventually, marriage.

In some other woman's story, maybe she'd turn her fake engagement into a real one without stopping the progress, but he knew, and I knew, this was what *we* needed.

"I'm right with you, *mon amour*. We're right with each other. We'll get there. And now I need only hear what it is you want *now*."

He dipped his head, touching his forehead to mine in a soft, sweet gesture that made my heart absolutely fly.

"You, Luc. Just you."

EPILOGUE

Elise

Six Months Later

I flipped the sign to *Closed* and sank back against the cool glass. The temperature had dropped with the October weather, and business was suddenly booming. Between the *Almabtrieb* and Harvest festival, the film fest coming up, and excitement for ski season brewing, Silvertonians and tourists alike were straight up gobbling down the donuts.

Thank goodness.

The exhaustion was real, but I felt only gratitude and joy. With Luc's insistence, I'd cut down my virtual assistant job to part-time this fall and soon, I'd whittle down to even less. I might even quit. It still made me nervous, but I had a safety net.

And no, the net wasn't my millionaire boyfriend. He'd kept the part of the business he'd bought from Callum, but I'd been slowly paying him back. Assuming the ski season did even seventy percent of what it did last year, I would pay him back in full by the end of January. I'd had the same plan with Callum... if he'd only let me.

Happily, I didn't need to think about him since he'd been in jail since kidnapping me. The best part was how shocked he was at the sentencing. He'd gotten the best lawyer he could buy and still ended up with six years in jail. His many pleas that he'd been coerced or bribed by Bernard and Cynthia de Valois had fallen on deaf ears. They'd been sentenced in federal courts for some reason, but they both got some jail time and then they'd be on house arrest... sorry not sorry.

The only person I felt for was Odette, but she'd been emailing and she and her partner were delighted to be free of her parents and their delusions for her future. They were planning to come visit this winter and do some skiing.

A knock on the door in the kitchen pulled me from my mental wanderings and I hustled through to the space I loved, then opened the back door.

"Um, hi." My friends were standing outside the door in a weird little semicircle, each bundled up in jackets to ward away the winter chill and holding flowers.

"Your tenacity," Nikki said, then handed me two gorgeous bright pink roses, the same shade as my little Glazed mascot logo.

"Your heart," Winnie said, giving me another pair of perfect pink roses.

Jo beamed and held out her two matching flowers. "Your love for your friends."

I sucked in a breath, not entirely sure what was happening, but feeling... something big was afoot.

"Your empathy," Catherine said, smiling as she added her stems to my growing collection.

Jess grinned. "Your grit." She pressed two flowers into my growing bouquet and patted my shaking hands.

Liz gave the opposite of spy face as she beamed, handing me two more bright pink blooms. "Your resilience, and I'm sorry but I have to add, your donuts."

Everyone laughed and smiled. My heart felt like it might grow too big for my body, so filled up already.

Dove stepped up then raised her roses and her bright blue eyes found mine. Of course, there were tears clinging to her lashes as she said, "Your beautiful heart."

She pulled me in for a hug and then stage-whispered, "And don't mind if I say so, but *dat ass.*"

More laughing as they wiped away tears. "This was so lovely, you guys, but—"

They parted, and behind them was Luc on one knee.

My heart stuttered, then sprinted. Dove took the flowers from me and guided me forward until Luc held my hand in his.

"Elise, *mon cœur.*"

He smiled that heartbreaking smile of his and I couldn't help but loose a laugh-sob, so much happiness and love flowing out of me.

"Luc," I said, not knowing what else to do with myself but grasp his hand and listen as he spoke.

"These months with you have been the happiest in my life. There are so many reasons I love you. Your friends helped me express a few of them—even the ad libbed additions."

Everyone laughed, and I became aware that more

people were here, witnessing the moment. Behind Luc were a crowd of faces I knew and loved—my friends' partners, his sister and Michele, some of my other local friends... so many beloved people.

"It hasn't been all that long, but I'm sure. Honestly, I've been sure since I asked you if you wanted more—I was just too scared to acknowledge what I wanted. I've wanted you in one way or another since the first time I saw you and my desire to know you and be yours has only multiplied with the days that've passed. We aren't perfect together, Elise, but we're right."

I nodded, because every word he said, I echoed.

He reached into his pocket and pulled out a small box, clicking it open with his thumb and showing me a gorgeous, sparkling, very familiar ring.

"Take me as your husband and let me be yours until our hearts give out. Let's share this life. Let's get married."

I couldn't control the tears as they slipped down. This man had said everything right, just like he'd demonstrated he'd do day in and day out since this wild ride started. We disagreed, sometimes even fought, but it was never mean-spirited. It wasn't the kind of purposeful hurting or gaslighting. It came from genuine mistakes, confusion, or miscommunication. Because we were two imperfect people, and he was so completely correct.

"We're right together. I'll be yours if you'll be mine," I said, hands shaking and desperate to hug him.

"Yes. I'm all yours."

I grinned through the tears now. "And I'm all yours. Yes. I'll marry you."

I launched into his arms as he stood, and we kissed as he twirled me around. The whole crowd was whistling and laughing and cheering.

After a moment, he pulled away. "I wanted them all here because they all love you. They support *you*, Elise, and they love you. You are never alone, and neither am I. We have each other and this whole messy family."

More tears and laughter, and another soft, perfect kiss.

He slid the ring on my finger. It was still huge, but I couldn't pretend I didn't love it. His smile practically exploded off his face at the sight of that ring back on my hand, and he hugged me close again.

Our friends—or better yet, the family we'd made—began circling around, hugging us, laughing, clapping, and congratulating us both. I was so happy, so full of joy I never would've imagined, and so deeply grateful.

And as Dove wiped another round of tears from her cheeks and Liz hugged me again, as Kenny pulled me and Luc into an obnoxiously tight group hug, and Dorian stepped out from the shadows to shake my hand and hug Luc... there it was. A thought I'd had more than once these last few months, but one that was loud and clear now.

This was better than any fantasy I could dream up.

I hope you loved Luc and Elise's story! Don't miss a bonus epilogue from Stone's point of view next, and get your copy of his book, Anything For You, today.

BONUS EPILOGUE

Stone

There was a person in my bed.

Scratch that, a woman person.

Woman.

There was a woman in my bed.

My brain stutter-stepped over her bare feet, the deep blue of her pants, the way she folded into a v-shape with her middle making the dip and her feet and head the peaks.

Her blond waves spilling over my pillowcase and the way one petite arm tucked under my pillow—*my* pillow—and... her face.

I swallowed, bouncing my eyes away.

Bear sniffed along the bed gently enough he didn't wake her. He whined slightly, expressing concern.

Pressing a hand to his head, I reassured him without a sound. Bodies in repose concerned him, thanks to our past. But she was fine. I'd seen her breathing when I first walked in.

"We're fine," I mumbled low.

Another hard swallow, then I took in her delicate features. Brow relaxed, straight slope down to her pert nose, darker lashes fanned against her cheeks. Pink lips closed, a cupid's bow like a soft kiss. Pale skin with enough color to signal life, even in the dim light coming from the hallway.

No need to see her open those eyes to know their color —a brilliant blue hid behind her lids which were moving a bit now.

She wasn't supposed to be here. She was supposed to be next door in the apartment above the garage. How she'd ended up not only in my house but in my bed?

Maybe Kenny was behind this, though he wouldn't have done this to *her*.

Just as I had the thought, Bear shifted, and his tags clinked together. Dove's eyes fluttered, then opened. She blinked long and slow, and she scrubbed at her eyes like they might be blurry.

I stood in the corner like a hulking creep in the shadows hoping to give her enough space, not sure if I should run away, or stick it out and see what had brought her here— *here*. I forced my gaze away, knowing nothing had changed since I'd seen her a dozen times before. She was the most beautiful thing I'd ever laid eyes on.

She stirred, turned, and gasped, sitting up and scrambling around until she came to her feet.

And then she screamed bloody murder.

Read Stone's book, Anything For You, Today.

AUTHOR'S NOTE AND ACKNOWLEDGMENTS

Thank you for reading Right With You! This book proved to be a genuine challenge. There are lots of reasons for this, but in the end I can say I'm so happy with their story, and so grateful to the people who helped shape them. Since these two have kept to themselves, stayed tucked away and haven't been as OUT THERE on the page as some (ahem-Kennyahem), discovering who they are was a different process than the other books in this series. I hope you loved spending time with them!

I always have to say thank you to my husband and family. With everything around us feeling unsteady, I am deeply grateful for each of you.

Thank you to Genny Carrick for getting me through this one. For real. Thanks for your honesty and heroic efforts to help me find the path for these two.

Thanks to Amanda K for your insights, too!

Thank you to Jess Mastorakos for this gorgeous cover—I just love it!

Zee Monodee, thanks for sticking it out on this one! I appreciate your tenacity, kindness, and wisdom! This book is one I know we're both proud of in the end!

Huge thanks to Jamie McGillen editing for your line edit and help! I so appreciate you!

I know I say it every time, but thank you to the ARC readers and bookstagrammers who support me and my books, and particularly those who've shared so much enthusiasm for this book's cover! I appreciate you so much!

Thank you to the readers who'll read early, and those who read years from now. Thank you for spending your time with my characters in Silver Ridge. Thanks for being here—truly. I know there are always things grabbing for our attention, and I'm honored you'd find some escape or reprieve of joy in one of my books.

Gosh, I can't believe it's time for Stone and Dove! Let's do this!

ABOUT THE AUTHOR

Claire Cain lives to eat and drink her way around the globe with her traveling soldier and three kids, but is perhaps even happier hunkered down at home in a pair of sweatpants and slippers using any free moment she has to read and cook. Or talk—she really likes to talk. She has become an expert at packing too many dishes in too few cabinets and making houses into homes from Utah to Germany and many places in between. She's a proud Army wife and is frankly just really happy to be here.

You can also join Claire's facebook reader group for exclusive content and fun: https://www.facebook.com/groups/clairecain/

Website: http://www.clairecainwriter.com

E-mail: Claire@ClaireCainWriter.com

Newsletter sign-up for new releases, exclusives, and freebies, including a free book:

http://www.clairecainwriter.com/newsletter

www.ingramcontent.com/pod-product-compliance
Lightning Source LLC
Chambersburg PA
CBHW021247190726
48289CB00005B/1523